"HIT THEM NOW! MOVE IT OUT."

He led the way, weaving and firing short bursts from his FAL. Not looking behind him, he could feel the men with him. From somewhere there came a cry, low at first. Then it rose to a skin-chilling crescendo as more voices joined with it. For a moment Hendricks wondered who it was that started it. Then with a shock he realized it was he. He and the assault group were screaming like the berserkers of old as they rushed at the Askaris, each man's weapon firing.

The Askaris taking cover from the first rockets raised their heads in time to catch part of the blast from the second barrage. They raised their heads again in time to see Hendricks and the mercs were on them, weapons firing. When the magazines went empty, boot and combat knives were drawn . . .

Books by Barry Sadler

CASCA, THE ETERNAL MERCENARY SERIES

BARRY SADLER
RAZOR

CHARTER BOOKS, NEW YORK

RAZOR

A Charter Book/published by arrangement with
the author

PRINTING HISTORY
Charter edition / February 1988

ISBN: 1-55773-002-4

Charter Books are published by The Berkley Publishing Group,
200 Madison Avenue, New York, NY 10016.
The name ''Charter'' and the ''C'' logo are trademarks
belonging to Charter Communications, Inc.
PRINTED IN THE UNITED STATES OF AMERICA

10 9 8 7 6 5 4 3 2 1

ONE

OCTOBER 10

THE RIDE UP from Guatemala City left the man cold. The mixed signs of affluence and poverty didn't touch him; he had more important articles of consideration. Perhaps later, if the situation became more critical for the Central American country, he might give it a bit more attention; but for now it appeared to be relatively stable, and the restaurants were quite good, especially over in Zone Ten. Not at all what he had expected. At least there was a reasonable substitute for the endless black beans and rice he'd had to endure for three days on his last visit to this part of the hemisphere.

The memory made him cringe in distaste. No wonder Latin Americans—what did they call them? Oh yes! campesinos—were always revolting. If that was all they had to eat then they were certainly justified in doing something just to break the monotony.

Phillip R. Anderson II was totally lost in his own problems and the importance of the mission entrusted to him by his superiors. It took him out of the ranks of merely being

1

a high-paid gofer into the antechamber of the inner circles where decisions were made and acted upon. If this situation was handled properly, full admittance to that circle would at last be within his reach.

Not even the incredible greens of the mountains and valleys or the sky-touching volcanoes distracted him from his thoughts. He was barely noticed when the car, chauffeured by a Guatemalan employee of the American embassy, turned off on an overpass for the road to Ciudad Antigua at San Juan Sacatepéquez.

He rubbed soft hands together in satisfaction. There should be no problem in dealing with his appointment. In the past he had handled quite deftly—if he did say so himself, and he did—some rather sensitive problems concerning members of the congress and senate, and even a general or two who had tendencies to run against the grain. If he could deal with people of that caliber, then there should be only minor irritations in handling a man who was no more than a hired gun.

The driver took a right turn up a narrow road. Barbed-wire fencing was barely visible between giant avocado trees and the lush undergrowth. Not obvious, but definitely there. Coming into a glade where the grass was neatly trimmed back for about a hundred meters, they stopped in front of a steel-and-concrete gate in a ten-foot wall, which disappeared around to the rear of the finca. It was topped in the Latin manner with broken beer bottles. No one came out to greet him, though he knew they were expecting him. The fool at the gate just stood there staring at him and did nothing to allow him admittance.

After a few moments of the ridiculous staring contest he groaned wearily. It was always so difficult to deal with half-developed intellects. Well, he had come this far and at this point there was no going back. He made the sacrifice and got out of the car. The chauffeur had started to get out also when another man appeared at the gate and gestured for him to return to his car seat. The gesture was obeyed instantly. Anderson noticed that the man had signaled with an ugly-looking thing with a curved magazine. He knew enough about weapons to know that it was not of American manufacture. Somehow that disappointed him. Another lost sale for American industry.

After inspecting his briefcase the sentries permitted Anderson—by now visibly uncomfortable—to enter the compound, where Martin Hendricks was waiting for him. At first glance Anderson didn't think Hendricks matched his concept of what a mercenary, or so-called soldier of fortune, should look like. Really not very impressive at all; in fact, quite ordinary.

Martin Hendricks was of average height, slender build, and wore his sandy gray hair short, but not as short as a Marine would wear it. He wore a plain white shirt tucked into well-worn, faded jeans. It wasn't until they shook hands that Anderson found his viewpoint changing. There was steel in the mercenary's hand, and it was calloused like that of a farm worker. His face was drawn skintight over bony prominences and he had a mouth that seemed long ago to have lost its sense of humor. And the eyes. Anderson couldn't quite make out what color they were. Hazel or green? They seemed to change from second to second but they were steady, calculating. They were eyes that had seen more hell than he would care to speculate about. Anderson released his host's hand as soon as possible. For the first time in his life he felt as though he had touched death. This man would kill and do it instantly.

Amenities were brief. Indicating the way with a sweep of his hand, Hendricks escorted his guest past the guards to the main house, taking him down a pathway lined with avocado and fruit trees. Anderson's car and driver had to remain outside the walls.

Clouds moved and wavered overhead, quickly changing sunny spots to shade, as always happened in October when the end of the rainy season approached.

On the way down to the house they passed two more of Hendricks's men with Israeli 5.56-mm Galil assault rifles slung on their shoulders as they went up to relieve the guards on the gate. Anderson was breathing heavily by the time they entered the house. Here above Guatemala City at San Juan Sacatepéquez the altitude was over six thousand feet. For the last three months Hendricks had been working with the Guardia de Hacienda, bringing up their training standards to deal with the current influx of narcotics passing through Guatemala on their way to the Stateside markets.

All of the guards at Hendricks's house were gringos, his own men brought in to assist with the training program. They were less likely to be bribed than local security. It was unfortunate but true that the drug traffickers were often better equipped and certainly better funded than the local enforcement agencies.

The Guardia de Hacienda was the equivalent of the American Border Patrol, Customs, and the DEA all in one. Most of them were good men but, just as in the States, some of them had a need for money, which the dealers could easily supply. It put a bit more strain on his men to have to handle their own security as well as their regular jobs, but it was safer, he had worked with all of them before.

Hendricks led the way into his office, a small, nondescript room with only a cabinet of native wood, a desk, and a single wicker chair for company as furniture. The walls were brightened somewhat with two posters of Spanish bullfighters. He invited his guest to be seated as he removed a carafe of water, two glasses, and a bottle of Johnnie Walker Red from the cabinet. He placed them on the desk before seating himself.

"It's your nickel." Always, Hendricks placed the burden of initial dialogue on his opponent. He had made his opening move.

"Mr. Hendricks, I have been appointed to represent a number of interests who have deep concerns about a most distressing matter."

Hendricks's friend at the embassy had informed him of the subject to be discussed. He had brought himself up to date as much as possible before Anderson's arrival.

Martin Hendricks eyed his guest sitting across from him. Distinguished, gray hair at the temples, the rest carefully trimmed to conceal a growing thin patch, his manner was that of a professional man of about fifty and in good condition. He was the kind that comes from well-supervised courses of instruction at expensive health spas. His tan obviously came from one of the new tanning beds. Still, he had a firm, if not overly tough, look to him, and his clothes cost more than most families made in three months.

"If I may encapsulate the situation for you," he continued, not waiting for Hendricks to comment.

Settling his tailored form into the stiff-backed wicker chair, he leaned forward, his words dripping with sincerity and import.

"As you know, there has been a civil war going on for some months now in the Republic of Bokala. The current regime headed by Afaiam Mehendi is in deep trouble. The opposition commanded by Leopoldo Okediji is rapidly approaching the capital. Due to the excessive repressiveness of Mehendi's regime, he has in effect made his country an outlaw nation, so bad that not even the Soviets or the Chinese want much to do with him. In essence, all of the world powers have been exceedingly reluctant to give him any support in terms of weapons or logistical aid.

"At this stage of developments he is in a panic and has resorted to mass executions of suspected dissidents. In the last month alone more than ten thousand have gone to the wall or been hacked to pieces by death squads in the bush. As with most African problems this is a conflict between different tribes. For years Mehendi has oppressed the Luda tribesmen who are the majority and placed only members of his own Shanga tribe in positions of influence.

"Okediji has rallied the Luda to him and they have at this time effective control of over seventy percent of the countryside as well as holding the second-largest city. They are now in the preparatory stages of advance on the capital."

He paused and looked questioningly at the carafe of water of Hendricks's desk. Martin poured him a glass, still saying nothing. As yet, nothing had been said that he did not already know, but if it made the man feel better to rehash it he would wait. Sooner or later his guest, who had only identified himself as Mr. Anderson, would get to the point.

Hendricks leaned back in his chair sipping on a thin scotch and water, outwardly giving his guest the impression of his total attention while inwardly his raw-boned frame stewed in a state of boredom. Most of his clients felt they had to go through this same ritual, but that was part of the game.

"President Mehendi, in his state of panic, has resorted to a rather drastic measure in an attempt to force the United States and Great Britain into giving him aid to enable his forces to defeat the insurrectionists.

"This latest action, which took place two days ago, has

not yet been made public. And as Mehendi has closed his borders and expelled all foreign embassy personnel—with the notable exceptions of the Libyans and Iranians—as well as all news correspondents, it may be some time before it is public knowledge.''

Hendricks leaned forward. This was something he had not heard. Anderson was getting close to the heart of the matter.

Anderson took another sip of water and leaned forward, his voice dropping in register to a theatrical conspirator's whisper.

''He has taken hostages. WE''—the ''WE'' whispered as if in capital letters— ''WE have reason to believe that he has taken into custody at least fifty British and American citizens. All other foreign nationals were deported. The Americans and British citizens are currently being held in the Presidential Palace under strong guard. By personal messenger he has informed US''—there were those capitals again—''that if he does not receive aid to throw back the forces of Okediji, then he will not die alone. All the hostages will die with him. We do know that his personal guard is fanatically loyal to him. They will without hesitation kill every one of the hostages, including an undetermined number of children.''

Hendricks put down his drink. Speaking in a quiet monotone, his voice was flat, dry. ''And what do you wish of me?''

Beads of sweat had appeared on Anderson's forehead and nose. He wiped them away self-consciously with a silk kerchief. ''We wish for you to prepare a contingency force for the rescue of the hostages.''

Hendricks avoided the temptation to ask who ''WE'' were. Instead he locked eyes steadily with Anderson, forcing the man to look away nervously.

"Why do you wish a private force to do the job? Surely the United States and the British had enough experts in their Delta Force and SAS to handle the job without outside help."

Anderson squirmed uncomfortably in his chair, not knowing why the seat was so awkward to get comfortable in. It just didn't feel right. There was a good reason: Hendricks had had the front legs of the chair shortened by half an inch, just enough to make whoever sat in it feel ill at ease. It gave him a slight edge in many negotiations to have his guest less than fully comfortable. He figured that single chair trick had added nearly twenty percent to his profit profile over the years he had been using it.

Anderson cleared his throat nervously as Hendricks picked up the Browning 9-mm he habitually kept on top of his desk and toyed with the safety catch.

"The truth, and no bullshit, Mr. Anderson. I have been in the game too long and have too many friends not to be able to check out your story. So, why do you want me to go in after the hostages? Understand I am not averse to the job, but if I am to take it then I have to know all the ramifications. I'm not going to stick myself or my men out on a limb so some security agency can cut it off behind us. I've lived on the edge too long not to smell something rotten, and I want to know what it is or else get your ass out of my chair and off my property!"

Anderson squirmed under Hendricks's steady gaze, which had passed from indifference to definite hostility. That and the familiar manner with which his host handled the pistol made up his mind for him. He had, after all, been given permission to deal with the situation as he saw best and that included giving Hendricks all the information he wished.

"Why of course, Mr. Hendricks. I had every intention of telling you of all the ramifications if you would have just been patient a moment more."

"Very well, Mr. Anderson, a moment more has just passed."

Ignoring the comment, Anderson went on in his same half whisper.

"The situation is so delicate. Mehendi has stated, and we believe him, that if any rescue attempt is made by the United States or Britain he will kill all of the hostages immediately. From our intelligence summation it is believed that any attempt to rescue the hostages would definitely involve a great deal of killing and most probably result in the death of some civilians. The layout of the city is such that a straightforward raid and exfiltration of the hostages would be impossible. And to be frank, it would take the United States and Britain too long to coordinate an effort with the required logistical support to go in before the rebels take over. Therefore, what we propose is for you and a number of your associates to go in, remove the hostages, take them to the airfield outside the city, and have them picked up by aircraft and transported to safety. That is all."

"That's all, my bleedin' ass!"

Anderson winced at the indelicate description.

Hendricks continued, "What you mean is that it is most likely that the Brits and Americans would take too many casualties in the operation and if anything went down wrong the governments would have their asses hanging out to dry. Whereas, if we go in and do the job and get our shit blown it will be no great loss. They will disclaim us and still perhaps be able to convince Mehendi that it was just a private job sponsored by the families of some of the people held hostage. And if we do get away I am sure that the fine print of our contract will read that neither I nor any of my men can make a public or private statement about it. So the Americans and British will play the strong, silent types and just nod their heads knowingly as they take credit for the operation. Is that a bit closer to the truth, Mr. Anderson!''

Hendricks's voice had not risen, but the intensity had increased tenfold. Anderson wiped his face again. It was getting warm and the chair was so damned uncomfortable.

He started to deny the allegations, but the pistol had casually moved to where it intersected his eye and the bridge of his nose.

''Why, uh, yes, Mr. Hendricks, that is not a totally inaccurate summation.''

The muzzle of the pistol lowered to where it was no longer centered on Anderson. His eyes followed its progress with fascination.

''That's better. Now, if we take the job what kind of logistical support can we get? We are going to need some hard-to-get items and need them fast.''

Anderson suddenly felt much better. Hendricks had not turned down the contract. ''We will see that you are supplied with whatever you request in terms of matériel or special equipment. But please remember that time is of the essence in this matter. I know that you will wish to have some training time, but how long do you think it will take for you to put your personnel together?''

''Fifteen days . . . after.''

''After?''

''After we agree on the price. And remember, only half the deposit I require is refundable if I find that we can't do the job and cancel out. You will have that information in ten days.''

Anderson was in for some of the toughest bargaining of his life. Every time he thought he was beginning to get the edge, the awful, incredibly big bore on the Browning would begin to swing his way and his control would falter.

Somehow it was done. The numbers were agreed upon. Now it was up to this incredible person to determine how many men he would need and what their matériel requirements would consist of. He had promised him everything that was available in both the British and American armories.

When they had finished with the bargaining Hendricks went back to the job. "Now, you have indicated that you have a source of information inside the country. Who is it, and where is he? I need to know how accurate your info is. Also, I want to be kept up-to-date daily. You can forward any information to the American embassy in Guate. I'll have one of my men pick it up there every day, and I do mean every day. If there's nothing but an expected change in the weather I want to know about it."

Pointing the pistol at Anderson's briefcase, he continued, "I presume that you brought that along because there is something in there that might be of interest to me. I hope so, because I need a lot of information before I can know for certain how many men will be needed and what special equipment will be required."

Anderson slid the case across the desk. "In here is our most current update along with maps of the city and photographs taken of the Presidential Palace in the last week. You are correct. We do have a source close to the palace. In fact he is an officer with the president's palace guard. He was born in this country, educated in the States, and has been working for us for the last five years. Ever since Mehendi came to power. It is through him that we know of the current situation."

"Are you certain he is reliable?"

Anderson sniffed. "We are not amateurs, you know. Of course he is reliable. His wife and child were killed by Mehendi during his rise to power. As you would say, he has his own ax to grind and would like nothing better than to do it on the neck of his president. You will find his dossier and several recent pictures in the case as well."

Hendricks liked that. There was nothing like spilled family blood to provide proper motive for treason. It made him a great deal more comfortable. It was a motive he could understand and trust, within limits.

The conversation was suddenly interrupted by a deep voice calling to Hendricks from the living room. It was his man Claude Becaude. With him, smiling behind his beard, was Duke.

"Boss, you better come out here. We gotta problem!"

Hendricks rose from behind his desk, taking his pistol with him. To Anderson he ordered curtly, "You stay here." And he went out to the front where a strongly built bearded man and Becaude were waiting for him. They didn't wait for him to ask what it was. Becaude pointed outside the window. Two Latins were being held at riflepoint. Their hands were clasped behind their necks with two of Hendricks's men guarding them.

He held a quick, hushed discussion with the bearded man and called for Anderson to come out of the office.

Anderson didn't notice the two Latins at first till Hendricks's finger pointed them out.

"Mr. Anderson. It seems that you picked up a tail on your way here. My men have already checked them out. No one from Guatemalan Intelligence or the Guardia has put anyone on you and neither has the embassy, which is probably where they picked you up. Whichever it is we will know shortly."

To the bearded man, he ordered, "Take them down to the old servants quarters. Check them out, then kill the toughest one and question the other. You have ten minutes. I want to know if what Mr. Anderson is talking to me about has been compromised or not."

Nodding his head, the bearded man looked at Claude, then back at Hendricks.

"You got it, boss. Ten minutes. Let's go, Claude."

Anderson's face grew even paler than it normally was. "Do you mean," he began to splutter, "that you are actually going to kill one of those men? Right here? Right now?"

Hendricks led him back to his office, putting him back in his seat before replying as he himself sat behind his desk, "Not at all Mr. Anderson. We are going to kill both of them, but not until the weaker one talks to us. Whether he was on to you or not, they have to go. I cannot have anyone speaking of your visit to me."

The muffled report of a .45 being fired inside a building soaked through the walls of the office. A man had just died. Hendricks said nothing; he was waiting. Five minutes passed, then seven, before there was a tap on the panel of his office.

"Come in."

The bearded man stepped into the office with a questioning glance at Anderson. Hendricks nodded his head. "Go ahead. We have no secrets from Mr. Anderson, now do we?"

"All right, boss. Like you said. They picked this gentleman up at the embassy on random scan. They know that he is political but that's all. They had no specific instructions to dog him. They just got lucky, or unlucky as you see fit."

Hendricks set his fingers under his chin, thinking for a moment, completely ignoring Anderson. "Very good, Duke. Get rid of the other one and dispose of whatever form of transport they used to tail Mr. Anderson."

Duke nodded his head and quietly left. Less than a minute later there came another of the muffled reports from outside.

Anderson felt his mouth go dry and sticky. It was hard

to get his vocal chords lubricated. This was becoming more than he'd expected, but he had to see it through no matter what form of low-life barbarians he had to use. His career options depended on it. He tried to speak but his words were stuck somewhere in the back of his throat.

Hendricks made it easy for him. "It's all right, Mr. Anderson. This incident will never be mentioned again, by me or any of my men. It was just one of those unfortunate things that occur when one gets careless. You killed those men, not us. Though they probably deserved it anyway."

Anderson's voice returned. "I do hope you are not going to try to blame this on me."

Hendricks shook his head. "As I said, Mr. Anderson. Nothing has taken place. It is, you might say,"—he paused, locking those strange eyes on Anderson's—"a dead issue. Now, do you have anything else for me pertaining to our earlier discussion?"

Anderson rose, anxious to be away from this unpleasant person. "I believe you will find most of what you require in the briefcase. If you have any other question you can reach me at my hotel. I am staying at the—"

He didn't finish. Hendricks did it for him. "—the Camino Real, room 816.

"One thing more. What about Okediji? Is there any way to get some ground support from him? It seems that what we're doing would work in with his plans."

Anderson wiped his brow again. "My heavens, no! The man's an absolute maniac. He has sworn to purge the country of all outside influences. He is a fanatic of the worst sort."

"Then where does he get his support?"

"Okediji is a Moslem, as are most of his tribe. At this time we believe that a small portion comes out of Iraq, but the vast majority of his aid comes from the People's Republic of China. As for Mehendi, what support he gets comes out of Libya. You know how Qadhafi likes to keep things stirred up. At any rate there is a complete rundown on him as well in the case. Now, if you will excuse me, I have to get over to the embassy for lunch with the ambassador.''

Hendricks didn't really give a rat's ass who he was having lunch with. He had already shelved Anderson and was giving his attention to the contents of the briefcase, separating the folders, papers, and photographs into neat stacks on his desk. Without looking up, Hendricks called out, "Becaude! *Ici.*"

Claude Becaude stepped into the doorway of the office stamping his heels together. His jeans and bright-colored red-and-blue shirt took nothing away from his military appearance. The man would look as though he were in uniform even if he'd been standing there stark naked.

"Oui, Chef."

"Escort Mr. Anderson to the gate and report back to me. We have a lot of work to do."

"Oui, Chef." That was all. Claude had been with Hendricks for many years, ever since retiring as sergeant chef with the Thirteenth Demi Brigade of the Légion étrangère. He knew there was a time to ask questions and that would come later. Right now he controlled his emotions at the prospect of action. The training job for the Guardia de Hacienda was all right, but not very interesting. Perhaps this new contract would put them back on the edge.

Just whom Anderson worked for, Hendricks didn't know and really didn't care. At the end of the negotiations the prim man had placed a cashier's check for one hundred thousand dollars into his hand as an advance on the job. That made it real. Until money changed hands everything was purely speculation and wishful thinking. A hundred thousand dollars took the job out of that category. Now he had his homework to do. Nothing was ever as simple as it seemed; if the United States and Britain didn't want to tackle the job then it must be a bitch.

His conversation yesterday with Vic at the embassy on the Avenida de la Reforma had prepared him for Anderson's arrival. Vic had said, "I don't know just what his function is, but he is definitely connected—and connected strong. I had a call yesterday from a very high office in D.C. asking me to arrange the meet with you. I have no idea what it's all about so don't bother asking. Just be careful. There's not too many of us dinosaurs left, and I'd hate to be the last one."

When he'd left Vic's office, his friend—a former Ranger—was absently rubbing the area of his left kneecap where his flesh ended and the prosthetic leg began. As far as Hendricks was concerned Vic was the only one with any real balls left at the embassy. He had the feeling that Vic Broadman might not be in the country much longer. He'd been making too many waves by telling the truth. That was often fatal behavior in the foreign service.

He was still sorting things out when Claude's short, square body reported back to him. Everything about Claude was square, his head, his hair, his shoulders, and hands. Hendricks often thought the man probably had square-shaped genitals too.

"Pull up a chair, Sergeant, we have a lot to do." Hendricks tossed him a notepad. "I want you to get on the line to Europe. We are going to need some people, at least fifty for this one, and we're going to need them fast. So start running down our old friends. Get me twenty-five or thirty from our sources there. They must have a common language. I don't want any fuckups because of a breakdown in communication. As much as possible, I want men we've worked with before. This isn't going to be a job where we have the time to get to know each other. Check with the Dutchman. He usually knows who's around that's worth a shit. And see if you can't run down one or two SAS men. Men with hostage-recovery experience. Remember, though: no one goes on this job who doesn't have combat experience. Things might get a bit rough before we're out of it. And have a safe house in the country arranged. That old horse farm we used two years ago outside of Liège will do if it's still vacant.''

Becaude bobbed his square chin up and down. ''*C'est bien*. May I inquire what will be the duration of the contract?''

Hendricks leaned back in his chair. ''There will be a short, tough rehearsal, and once we go in the job won't take long. Those that wash out will still have to remain in isolation till the job is on the deck. They'll be given one thousand dollars to compensate them for their time, and nothing else. For those we take with us, tell them the entire job will take less than a month. There's no need to give away any more information at this time. Of course they'll be briefed once final selection is made. The pay is fifteen thousand American dollars for every man, or the equivalent in whatever currency they prefer. And there will, of course, be the usual casualty bonuses.''

Sometimes he felt like an insurance salesman. Casualty bonus. If you lost a hand, eye, arm, or leg, you got so much money. However, if instead of just being maimed or mutilated you got your shit blown away, then there was a lump payment to your next of kin or stated beneficiary. In the past he'd paid out many next-of-kin bonuses and knew that he would be paying a lot more before this job was done.

The short look he'd taken at the layout of the job site and the setup of the city and the airfield made it clear this was not going to be a walk-through. People were going to die, but he would do his damnedest to see that the numbers were as small as possible.

"Sergeant Becaude. Tell our friends to keep their mouths shut or we'll take the necessary actions to see that they don't let their tongues wag anymore in the future."

Again the square chin bobbed up and down as Claude's dark brown eyes burned with new fire.

"Shall I open the lines of communication for equipment, *Chef*?" They had gone into the somewhat formal profile that they always adopted when a hardball job came down.

"No. Our employer will see to all our needs in this case. Just find the men, and once you have, arrange for them to be isolated immediately. No good-byes to girl friends or wives. No last-farewell parties. Once they sign on they are ours. Make sure they know that, before they come in for the interview, they should have their personal effects with them, because if they're accepted they won't be going back home."

TWO

OCTOBER 10

THE JOB WAS going to be a bitch. The first look at the layout and diagrams of the palace told him that. In addition he would have to take and hold the airfield long enough to get the hostages evac-ed out. He knew instinctively after the first look at the contents of the briefcase Anderson had given him the approximate number of men he would need. Of course he'd have to stay flexible on that till he had more information, but for right now it looked like two teams of twenty-five each: one team going in for the hostages; the other to secure the airfield for them. Any more men and he'd run into logistical and transport problems.

Fortunately his contract with the Guardia de Hacienda would be completed in the next week and he had some good men with him right now. They would give him the core of his new commando. Commando! He still used the title for his commands. Guess it was hard to get rid of the past. He'd been a smooth-cheeked youngster when he'd served with Mad Mike's 5 Commando in the Congo in

'61. God, that seemed an eternity ago. Eternity had come for many over the years, and would come soon for more. What had Vic called him, a dinosaur? Not completely inaccurate, but every now and then there was a need for them.

The front door opened. From the sound of the man's walk, he knew who it was. "Duke! Come in here for a minute."

A shadow filled the doorway. Duke Falger waited for permission to enter.

"Come in. There's a few things I want you to take care of for me. We have a new contract coming up. You were pretty tight with some of the Special Forces people, weren't you?"

Duke knew better than to ask what the job was. He'd be told when it was time. "Yes, sir. As you know, I was with the Lurps, and we spent some time with the Berets. Also I was stationed at Fort Bragg for two years. So I do know a few pretty well."

"Good. I want you to make reservations and get to Bragg tomorrow. Find me two Special Forces medics that want to take a short trip. If you can I also want some types who have been through the counterterrorist program. There ought to be a few collecting their pensions." He gave him the same ground rules he had given to Becaude.

"Anything else, sir?"

"Yes, but it'll wait till morning. Then I want you to go by the Camino Real and deliver a folder to someone there. For now just make your reservations and arrange with Becaude for someone to take over your part of the course."

"Very good, sir." He almost did an about-face but caught himself in time. Hendricks smiled. Duke was a good, stable man. He'd be where he was supposed to be when he was supposed to be. Steady, he taught the course

in quick-kill shooting technique—rifle, pistol, shotgun—
and was a damned good hand-to-hand combat instructor as
well. If he had any bad qualities it was that he didn't *have*
any really bad qualities—other than being a semi-health
nut and cunt junkie. But that didn't make him all bad.
Putting Duke out of his thoughts, Hendricks went back to
the job.

For the next ten hours he went over the contents of the
briefcase, sifting through reams of information, staring at
the diagram of the palace interior and grounds till he could
close his eyes and see every room. Intimacy was what he
needed now, to feel the place in his mind.

Becaude came in once and Hendricks handed over the
schematics to him to make an enlarged sketch to go on the
wall. It took two hours and he was still going over options
in his mind, of which there were damned few. As far as
finesse went, there wouldn't be much of it. It was a raid.
Get in, get out, and try to keep casualties to a minimum.
The medics he asked for would be needed. That's why he
wanted Special Forces men. They were the best field
medics in the world and each was cross-trained to handle a
variety of weapons expertly as well. If they couldn't cure
you, they could kill you.

As was normal, the sun began setting at six P.M. The
men in the compound knew something was up. Not exactly what, but Becaude had been doing a lot of grinning
lately and had even told a joke or two—something he
never did unless he was happy. They weren't stupid. The
arrival of Anderson, Becaude on the phone for two hours,
and Duke packing his bag to go Stateside: something was
definitely up.

After dark the lights went on in Hendricks's office.
Claude stoked up the fireplace and put coffee on. He knew
it was going to be a long night for *le chef*. From the other

two chaletas in the compound the normal sound of music was diminished. They knew the boss was working and what he came up with might have a direct effect on them. No one wanted to break his concentration.

Becaude kept the coffee coming, a couple times with a dash of Henessey in it. He wished he could have participated, but for right now *le chef* would work until he came up with a basic format; then he would ask for opinions and comments. He would listen, too. Often during the past eight years he had been with Hendricks he had seen him make major modifications or even total changes of their plans when a fault was pointed out. His thinking wasn't locked up.

In the briefcase was most of what Hendricks needed: maps, charts, time of guard changes, names of commanders, numbers of men on duty around the palace. Anderson may have been a bit of a prick, but he did bring a pretty complete file. His agent on Mehendi's staff had done a good job. He would have to check with Anderson later for an update. The palace itself looked like a straightforward hit. It was the getting in and getting out in one piece that gave him problems. He knew they could get into the palace and probably take out the hostages—or at least most of them—alive. It was that damned distance to the airport they had to travel. This was going to have to be fast, very fast.

He left the dossiers on Okediji and Mehendi till later. For the rest of the night he made lists of options. Tried to work out time frames and reviewed the weather reports for the different times. Not much change there. If Anderson was right they didn't have but about thirty more days. The weather story for the Republic of Bokala at that time of year was normally clear and dry. Once in a while a storm would have enough strength to blow in across Nigeria, but not very often. The worst luck. A little foul weather could have covered the movement of his men for a time.

Reconnaissance photos gave him a composite picture of the terrain around the capital for a distance of about forty kilometers. He would have to insert his force somewhere in that area and then get transport to the city. He didn't like it. His eyes kept returning to the photos of the airport. Goddamn it to bloody hell, he wished he had more time, but decisions had to be made—and fast—or the job would be blown. The airport was the key!

Slowly, around 0400 hours, it started to come together. The jelling process. They say that 0300 hours is when a man's faculties are at their lowest. But for some it is the small hours of the morning, when they are on the fringe of mental exhaustion, that creativity sets in.

"Becaude, bring the bottle and glass for yourself. We have some things to talk over!"

Grinning happily, Claude did as he was asked. He knew when to give *le chef* a little time. He had been awake and waiting for this moment. This was not the first time that inspiration had come at this hour. He had expected it, though sometimes it took a great many more days to break through.

"*Oui, Chef.* Brandy for two on the way."

Becaude knew just what to do. He poured two stout drinks for both of them, set soda on the side, took a seat directly across from Hendricks; and then he waited as Hendricks shuffled through the papers and photos, selecting the ones he wanted. Then he cleared the rest of his desk with a sweep of his hand. Becaude knew he had reduced the material down to what was immediately pertinent.

"Now here is what the job is, but remember we are going to have support on this one. We can squeeze their balls to get everything we want and then some. They don't have any other choice in the matter; time is running out for them. I think they'd let us have anything short of a tactical nuke.''

Becaude almost whistled between his teeth. He knew the area, having served there at one time with a Legion detachment on exercise many years before. This was going to be what Hendricks referred to as a ''great, bloody, hairy bitch.''

Hendricks went over his primary plans at this point. There was no mention of the logistics required. First was to determine that, if everything was in their favor, would they have a chance? Then, what were the odds? That is what he wanted Claude for. The former legionnaire had a good mind. He wasn't just another pretty face in the crowd. If there was a basic flaw in his use of the men or equipment, Claude would instinctively know it. He had a gift for small-unit operations, if not for strategic planning. He knew his men: exactly how far they could be pushed and still function; Weapons, vehicles, maneuvers. Claude had the touch of a natural for all of them. As Hendricks spelled out his basic format, Claude shook his head from time to time in agreement. The basic plan was sound. Something similar had been tried before on a more re-stricted level, but as Hendricks pointed out they did not have many choices. The key had to be Kamara Airport.

''I think you are right, *Chef*. That is the only way to approach it at this time. It will be very risky but it can be done if we are quick and lucky.''

''Do you have any suggestions? We don't have much time to put this together.''

Claude did. He wanted certain specialists and knew where to find them. Also he wanted a few hard-to-get items. He gave Hendricks his suggestions, which were added to the growing list. Hendricks nodded in agreement. "Good, good. Keep thinking. I'll pass these on to Duke to give to Anderson at his hotel tomorrow."

Satisfied for the moment, he leaned back to savor the taste of his drink. The soft dim glow of the lamplight on his face took years away, smoothing the lines around the corners of his eyes, the indentations at the edge of his lips. His body relaxed. It would get tense again, but for now at least he had a basic plan, something to build on.

Behind the rim of his glass Claude watched his face casually. He knew all the signs. The chef was a good man. Always careful about whom they worked for, their money had always been paid and he had always kept casualties to a minimum.

Hendricks said, "God, I'm stiff. Too many hours of sitting make my bones lock up. Let's take the drinks and go outside. Maybe some fresh air will wake me up a bit, get the brain moving again. We still have a lot to do and time's our greatest enemy right now."

On the porch they found aluminum chairs to sit on with faded red and blue backs. Overhead, sharp and clear, the constellations moved as they always had. Here in the mountains outside of Guatemala City the air was clear of the cloying diesel fumes of the city. In the distance, on another hillside to the northeast, he could see the lights of other houses and farms. The homes of the campesinos were different from those of the landowners. There the lights were long since turned off to save money. But at least they had lights. The Guatemalan government had done a pretty fair job of getting electricity to most of the people. Even in the highlands and most of the Petén, homes had discovered the electric light.

Breaking the silence as his eye caught the soft movement of one of his men walking the grounds, his Galil slung parallel to his body, Hendricks said, "I want you to make arrangements to leave for Europe and take over the recruiting and selection job there. Your work here will be finished in two or three days. That will give your man in Brussels time to have some candidates for you to inspect."

Claude took the last sip of his drink. "Very well, *Chef*. I will make the necessary arrangements. How long do you think you will be here?"

"I don't know for certain, but I'll leave someone here to take messages. We might as well use this as our commo center till we get more settled."

Smiling in the dark at Claude, he said, "Now, you old watchdog, go on to bed. I'm over the worst of it. You get some sleep. I'll need you fresh for the morning if anything starts to come down fast. One of us has to be able to move and I'm going to be stuck here for some time yet. So take yourself away and leave the rest of the night to me. I still have a few things to go over."

Unseen, Becaude returned the grin. "As you command, *Chef*. This old dog will go to its kennel." Genuine concern in his voice touched the next words. "You get some rest also. We are not as we once were, *mon vieux*."

Once he had gone, Hendricks thought over the familiar phrase used only by close friends, *mon vieux*. My old one. You're right, Claude. We are the old ones here. Even Duke, with quick manner and energy, had that distant quality to him which was somehow timeless or perhaps time trapped.

It was good to sit alone in the dark for a moment. The cool night air opened up his nostrils. He breathed deep, sucking in the crispness. It wouldn't be like this for much longer. Soon the rains would come and the days and nights would be heavy with moisture.

He tried to think of other things, of women he'd known,

of places he'd been. But the past was pushed away by the job. The next month kept coming to the front of his mind, pushing yesterday away. Facts and more facts. Details, weapons, communications equipment, medical supplies, night-vision devices, Kevlar vests. And the men he would need.

That was the most critical, but he'd get them. There were thousands of them out there in the real world, hiding behind desks or under cars repairing clutches. Men who kissed their wives and kids good-bye in the morning and went off to a nine-to-five job in the city.

He knew that when they were alone in their garages or dens they'd take out boxes or open old footlockers. Taking out the items one by one, they'd run their hands over them, feeling the past come alive again. A captured Tokarev automatic pistol or enemy flag. A faded picture of young men in tiger stripes or jungle fatigues standing together with bright eyes, arms around each other's shoulders, toasting themselves and the world with a local brew. And in each photo there were some who had not returned. Each memory carried its own loss with it. The bright faces of the dead would haunt them in their sleep or on the street when they saw a youngster in uniform who carried himself the same way or had a laugh that took them back to nights of shared terror when all they'd had was each other. Then finally the relief and surprise when dawn would come and they found themselves still alive.

They would also remember the young faces becoming old before their time with deep, grime-filled creases where laugh lines used to be, and the eyes that were incredibly deep in their sockets. Instead of the dim glow of hope or the pain of loss, some of those eyes held a hungry spark that burst into flame with the first flat cracking rounds came overhead. And they remembered when they waited for hours in ambush, anxious for the faint snapping of a twig, the smell of African ganja, or the odor of a body that lived on rice and nouc man sauce to drift to them slowly on a jungle breeze. These came alive as with practiced hands they gently moved safety switches over to fire, their fingers taking up the slack on the triggers.

These were the ones who hid themselves in everyday civilian life, laughing at shallow jokes, trying to avoid becoming trapped in the world of making a living, going out on a Saturday night and getting drunk with the boys and talking about the job or the boss, then stumbling home to a wife whose biggest concern was whether he'd been fucking around on her or not.

But if he was really lucky, at least once more he would have the chance to feel the rush of adrenaline to his heart, the quickening of breath and reflexes that responded to the smell of cordite hanging on the morning mist. For them, that was the real world. The other one, the one they left behind, was only something with which they bided time until they could taste their own reality again.

If he could have advertised in the paper or on television Hendricks had no doubt that in the first twenty-four hours he would have over a hundred thousand responses.

There was no doubt he would get his men in the time required. He knew where to find them. He did need one or two special types, though. Perhaps Vic could give him some help on that. He did have access to more computer banks than Hendricks did.

THREE

OCTOBER 11

RESPONDING TO THE knock on his door, Anderson opened it. He found a bearded, heavily muscled man in his thirties standing there with a sealed manila envelope in his hand.

"Mr. Anderson, I have something for you from the boss."

That was it. The neanderthal handed the envelope over and left without another word. Anderson began to have doubts about the quality of people he was forced to deal with. They had no manners at all. He'd be glad when he could get back to D.C. and some civilized behavior. Well, at least they did seem to get on with things a lot faster than the military establishment. But then again, when you just work for money and don't have superiors to answer to for every minor item or request it was certainly a lot simpler. Now, he mused, let's take a look at what they think they need.

Going over the first sheet quickly, then the second and third, his face went pale. My God! What do they think they're doing? Restaging the Normandy invasion with the original cast? This is totally unreasonable.

It might have been unreasonable but he didn't want to go back out to San Juan and face Hendricks to tell him so. Therefore, as most good diplomats and politicians would do under similar circumstances, he called someone else to run interference for him and keep him away from the discomfiting man with the large ugly pistol.

"Hello, Victor?" he said, his voice dripping with goodwill. "I would like to come over and talk to you this morning if it's convenient."

He knew it would be. His credentials guaranteed that. But it was best to spread a little oil if one wanted cooperation from the lesser ranks.

"Fine. I'll see you at eleven, Victor."

At ten minutes to eleven he showed up at the front entrance to the embassy on the Avenida de la Reforma across from the Museo Popol-Vul. After showing his passport for identification to the Guatemalan security guarding the gate and having his briefcase opened for a cursory inspection, he was permitted inside the gate. Then, once inside the glass doors, he had to hand his briefcase over to be opened once again and then passed through a metal detector. This was all such a bore but he had been reluctant to show any other identification that would have established him as a State Department representative. It was best to go in as a private citizen and thereby not attract undue attention.

In the lobby, under the disinterested gaze of two marine embassy guards behind their bulletproof glass shield, Anderson waited for Vic's secretary to come down and get him. Also waiting were several Guatemalans hopeful for visas to come to the United States. Studiously he ignored them as lesser beings. Of course they wanted to come to the U.S. Anyone with any sense at all wanted to come to the U.S.

Three minutes after he had announced his presence by house phone, Vic's secretary came out of the elevator, greeted him tersely but correctly, held the door to the elevator open for him, waited till he was inside, then pushed the button for the second floor. Leaving the elevator, they passed another security point. This time he was passed through with no more than a glance since he was with Miss Morales. Guiding him down a hall lined with bulletin boards listing official policy and codes of behavior while in foreign lands, she guided him to Victor Broadman's office in the political section.

Anderson eyed her. She was a good-looking woman with dark wavy hair and gray eyes, a mature ripe female with lush figure movements to her hips that only came with confidence and natural femininity. He detested the thin stilted jiggling of most of the plastic, domestic girls Stateside who all seemed to have bought their cosmetics from the same Avon salesperson. Licking his lips with just the tip of his tongue, he eyed her with both a touch of lust and suspicion. She had a definite hot-blooded Latin look to her and spoke English with a slight accent. It never paid to become too trustful of local employees.

Claudia Morales could not have cared less. She had four more years to retirement and had seen his kind come and go. Four more years and she'd go home to Tucson and lie in the sun at her home in the Rincon Mountains.

Knocking on the door to the right of her desk, she stuck her head in the office and said, "Your appointment is here, sir."

Obviously she received permission to show the appointment in. She held the door wide open for him and he passed by her into the office. He had the strangest feeling that she hadn't seen him. The door closed immediately behind him with a sharp *click*.

"Victor. So good to see you again. I do hope you don't think that I am abusing your hospitality by taking up so much of your time on this matter, but you do know how important it is."

Victor Broadman did know how important it was and for once agreed. There was a need for something to be done fast. As diplomatically as possible, he controlled his distaste for Anderson, saying only, "Of course I understand. What is it you want?"

Anderson pursed his lips together, sucking on his teeth at the back of his jaw as he rested his fingertips thoughtfully under his chin. My, he is a bit testy today. He wondered why so many veterans who just happened to get a limb or two shot or blown off always seemed to be so terse. They seemed to think somebody owed them something. It wasn't his fault that he'd had a college deferment. If his country had called, he would have certainly gone into uniform. He'd always thought he would have been quite impressive in one. Though of course he couldn't have possibly considered going into anything so common as the infantry. His expertise and creative talents would have been put to much better use in, say, one of the Pentagon's public relations divisions.

Broadman sat waiting patiently for Anderson to collect his thoughts. He was one of those who always had to appear thoughtful, intellectual, as if it was a chore to find a common ground in which he could communicate with the less advantaged.

"I would like to say first how much I appreciate your help and cooperation in this matter. It has been most valuable and time saving, which of course is of the essence."

"Of course."

"I will have to say that your acquaintance does move rapidly and makes up his mind quickly. However, he has made some requests which are extremely sensitive, and I would hope very much that you might be able to assist me in determining just what they are and why they are needed. In addition, he has demanded that all equipment used by him or his men in this operation remain his property after it is completed. Is that normal for this sort of thing?"

Broadman avoided the desire to shake his head in frustration. "I don't know. You'll have to be more specific about what his requests are. But I, as you know, have been acquainted with the man for some years now. I believe that whatever it is he wants you'll have to get or else you'll have to find someone else to do the job. He doesn't fuck around."

Anderson winced at the expletive. Yes, there was a definite similarity between the two men.

Vic subdued a grin at the pained expression that passed fleetingly around the corners of Anderson's mouth when he'd said "fuck."

From his briefcase Anderson handed over the list of items Hendricks wanted.

Quickly Broadman turned the pages. From the inventory he was able to put together a rough idea of what Hendricks had in mind and the number of men he planned on using. "Get him what he wants. Everything here is justified and necessary for the job."

"But where can I find these items? You know that military equipment is not my specialty!"

Bet your rubbery ass I know it. Your specialty is ass kissing. Keeping his thought out of his eyes, Broadman explained to him as he would a child, "Don't make it complicated. I know that this has a high priority and the less people involved the better. Therefore I would suggest that you communicate with the JFK Center at Fort Bragg. That's where you'll find most of the items listed here and the people with the proper security clearances to help you transfer it without it becoming general knowledge."

Anderson still had a worried look around the corners of his fleshy eyes. "Oh, yes, certainly. I should have thought of that. But it would help if I knew what some of these items are. For example, just what is an RPG-7 and why does he want ten launchers and one hundred rounds of something called HE?"

Victor was beginning to have fun. "RPG-7 is the nomenclature for a Russian or Chinese-manufactured light antitank weapon."

"Really! But why doesn't he want to use some of ours instead of these Russian or Chinese things?"

Vic could not control the grin now. "Because they work better and are more reliable under stress conditions."

That offended Anderson. Just the idea that anyone could produce better equipment than the USA was distasteful in the extreme. Trying to keep his own estimate of himself up, he probed a bit further, eyes narrowing to show that he was grasping the situation. "But what could he want with a hundred of the rockets? And what is a C4 or laser sight?"

Broadman leaned back in his chair. For the first time in days the pain from his stump was far away. "If I may venture a suggestion, Mr. Anderson, I think that you should ask him. It's his plan. But I'll give you some sound advice. Get him what he wants. Don't question it. Make it easy on yourself, and a lot faster for Hendricks, and just turn the list over to the Special Warfare Center and leave it to them. I don't think there's enough time or need for you to go through a course in Soviet-bloc weaponry or demolitions.''

That made sense. He certainly had enough other things to do, and there was, as Broadman had suggested, the Special Warfare Center. That would simplify things. All he had to do was have the proper requests made by the Pentagon and that would put an end to the matter. It would be taken from his already burdened shoulders. Besides, he didn't even like the sound of the things on the list. They had a flavor to them that put his sensibilities on edge even if he didn't know what most of them were. Twenty Uzis with integral sound suppressors, night-vision devices, two thousand rounds of subsonic nine milimeters. And what in the name of God was a Kevlar?

It was too much. Broadman was right; his time would be better spent working as liaison and turning details over to subordinates to deal with. Then it would be their responsibility, and if anything went wrong he could then, with righteous indignation and total justification, put the blame on someone else for nonperformance.

Rising, he stepped over to Broadman's desk in a gesture of good fellowship and put his hand out to be shaken.

Broadman looked at it like it was a clump of fat worms, but he shook it.

''Thank you very much for your good advice. I shall certainly inform my superiors when I return to D.C. of your valuable and timely assistance.''

Vic experienced a tight grimace. Bet your chubby ass you tell how much help I was. There won't be anyone's name on any report but yours.

Out loud Vic said, ''Not at all. I was glad to be of some help. Good-bye, and good luck.''

His door opened. Miss Morales was standing there ready

to escort Anderson back to the lobby. For a brief moment Anderson wondered how she knew he was ready to go but dismissed the thought that she could have been eavesdropping. But then again perhaps she was. He would have to run a check on her when he got back.

Sometimes Vic wondered, too, how she knew when people were ready to leave. He'd asked her about that before, but she'd just smiled sweetly and said she was gifted.

FOUR

OCTOBER 11

BROADMAN'S RECEPTION FOR Hendricks was totally different than that he'd given to Anderson, the little ass-sucking prick. Vic was sure that he'd go far up the ladder of success. He had all the attributes, not excluding pimping for his sister if it would help him. Even Claudia was more open. She had worked for and with Vic in El Salvador for three years before his reassignment to Guatemala. They had moved under protest. State said that it was for his own safety. Obviously some of the programs he'd been sponsoring were beginning to see results, and that made him a target for the terrorists.

Claudia showed Hendricks into Vic's office, stepped outside without closing the door, then returned instantly with a cup of steaming rich Guatemalan coffee touched with a hint of chicory. Only then did she leave, making a small pucker with her mouth as she closed the door behind her.

Hendricks grinned at Vic. ''That is one hell of a woman.

If I thought I had the energy, I'd steal her and run off to hide on some mountaintop for the rest of my life.''

Holding his coffee between cupped hands, Vic sniffed the aroma. "Forget it, she'd ruin you. Put a dorsal fin on the woman's back and she'd put Jaws out of business. She's definitely a man-killer. Besides that I'd have to come after you to get her back and you know how hard it is for me to climb mountains. We've been friends too long for you to put me through that much effort.''

It was true they had been friends for a long time. Vic came from a family with a long history of public service, much of it in foreign offices and embassies. They'd first met in sixty-four in Africa. Vic had gone over as an observer with the UN forces. They had run into each other in a cane field outside of Stanleyville as they watched UN-sponsored planes bomb a village. Vic had always been a bit more cynical about so-called good works after that. Vietnam did nothing to make him change his mind.

They had shared a bit of cover as the "friendly" aircraft went in with a load of napalm. Vic had rolled over to face the young man in French camos, a strange patch with the number five embroidered over a flying blue goose. Vic recalled thinking that it was a strange emblem for a mercenary to be wearing. Beneath the wide brim of a forage hat his companion's face was covered with dirt and sweat streaks. The rest of his platoon of 5 Commando were taking cover from the eyes of the circling mechanical vultures overhead.

Vic looked at their weapons, mostly light machine guns and automatic rifles. "Well, goddamn it man, aren't you going to do something?''

"Like what?''

"Shoot the bastards down.''

Martin Hendricks had turned his grime-encrusted face to him and croaked out between cracked lips, "What's the matter with you? Those guys up there are on your side. We're the bad guys, remember?"

They were the bad guys in those days, though not all of the time. It just depended on how the winds of international politics and business were blowing, and they changed directions all too frequently. When they did, innocent people died.

From that point on they had somehow run in to each other at odd times wherever there was trouble in the world: South Yemen, the Gulf Emirates, Biafra, Angola, the Argentine, and others. Hendricks had grown older, too. Now, instead of being just another tough young gunfighter, he'd become nearly a legend in his own right. He had . . . what was the phrase? Expanded his horizons. Now he orchestrated projects in what some magazines now referred to as the private sector. For a fee he would put teams of professionals together to train and advise, and in some cases do the actual fighting. But he had always been careful about the clients he chose.

In those years Vic had found out that the American government, through intermediaries, had also put his services to work. Twice that he knew of it had been in hostage-recovery situations. For one of those jobs it had been he who had made the contact with Hendricks. His association with the whatever-you-chose-to-call-him—mercenary, soldier of fortune—was of course well known and established by the security agencies who kept an eye on such people and those in his own line of work. Eyes spying on eyes. Sometimes he thought they had his artificial leg bugged.

"Well, what is it you want? The only time you come

around anymore is when you need me to pull a string or two.''

Hendricks put his cup down. ''Now love, don't get your ass in an uproar. You know that if I hang around you too much several of your esteemed colleagues will start to think they smell something and from what I hear you have enough problems already without that. But you're right. I do need something if you can do it.''

''Does it have to do with the job Anderson wants you for?''

''Yes.''

''All right, give it to me.'' Picking up a black federal government–issue ballpoint pen from his desk, he waited to make notes.

Taking another sip of the aromatic blew, Hendricks leaned back. ''Not too much really. I just want you to find at least two men in the States who are combat veterans in good health that need a few dollars, like to travel, and also speak Shanga.''

''Speak what?''

''Shanga. It's a—''

''I know what it is!''

Placing his empty cup back on a table, Hendricks ran a hand, through his short-cropped hair. ''That's it, comrade.''

Vic groaned. ''When do you want them?''

''No later than one week from today.''

''That's not very much fucking time, is it?''

''No. But then I don't have much time, do I?''

Eyeing his guest, Vic hit the intercom button. ''Claudia. Could you come in for a moment please?'' His door opened and he handed her the slip of paper on which he had written Hendricks's request. ''Run this for me, priority one. You know who to run this through." It was a statement, not a question.

Glancing at the paper, she didn't raise an eyebrow, as if it were every day she was asked to find two black veterans who spoke something called Shanga. Maybe it was a new street dialect from Weehawken.

"All right, Martin," Vic declared, "it's done. If there's even one on file anywhere in the States I'll have his name for you, but you're going to have to recruit him yourself. We can't get involved on that level." There it was again. The proverbial *We*. Even Victor was victim to whatever syndrome it was that affected diplomats, politicians, and devoted company people. They had become part of something more than themselves.

He knew that Vic had long been bitter about the way things were managed—or usually mismanaged—in the diplomatic field and the military, but that did nothing to lessen his loyalties. If anything he saw himself a lone crusader out to bring some balls and common sense to the jobs he was given.

"No problem, Vic. You locate them and I'll go get them."

Vic finished his cup and then answered the blaring of his phone with a bland expression. "Yes, sir. Twenty minutes. Very good, sir."

"We've got to wrap this up. I have a country team meeting with the ambassador in twenty minutes. By the way, Anderson was here earlier today. I told him to give you what you wanted or you wouldn't play the game."

"Thanks, Vic. He's a bit of a bloody prick, isn't he?"

"You got it. Now get your high-paid assassin's ass out of my chair and my office and let me get on with what they pay me for!"

Hendricks laughed softly. "Yes, sir. *Zum Befehl, Herr Gruppenführer.*"

Vic pulled his body painfully out of his chair, escorting him to the office door. "Don't give me any of that old-time Nazi shit. I know you better than that."

He reached for the door handle only to have it whisked out of his hand and opened from the other side. Claudia stood there with Hendricks's hat and a smug smile.

"How does she do it?" he asked Hendricks as much as himself.

Taking his hat, Martin held Claudia's hand for a moment, admiring the strength and softness of it. "I know how. It's obvious to anyone with a lick of sense."

"You know? Then for God's sake tell me before she drives me mad!"

Looking first at Claudia, then at Vic, he said softly to the smiling female, "Should I tell him the secret?"

She nodded in the affirmative, a little tic of amusement playing at the corners of her red lips.

"All right Vic, the secret is: woman's intuition!"

"That's it? Both of you get away from me. I have work to do."

Taking Hendricks down as far as the elevator, Claudia held his hand before he got in. "I don't know what's going on, but take care of yourself. He doesn't have so many friends that he can afford to lose one." Then she kissed him on the cheek with warm soft lips, friendly and caring, and said, "And neither do I."

The elevator door closed before he could respond.

In his office Vic went to the file, taking out the documents the ambassador had requested. Gathering them together, making certain he had them in order, he wondered idly, as he had many times before, where Hendricks had acquired so many British expressions in his speech.

Then he realized that after all these years he still didn't even know where Hendricks was from or what passport he currently carried. When be broached the matter, Hendricks deftly changed the subject, avoiding any reference to the time before they first met in the Congo. And Vic let him.

Whoever he was, Vic knew one thing: At least he'd smelled cordite. That gave them a common ground. Hendricks was a good man and that was enough.

FIVE

OCTOBER 11

TIME WAS PUSHING. Even though they'd just started, he knew that every hour was critical. He scarcely noticed the ride back to the compound. His mind was moving ahead. Logistics, manpower, specialists. Equipment, transport, weather, terrain, training. What would seem to the novice to be a simple matter of getting a bunch of hard cases together and just going in and kicking ass was definitely not the story, though he knew that gathering men willing to go in on a job such as this was not going to present any difficulty. One phone call and the word would be out spreading like wildfire through the mercenary world's own form of the jungle drum. One would tell another and the word would spread. The problem was not in getting men, it was in getting the right men and having the time to prepare them for the job.

When he got back, Becaude was packed and ready to go.

"I will call you as soon as I arrive, *Chef*. I talked to the Dutchman and he is putting it together. I think that he keeps a computer list of people and specialties. At any rate he said he can probably have the men we wish within seventy-two hours. The economy has been bad in Europe and there are many looking for work.''

Hendricks went in to his office. "Good. I'll be moving out of here as soon as I get confirmation from you and Duke that you have the men. Are you ready to leave now?''

"Oui, Chef."

"All right. Take care and try not to get into any trouble.'' Opening his desk drawer he removed a stack of bills. "Here's five thousand for expenses. By the time you get in I'll have transferred another ten to your account in Brussels. Bon Voyage.''

Without further ado, Claude left Hendricks alone. He had many miles to go and didn't look forward to the trip. Jet lag always played havoc with his appetite and his stomach.

Sitting down, Hendricks once more went over the packet of data Anderson left him. There was so much to do but he had to wait until he heard from Duke and Claude. Until then all he could do was make contingency plans and finish up his job for the Guardia de Hacienda. He'd better take care of that right now. He got Antonio Sarda on the phone and explained to him that he had an emergency situation and would be turning over the few days remaining on the training program to the instructors and that he would most likely be gone within two days.

"No problem, my friend. Really, your job is done. I think that I could handle the rest of the program, which is nothing more than the use of infrared devices for surveillance. Do not worry and come home safe from where ever you are going. *Vaya con Dios, amigo.*''

"*Gracias,* Don Tony."

Well, that was taken care of. He hadn't thought there would be any problem. Tony was a sharp, energetic, good-looking man who went at his work with enthusiasm. He'd arranged for Hendricks to get the job with the Guardia. Personally, Tony didn't need much training. He had been to a number of schools Stateside, but as he'd explained when Hendricks asked him why he wanted instructors, "My friend, there is a large difference between knowing how to do something yourself and being able to pass that skill on to others. I am no teacher. That is why I need you. Besides, I have much work of my own to do, which would suffer if I had to take the time to set up the entire program myself."

He assigned the remaining instructors their duties, paid them off in full for when the job was over, and began his wait. In two days the input began to come in.

Duke first reached him at 1900 hours.

"Boss. I'm on the job and it's going down easy."

"Good. How many have you got lined up now?"

Laughing over the crackle of the international line, Duke replied, "Hell, Boss! The problem is who not to take. This place is like a mercenary's smorgasbord. The only problem I had was in finding the medics. But I got one. He's got a track record and has been operational in the private sector. Did some work for Schramme."

"Good enough. I'll call you back at your hotel. By the way, where are you staying?"

"I'm over at the Travelers Inn off Yadkin Road."

"All right. I'll call you back tomorrow at 1700 hours your time with more instructions. Can you fill the requirements by then?"

"I got 'em filled now. Twenty-five. All either ex–Special

Forces or Ranger types. I've had the medic go over each of them and they're in good shape, ready to go and go now. Most of them didn't even ask what.the money was.''

Hendricks wasn't surprised. Fayetteville had more than its share of veterans, a large number of which were fed up with civvie life.

"Very good, Duke. I expect to hear from Claude tonight or in the morning. Take care and don't get in any trouble. We can't afford to have you locked up right now. So keep control of your temper.''

Duke sounded a bit wounded. "Aww Boss. I'll be good.''

"All right, till tomorrow evening then. Good-bye.''

Breaking the connection, Hendricks next dialed the number given him by Anderson. It took two tries to get through; the overseas lines were busy. At 2113 hours he got through. The voice telling him the last four digits of the number he had just dialed had a stuffy nasal quality to it that said upper-class New England.

"1968.''

"I wish to speak to Mr. Anderson. Tell him it is about the hunting party he wished to arrange.''

"Just a moment, please. I will see if he is in now.''

Anderson came on the line in ten seconds. "Is that you, Mr. Hendricks?''

Dumb fucking question.

"Yes.''

"One moment please.''

Hendricks heard a thin buzz on the line and knew that Anderson had switched the call over to a scrambler.

"Now, Mr. Hendricks, I presume you have a progress report.''

A bit wearily, Hendricks replied, "Yes. I need for your

people to get moving. I have one team ready to go as soon as transport can be arranged.''

There was an audible pause on the other end. ''That is fast. You mean you have already found the men you need?''

''Most of them, yes. Enough to start things moving. Now, what about transport? You said during our first meeting that a safe area had already been selected for us in Egypt. I can have my first team ready to go in forty-eight hours. And I'm waiting to hear from Europe as to the other. But I'd like to get the first team on site as soon as possible. It's not good to leave them hanging around where they can draw attention to themselves. Men like these are just hard to conceal.''

''I agree completely, Mr. Hendricks. Tell me where they are located at this time and I will be better able to arrange their transport.''

''Fort Bragg.''

''Fort Bragg?''

''That's right, actually in Fayetteville.''

Another long pause. ''Well, my goodness, that will work out nicely.''

Anderson gave him a number on post, which Hendricks recognized as that of the Special Warfare Center code.

''Call this number in the morning, and when you're ready to move out the man there will arrange for your unit to be taken to Pope Air Force Base and from there to Andrews Air Force Base, where they will be transferred to another Air Force plane for transport to Egypt.''

Hendricks nodded his head. Maybe Anderson was a prick but the little bastard did seem to get things done.

''What about my special requests?''

''By good fortune, Mr. Hendricks, most of those items are going to be supplied from Fort Bragg. They will go with you on the trip. Some of the other items will come in later, but I promise you will have everything you requested."

"Good enough. Now, if you can give me the number of your contact in Europe and the debarkation point for that unit when it's assembled, which I expect to be in the next seventy-two hours."

He could almost hear the wheels turning between Anderson's ears."

"Please stay on the line, Mr. Hendricks, I shall be back in five minutes."

Hendricks checked the time. Anderson was back on in four.

"All right, Mr. Hendricks. Have your man call this number." He gave Hendricks a number, which he said would be manned twenty-four hours a day beginning now. The takeoff point for the Europeans would be Rhine-Main Air Force Base in West Germany.

"Very good, Mr. Anderson. When my man calls, he will identify himself only as Claude. Then I want your people to arrange the transport from our safe house in Belgium to the Air Force base."

"No problem, Mr. Hendricks. I think that we would also prefer to handle the transportation requirements. We are better able to get a large group of men across the borders with no problems."

That was it. Now for Claude to call, and he'd close down here and go to Fort Bragg to join Duke. He wanted to be on site with the first contingent, to get the feel of the men and the location.

At 1500 hours the following day Becaude called from Brussels.

"*Chef.* We are in business on this end. The Dutchman has done well by us. Do you know that he does have a computer system and takes a ten percent agent's commission?''

''Good, Claude. Duke called. He's ready on his end. Now listen and take this down. I want you to have all your people ready to go in two days. Call this number and transport will be arranged by the contractor.''

''*C'est bien, Chef.* By the way, I have also hired another medic. Remember Doc Smyth-Wilson?''

Hendricks smiled. ''Yes I do. And if he's available, by all means take him on. Did you get your money transfer?''

''*Oui, Chef,* all is in order and the Dutchman has been paid in full. I am now shipping my party in small groups to the house in Liège. I should be in residence by this time tomorrow.''

He hung up with Claude then immediately called to make his reservations to Fayetteville, North Carolina, cringing at the thought of having to fly the local airline again. It was the nearest thing to a kamikaze squadron the States had. But he would be with Duke on the flight to Egypt. Becaude could handle the European thing with no help from him and he had no doubt as to the quality of the men he would get. They would do the job.

His planning was interrupted by the clanging of the phone.

''Hello.''

''Martin. Vic here. I got some word on those bodies you wanted. It wasn't very hard to do. I know you wanted two, but I got you four. Our people already had them under study for their own use. Two of them are brothers. One is a bit of an asshole. He's been involved with everything from the Black Panthers to Save the Whales. The older one has been pulling the younger one's ass out of the fires for years, but both were in 'Nam. Right now they're on ice. The younger brother was caught holding some coke.

They were told the charges would be dropped if they do a special job. The other two I don't have much on but they're all under Uncle Sugar's thumb one way or the other. A bit of inducement for all concerned and they agreed to cooperate. So all I need now is to know where to send them.''

Hendricks gave him Duke's location and number. That was good. ''Thanks Vic. I owe you one.''

''Damn right you do, and come back so I can collect.''

It was coming together.

SIX

OCTOBER 12

PRESIDENT-GENERAL MEHENDI was not too displeased with
the manner in which he had been dealing with a very
sensitive situation. He admired his reflection in a floor-
length mirror with gold-dust backing. His uniform was
tasteful, exquisitely tailored, and done in the British style.
He wore a dark green tunic over a khaki shirt of bombay
cotton with a dark brown tie and khaki trousers tucked into
desert boots. A Sam Browne belt with a Walther PPK in a
polished dark brown holster set off the ensemble. His
decorations gave it just the right touch of color without
being gaudy.

He examined his face carefully. The jaw was still firm,
if a bit fuller than a couple of years ago. Pulling his lips
back, he showed his teeth, as he often chose to when
addressing his public. They were strong, even, very white.
They had cost a fortune and he was quite proud of them.

While the rest of his body was not as hard as in those
difficult days gone by, it was still well fleshed without
having yet gone to fat, though there was a promise of it in

the way in which his uniforms had to be let out every few months to maintain a proper fit. But that didn't bother him. A stout man was to be respected in this land. It was a sign of affluence and power. He like his women that way, too, well fleshed with large silky buttocks sleek with good fat.

All in all, he thought he looked quite fit considering the problems he had to deal with day after day. But that would pass. A bit more time and he was certain the Americans and/or the British would come to realize that he was in control.

Today he had responded to their demands that all of the "detainees," as they liked to refer to them, were to be taken to the capital airfield where they would be evacuated. He had responded to their pleas with an official letter stating: "Your request is not feasible at this time due to the unrest in the countryside. It is entirely too dangerous for any white people to be moved as the rebels, under their insane leader Okediji, are well known to kill, rape, and torture any whites who come into their hands.

"For their own safety, I, as head of the elected government of the Republic of Bokala, have determined that the best course of action is to keep them under my protection until the situation in the countryside has stabilized."

A very fine letter. But the more interesting aspects were the responses from Washington, D.C., and London to his request for aid, without which he could not for long guarantee such safety. He liked to think of his approach as the "Velvet Glove over an Iron Fist:" Most descriptive.

Turning from his reflection after admiring his many awards and decorations for valor, most of which he awarded to himself, he gave a deep lingering sigh. Still he was most disappointed with the reactions of his good friend Colonel Muammar Qadhafi. Of late he had been very distant.

He knew the colonel had problems of his own and there had been several attempts on his life in the last year. But he had not delivered the promised aid, only an occasional shipment of small-arms and rifle ammunition. If it had not been for that, he would not have been forced into taking the whites hostage. Instead he could have simply killed them all and blamed it on Okediji, as he had done in the past. Though there was no doubt about their fate if they had indeed happened to fall into Okediji's hands: They would have been killed to the last snotty-nosed child. About that there was no lie. It was the hard truth. Okediji was an animal.

To think that he had once sat in a barber chair while the man shaved him. He had let him run a razor over his throat. Mehendi shivered. The ''barber.'' That was what he was called. Now he used his skill with a straight razor for other purposes. It was said that he could literally skin a man alive with one. He reflected upon that for a moment. That would be interesting. Then he recalled the thin hot face of the barber when he had sat in the chair and cold steel had slid across the stubble of his beard. That had been long ago. Three years.

Well, the barber had come far. But the game was not done yet. Okediji was low on ammunition himself, and his men were growing tired of life in the bush, away from their wives and fields. If Mehendi could just hold out a while longer he would be certain to win. Then he would be the hunter and the barber the prey. He would run him to earth, no matter where he chose to hide. With money one can achieve nearly everything.

Money, what a warming thought. He had millions in his accounts in Europe and the Caribbean. There was probably enough there to buy the arms he needed to push the barber back. But to use his own money for such a purpose offended him. He had worked too hard and too long. That money was his and he would not part with it.

The Russians, Chinese, and Americans were giving weapons away by the thousands of tons all over the world. Why couldn't they put him on their list as well? Why was the world against him? Even the Russians, who were well known to wish a foothold in this area of the world, had rejected him. Indeed, he suspected them most heavily of supplying his enemy with some arms and supplies. And the Americans and British had deafened him with their constant cries about human rights.

That single issue, more than anything else, had blinded them to the danger of an animal such as the barber taking control of the country. All they could ever find to talk about was how a few miserable Luda villages had been exterminated for harboring guerrillas or for other treasonous activities. If they were Ludas, then they were all traitors, every one of them. They deserved to be wiped out. Once that was accomplished then there would be no more trouble in Bokala. They would be of one tribe, one tongue, one nation.

"Human rights." He snorted. What did they think would happen to his people if the Luda took over? There would be a bloodbath that would make his small reprisals seem totally insignificant. No! They never looked ahead! All they could do was tear at their hair and cry great tears about the poor mistreated peoples of the world.

Why could they not leave Africa to the Africans, who knew how to deal with situations like this? If one is your enemy, you kill him and do so in such a manner that others who might come against you would think twice about it.

His face began to flush with the passion of his indignation. Taking a deep breath, he regained his control. He had

to set an example for his men, and he did have some good
and loyal men. He gave his military tunic one more tug at
the bottom to set the drape just right. He was satisfied with
his image. It was time to go. There was much to be done;
the oppressive weight of government sitting totally on one
man's shoulders was most heavy.

"Captain Kelo. You may come in now."

The door to his private chambers opened. Through it he
could see his personal guard at their posts by the large
double doors leading to the hallway of the palace. That
door would stop a tank. It was his security blanket. Once it
was closed it would take hours for anyone to break through,
by which time he would have long since made his escape.
One should always plan ahead. What do the Americans
call it? Ahhh yes, contingency planning. He rolled the
term over in his mind again. It had a good flavor to it.
Contingency planning. He would try to find some way to
use it in today's briefing.

Swiftly Kelo went to his duties. He took Mehendi's
briefcase under one arm and then moved to stand by the
bedroom door at rigid attention.

Mehendi watched him with approval. A good man.
Totally loyal. They had fought together in more than one
campaign when Mehendi was on his rise to power. Kelo
had always been there, as he was now. Steadfast, solid, he
was one of the very few whom he trusted with the most
valuable thing in his possession, his life. However, he did
wish the man had more of a sense of humor or at least
some visible human weaknesses. It would have made him
more comfortable to be around. As with all of his staff
officers, he had put Kelo under surveillance more than
once.

The man was a rock. Neither women, nor liquor, nor
power seemed to interest him. He had even turned down a

promotion twice. Mehendi had offered him the command of one of his crack Askari regiments, a post that would have given him great honor and a chance to acquire a personal fortune. Yet he had refused it, saying he could best serve the country by remaining at the side of its leader. He wanted nothing for himself save that honor.

Mehendi almost shook his head. An incredible man. So loyal. When he had refused his promotion and asked only to serve him by his side, he had felt tears come to his eyes. Such dedication was rare and to be cherished. He had granted his request. Still, he wished the man would smile more frequently, or at least get himself a woman.

"I guess that we are ready, Captain."

"Yes, General. The staff is gathered, awaiting only your presence to begin the meeting."

"Very good. Let us be about it then."

Straightening his back to the proper military attitude, he strode from his room, looking neither right nor left. The double doors were open wide for him as he came to within two steps of them. The guards came to attention, unslinging their AK-47s. He did not acknowledge them. His eyes were straight ahead. Outside his quarters two Askaris in camouflage battle dress with AKs stepped to the front of him. Behind came Kelo with his briefcase and two more guards from his private quarters, their weapons no longer slung but carried in both hands at chest level, rounds in their chambers.

Turning to the left down the hallway leading to his conference room, he glanced idly at the wall where a series of pockmarks showed where his guard had once slightly overreacted when a major of the Air Force, who happened to be in the hall, reached into his shirt pocket for a package of cigarettes. He had not seen the approach of Mehendi and his guards. His hand had moved a hair too rapidly and Mehendi's front guard had cut him nearly in half from point-blank range.

The stains in the Persian carpet had been nearly impossible to remove. He had thought for a time about having the pockmarks in the wall filled in, then decided that they were a good reminder to the rest of his staff to move carefully around him. The two Askaris who did the shooting were both given promotions to the next rank.

The entrance to the conference room was guarded by two more of his palace guards. Like the others, they were in battle dress. Stamping their feet, they came to quick attention, presented arms, then each took a handle of the door on his side and opened it outward to permit his unhindered entry. The sound of men inside scrambling to their feet was clear.

His personal guard dropped off to take up positions with the sentries at the door until he came out. Kelo came in behind him, advanced to the head of the forty-foot-long teak conference table, and set the briefcase down where it was exactly center to the high-backed chair of the same wood as the table. He then stepped behind it, standing at parade rest, eyes straight ahead.

Mehendi stood for only a second, casting his eyes over his assembled staff officers. All were in battle dress with full decorations. That was good; he liked for his officers to set examples for the men. He knew also that the only armed man in the room was Captain Kelo. The pistol holsters worn by his staff were empty, the weapons held at the cloakroom.

Mehendi loved these moments when everyone waited on his first words. It was good to take his time and move from one face to the other, searching for nervousness, the trembling of a hand, or eyes that looked away from his direct gaze too rapidly.

"Gentlemen, I have decided on a course of action in which we have built in a contingency plan." There, he did it. He felt inordinately proud.

"Our opponent has, in effect, control over a large segment of the countryside. We, of course, know that does not mean he has control over the country. If a piece of land has only one man in it with a gun, then he is in control. And there are large areas where our forces have been pulled back to consolidate their strength and shorten supply lines. We are going to let this barber have the countryside. Little good it will do him. He will have to detach men for security purposes to maintain fixed installations, much as we have to do ourselves. By these means we will force him into a conventional-warfare role where we will smash him with our better-trained and -equipped Askaris.

"I have been saving our air force for just such an occasion. By not committing them too early in this struggle I have made him overconfident. We shall draw him to us." Rising, he went to a large scale map of Bokala.

"We shall," he continued, "draw him to us here!" Pointing to the map, his finger touched on the capital.

"By holding main access roads and selected strong points we shall channel him into places where our air power can be used most effectively, and our troops, who are better trained, shall bleed him to death from prepared positions. These outposts of strength, as I like to think of them, will give our men much more confidence. By this stroke I have taken away his advantages in mobility and will have forced him to do as I wish."

A rapid rattle of clapping came from his staff officers as they applauded his genius.

Mehendi smiled broadly, his wide face glowing with energy. He was believing his own words. "It is true that we are the best in many areas and have enemies, not only inside our borders, but outside, who give this barber aid.

"However, I think that I can promise you that the aid which we require will be forthcoming within the next five or six weeks. Have confidence in your country and your leader and we shall prevail. I shall pass among you copies of my plans for the next few weeks. These concern the dispositions I wish you to make of the men in our individual commands. They will be followed exactly."

Opening his briefcase, he handed the papers to Captain Kelo, who placed them in front of each officer before returning to his position behind Mehendi's high-backed chair, still looking stonily ahead.

Mehendi gave them just enough time to scan over the orders; then he rose. They hastily followed suit, standing at rigid attention.

"Gentlemen," he intoned, his voice soft and warm, "as you know, the door to my office is always open. If you have any suggestions or complaints, bring them directly to me. As your leader and your father I will see that you are heard and your words given the consideration they merit."

That was it. He moved out from his chair, not looking back as Captain Kelo gathered up his briefcase and followed him from the room.

Behind him the officers gave a collective sigh of relief. No one had been ordered arrested. As to bringing suggestions or complaints to President-General Mehendi, that was not going to happen. They had seen what the future held for the few who had dared to do so.

In Bokala, Mehendi was master. They were his dogs and knew it. They would do as he ordered even to the death. At least a death in battle was preferable to one at his hands.

SEVEN

OCTOBER 14

"AT EASE, COLONEL, be seated."

Lieutenant Colonel Bob Robinson did as he was ordered. Feeling very ill at ease, the symptoms of jet lag still with him, he felt as if his mind had been stuffed with Asyût cotton. Only hours ago he had been at his field in Egypt near the junction of the border of Egypt and the Sudan. Now he was at what was often referred to—and not always jokingly—as the puzzle palace, the Pentagon, in the office of the assistant to the chief of staff of the United States Air Force.

Brigadier General Alex Forbes knew the confusion going through Robinson's mind. He had sat in that very chair more than once to receive orders he didn't understand. It was always tough for a professional to follow orders blindly when he was a thinking man, and this job needed a thinking man who would do just that.

He studied Robinson's face carefully. He was glad to see none of the fanatic in his eyes. There was intelligence and a certain wariness, which was to be expected when

one is called in for a meeting and doesn't know the reason.
The man was tired after his long flight, but that was all.
He was alert, curious but patient, leaving it to his superiors
to broach whatever the subject was to be.

"Relax, Colonel, and help yourself to some coffee. You
look as if you could use a cup. I know I would if I'd just
made the same flight."

He was giving Robinson time to settle down, get comfortable, and, if possible, be a bit more at ease. It was
always better to have a man like this feel as if he belonged
even if he didn't know what the score was—at least not
yet.

After Robinson was back in his chair and had taken to
sipping his steaming black coffee, Forbes gave him his
briefing.

"Colonel, this is going to sound very strange to you,
but it is necessary. You are going to have to do a job and
work with some people that you may find distasteful and
take orders that you will not like. I know that I wouldn't."

Another good solid maneuver. Make the man feel as if
you were sympathetic to the problems you were going to
force on him.

Robinson tensed a bit. He'd been in a hot seat before
and knew that's where he was now, no matter how pleasantly the subject was being broached. Usually the more
pleasant the host the worse the job.

"I understand, sir." Not understanding at all.

"Good, very good, Colonel. That helps a great deal and
I appreciate it. Now here is what I want you to do. You
are to return to your base this afternoon."

Robinson repressed a groan at the thought of climbing
back into the cockpit for another ten-thousand-mile jaunt
in less than eighteen hours.

"You are to return to your base and prepare for the

reception of a group of men. You will clear all of your people away from them and put them up in the Quonset huts that were last used by our Egyptian counterparts during the training exercise 'Desert Star.' In addition you will have all of your personnel remove all insignia and symbols of rank or nationality for the time these men will be your guests.''

Robinson couldn't help it, he had to interject: ''And how long will that be, sir?''

Forbes walked behind Robinson to the stainless steel coffee urn and poured a cup for himself.

''As long as they are there. In addition, all equipment, aircraft, and trucks will receive the same treatment. No markings of any kind and no communication between your men and them. *None!* That is essential. Any communications or requests will be made directly to you by their leader. You will therefore have to keep yourself available to him twenty-four hours a day. He will in all probability make some strange requests. You will honor them without question, consider them as coming from the chief of staff personally, and you will not be far wrong.''

Robinson was no longer suffering from jet lag. This was something big going down. ''What about our uniforms, sir? They are clearly American.''

''Don't concern yourself, Colonel. By the time you return there will be a completely new issue of clothing for you and your personnel already on hand. They are not to wear, under threat of severe penalty, anything other than the new issue.''

General Forbes lowered his voice to a conspiratorial level. ''Colonel Robinson, we have selected you to run this operation with your staff because of your past record and that of your men. A good portion of this, shall we say exercise, will be in the field, which we feel should only be handled by the Air Commandos. If I could tell you more I am certain you would feel that a great trust and honor has been given to you and your men.''

Robinson felt a shiver run up his back. The last time he had been told that his group was being so honored it had cost him eight dead men and three aircraft.

''Thank you, sir, I'll do the best I can.''

''I know you will, Colonel. And rest assured that your efforts will not go unnoticed. You're about due for a review board, aren't you?''

Robinson agreed that that was so, knowing full well that the general knew it, too. This was the bait. The more they stroked you the worse it was going to be. Robinson felt a definite sense of apprehension.

''What about the Egyptian personnel, and will I have any written orders, sir?''

The general never turned around, but his voice took on a different tone. ''You have just had your orders, Colonel. Your Egyptian counterpart has by this time also received his. He will know what he is to do. You will leave him to take care of his business, which will be to handle external security and patrolling, and you will tend to yours.''

Robinson knew when he was stuck. There were some bridges not to cross. ''Very good, sir.''

Turning around, Robinson saw a slight flush rise above the pale blue collar with the silver stars on the tips, as if the general were slightly embarrassed by what he was going to say next.

''One other thing, Colonel. If any of our men should enter the compound being used by these people it could prove very awkward for them.''

''How so, sir?''

Forbes cleared his throat. ''They could be shot.''

''You mean a court-martial?''

Forbes's face was definitely a bit red now. "No. They could be shot by these people, and if that happens you are to do absolutely nothing about it. Merely forward the information through crypto channels to me direct and take no action yourself. I tell you this so you may realize the seriousness of the operation."

That was the first mention of an actual operation coming down. Goddamn it! What could it be that restrictions of this nature were to be enforced?

He knew now why his group had been selected for the dubious privilege of playing host to a number of unknown personnel. All of his people had signed the security act statement and had secret clearances.

Robinson stood up. He'd had about enough of being told what he couldn't do. "How long is this condition to last, General?"

Forbes ignored the vaguely insolent tone. "Not long. Perhaps two weeks, not much more."

"And you cannot give me any more information than you have?"

Forbes shook his head. The blood had drained back down into his chest now that the worst of the embarrassment was over. "Not a thing more and neither can anyone else here except for the chief of staff, and I'm following his orders."

"Am I to assume, sir, that neither myself nor my men will have any actual part in the operation."

"No, Colonel. You are not to assume anything. You are to do as you have been ordered. That, and no more. If there are to be any further orders, you will, of course, be duly notified."

Glancing at his watch, the general said, "I know you will have a great deal to do when you return, therefore I shall not detain you further. The commander of the guest element will be arriving at your post tomorrow morning and I am certain that you will wish to be on hand to greet him.''

Robinson accepted the dismissal. Standing, he gave the general a high-ball salute, did an academy about-face, and left the office. He went down to the third floor, where a staff car had been put at his disposal. It was to take him from the Pentagon directly back to his plane, which had been serviced and readied for a quick turnaround.

In one hour he was on his way back to Egypt to await the presence of the man the general had identified only as the commander of the guest element. What kind of fucking description was that? Was the man military or not?

At least he didn't have to pilot the fucking aircraft and would be able to relax a bit in the rear. The KC-135 lifted up, leaving the smog and confusion that was the capital behind.

He had the strange feeling that there were bigger and better vultures in the District of Columbia than there were in the region of the southern Egyptian desert known as Bir Misâha.

The flight back gave him time to try to figure things out. Several things bothered him besides having to play nurse-maid to a bunch of people he wasn't even permitted to speak to. One of these was, why the change in uniforms? That meant that the men coming in were not to have any visual proof that they were on an American installation. To continue that line of thinking, it had to mean also that if for any reason any of these men were questioned they would not be able to state for certain that they had ever been on an American installation. He chewed that over for some time and couldn't come up with any other plausible explanations. Could that also mean that they wouldn't even know where they were other than in some great desert?

He was asleep when they cleared Egypt's Alexandria Movement Identification Control Center and turned to a solid 180 degrees. Their next and last checkpoint would be at Al Bahrayn, then almost another five hundred kilometers to their destination, the strip built by Robinson and his men at Bîr Misâha.

The sound of the hydraulics letting down the landing gear woke him. He was back. Groaning, he strapped himself in for the landing. He already anticipated the moment when he would have to leave the plane and step out into the eye-piercing glare of the desert and he was suddenly thirsty. Shaking his head to clear it of the drugged feeling he had, he knew he had to be a little crazy. Maybe that's what it took to do these kinds of things. Maybe he *was* a bit crazy. If he was, he wanted to get treatment in a hurry, a conference with his favorite analyst, a square-shaped understanding gentleman from the hills of Lynchburg, Tennessee, called Jack Daniel's who specialized in cases of fatigue and Weltschmerz. That was one of his acknowledged weaknesses. Good sour-mash bourbon.

EIGHT

OCTOBER 20

HEAT HAMMERED DOWN on him in lifting, heaving waves. It was a monstrous sea washing over the desert in shimmering, rising undulations. Shielding his eyes with a hand he strained to see through the haze. The last batch was coming.

The light colonel from the air commandos looked at Hendricks with interest mixed with distaste and wished he'd had a sombrero on instead of his small blue beret, which, while quite dashing, did little to keep the sun out of his eyes.

He didn't know who these people were, and he didn't like being in the dark, but his orders had come from the chief of staff of the Air Force, and he'd obeyed them to the letter—if reluctantly. Though that didn't show by the amount of work he'd had done in the past few days.

Across the field sat three C-130s. Their crews had been sent away. The planes just sat there as if in storage at a boneyard or awaiting some distant resurrection.

Out of sight, patrolling the perimeters of the outpost, were a combined force of Egyptian light armored infantry and American paratroopers from the Eighty-second Airborne division with live ammo in their weapons and orders to shoot. They patrolled a twenty-square-mile block of the desert behind a perimeter of barbed wire and mines covered by electronic surveillance. Inside this block was a two-story adobe building complete with a mock chopper pad on the roof.

Sitting right across the tarmac strip was another mud structure which had the feel of an airport terminal to it, a small one, but he'd been flying long enough to know an airport when he built one. Why his "guests" wanted another one built when they had a perfectly good one already in service was a mystery. That was what Robinson didn't like most about this job, the not knowing.

A distant drone reached them from over the dunes. They were coming. Resisting the temptation to check his watch, Hendricks knew they were right on schedule. His people were always on time.

Splitting the haze, the wavering shape of a desert-camouflaged C-130 came into view.

"Very well, Colonel, let's get things rolling."

"Very good, sir." Robinson led the way over to the jeep with the same pattern as the C-130. Waiting for his guest to climb in first, he took the backseat and ordered the driver tersely, "Let's go, Sergeant."

In silence they drove over to join the four two-and-a-half-ton trucks waiting at the far end of the strip. The pilot had orders to taxi back there even though his approach took him right in front of Robinson's air-conditioned Quonset hut terminal.

Hendricks was greeted by one of his men standing on the shady side of his truck. "Looks like they're right on time, Boss."

Hendricks nodded back at Duke, who had lately begun to think about shaving his beard. Sand was in everything: his food, his crotch, his armpits, and his beard.

Robinson had done his best to be civil to these interlopers and to the man whose own people referred to him so casually as "Chief" or "Boss." Just who were they? From what he'd been able to see they appeared to be Americans. That they were all soldiers was of no question. But what kind of soldiers, and whose? Robinson was an efficient, well-ordered man who didn't like having unanswered questions when he was theoretically responsible for the results of their actions while under his jurisdiction.

He had even been ordered to give the lean, hard-faced man who had been introduced to him only as Commander Hendricks everything he wanted without restriction, and to keep his men at least one hundred meters from the small compound which had been erected for them.

That compound was patrolled not by his men but by these rather disreputable-looking people, and he'd been told quite clearly that if any of his people entered their compound without the express permission of Hendricks they would be shot out of hand, no questions asked.

It was difficult to control his curiosity, but he did the best he could. His initial efforts at friendly conversation with the taciturn, lean-faced man had been ignored. He wasn't exactly rude; it was just as though Hendricks didn't hear the questions.

Touching down in a cloud of dust, the cargo plane reversed its props and slowed to a near stop. Then it turned around and taxied back to the waiting trucks, the tailgate opening.

Still a bit pissed, Robinson moved to where the plane would come to a stop. He was there only to act as liaison in the event any of his men came too close to the operation or if the pilots had any difficulties. He was playing gofer for a bunch of hoodlums, and he didn't much like it.

The transport had barely come to a stop when a man with the body of a halftrack leaped from the open tailgate and ran over, head down to protect his face from the worst of the sand thrown up by the C-130s still-whirling props.

For the first time Robinson saw a human emotion pass fleetingly over Hendricks's face; then it was gone.

"Becaude, *ça va?*"

"*Très bien, Chef. Très bien.*" The two conversed in French as the plane came to a full halt and others disembarked in a mixture of civilian clothes with small flight bags from Eastern Airlines hanging over each of their shoulders.

Just what the hell was this? These new men were not Americans. As they passed by, ignoring him completely, he heard French, German, and several other languages he didn't recognize. They passed him so fast he couldn't get an accurate count on them.

Duke began separating them into the trucks, keeping a dozen back to handle the gear.

Without wasting any time, the cargo master and his men hauled bundles and banded wooded crates off the rear end, where they were quickly picked up by Duke's detachment and loaded in the back of the center truck. The flaps were pulled down and the men who'd done the transfer climbed quickly, without speaking, into the rear of the tail truck with the rest of their contingent.

Pulling himself up onto the running board on the passenger side, Duke gave a quick up-and-down jerk with his right hand. One by one the trucks started their motors. Swinging into the cab beside his driver, Duke took the lead heading off to their compound. The whole thing had been done in less than ten minutes.

Sticking his head inside the transport, Robinson yelled at the cargo master over the roar of the props, "How many did you bring in?"

The cargo master was already sweating profusely from his short time on the ground. His orange flight suit bore dark, wet circles around the armpits. As he signaled for the tailgate to be brought up, shutting him and his crew off from the outside, he yelled back, "Just what you saw!"

Robinson had to turn his back to keep his eyes from being blinded as the props picked up RPMs. Insubordinate bastard!

As the C-130 began to taxi back for its takeoff, he started to take down the numbers on it. He'd find out who they were. When the plane was far enough away that he could look without getting an eyeful of grit, he saw there were no numbers on it.

When he turned back from the strip he found his driver and his jeep were gone. He was alone on the runway. The small convoy of trucks led by his jeep were out of sight, leaving only a thin dust trail rising into the searing sky. Cursing those who were supposed to be in his charge but over whom he had no control, he began walking the long way down the strip to the Quonset hut.

It had been a long flight from Rhine-Main Air Force Base in West Germany, but the new arrivals were given no time to relax. Time was on them like a mad horseman. The first arrivals, the American contingent, had already prepared the newcomers' areas for them. Bunks were made, nametags on each of them. New camo uniforms of the French pattern were laid out, neatly folded on each man's bunk, along with a single olive-drab footlocker containing the rest of his soon-to-be-needed gear. They were given ten minutes to change and be outside for roll call.

Duke hustled the new arrivals along, using a mixture of French, English, and German, liberally mixed with oaths in all three languages, some of which caused an eyebrow or two to be raised in admiration. As soon as they had all changed into their new fatigues, he double-timed them outside to join the American contingent who had earlier changed out of their civies. This was the first time since they had arrived two days earlier that they had been permitted to put on their new uniforms.

All ranks stood to as Becaude marched to the front of them, wearing a web belt with holstered pistol attached it it, and called them to attention. Some moved a little slowly. He noted them, each and every one. Once they were lined up and braced to his satisfaction, he gave the roll call, last names only. There was one case where two men had the same last names. These were referred to as Jones Number One and Jones Number Two.

Once he was satisfied with their appearance, he did an about-face, and arms swinging as if he were on the parade grounds at Sidi bel Abbès, he marched to present himself to Hendricks. Duke was already standing to Hendricks's left.

"Sir, the group is formed. All present and accounted for."

Hendricks had also changed. He, like Becaude and Duke, wore a khaki shirt over camo battle trousers and bore a side arm. The men on guard duty were likewise in fatigues. These did not leave their posts. Becaude and Duke would brief them later.

"Gentlemen, I am your commanding officer. At this time the two men beside me are my seconds. Any problems or questions go through them first." He stopped to look over the faces of the men standing before him. He knew several.

"I am glad to see there are some familiar faces among you, men with whom I have soldiered before. That will make things easier for you. If you want to know about me, ask them.

"You have all been briefed as to the rules. At this time I will tell you little more than what you already know. We are going to do a bit of rehearsal, then we are going to do a job. Follow orders, move quickly, and you will have a good chance of coming out of this to spend your money. Screw up either here or on the job and I promise you that you will not have that opportunity."

Turning back to Becaude, he said, "You may dismiss the group."

Giving a French army salute, flat of the hand forward, Becaude whipped back around to the formation. He barked at them in French and then English.

"Group! You are confined to your barracks for the night. Reveille will be at 0500 hours. Be prepared for a full day's work. Dis-*missed!*"

Robinson let the binoculars slip down to rest on his chest. He had gone to where a small rise over a wadi gave him the only good viewpoint of the compound.

"Well I'll be damned," he muttered to himself, "I still don't know what they're up to, but I do know that the buildings we put there are for a rehearsal of some kind. But for what and when?"

Click! The unmistakable metallic sound of a rifle bolt being pulled back made him freeze in his tracks.

"Don't move a muscle, sir, or we will blow you away. Just stay right where you are." The voice behind him was steady, calm, and matter-of-fact. Robinson believed the voice would do exactly as it said and blow him away.

Quickly, professionally, a practiced hand relieved him of his own side arm and his field glasses. He had been through all the self-defense schools and might have tried to take the man, except he had said "we." That was too big a risk. He stayed frozen as the voice behind him spoke over a walkie-talkie. He couldn't hear the response, only what the man with the gun said.

"Yes, sir. I said, I have taken into custody a man observing our camp. Shall I kill him?"

Sweat streamed down Robinson's back. It sounded as if the bastard wanted to shoot him.

"No, sir. Very good. I'll bring him in." He prodded Robinson in the back and said, "Straight ahead, sir, down to the camp, and don't look back or stumble."

Once inside the compound he was shown to what he took to be Hendricks's office. He had never been permitted back inside the compound since the newcomers had moved in. Hendricks waved the escort off at the door.

"I'll take care of it from here. if you see anyone else doing the same thing, kill them and then call me."

"Very good, sir."

Robinson never did get a look at the owner of the flat, matter-of-fact voice.

Rising from his chair behind a plain gray metal desk, Hendricks stood nose to nose with Robinson.

"My bleedin' God, man! Are you a complete fool or do you simply wish to get your bloody head shot off? I told you the rules when I got here, and they haven't changed."

Robinson countered with, "I am an officer of the United States Air Force and commander of this base."

Hendricks cut him off with an acid, "Listen to me. You know where your orders concerning us came down from, don't you? Understand me. If you interfere with my operation in any way, I can kill you and get away with it. And if

I have to make my point the hard way don't think for a moment that I won't do it. I will, and there isn't a thing you can do about it. Don't take it personal. This game is outside of your experience. So there is nothing personal in it. I have a job to do, and I will tell you this—it is an important one. And before it is over some of those men you saw in your glasses are going to be dead. Do you think your life has any more value to me than theirs?''

Robinson tried to control his emotions. Reality had come home hard; he was expendable. There had been other assignments in the past where details had not been filled in, but those had been different. He'd had some feeling of participation, but in this he was totally left out and the men in this compound weren't like any he had dealt with before. He was certain now of what they were, and he couldn't understand why his government would give them such a high priority. But he didn't for a second doubt the sincerity of Hendricks's words.

Hendricks knew the frustration of being left in the dark and therefore he had some sympathy for the officer. He eased off a bit.

''Look, Colonel. I will say one thing, and that will be the last thing I have to say on the matter. When the thing goes down you will have a part to play, and in a matter of days you'll receive a full briefing. Till then, let's keep off each other's backs and just do our jobs. It'll make things easier for everyone, including yourself.''

''You said I'll have a part to play?''

''Yes, an important one.''

Mollified, Robinson straightened his uniform and adjusted his blue beret to the proper angle.

''That's all I need to know. You guys are going in on something big and I've been sitting on my ass since Vietnam waiting for something to do. Guess I can wait a few days more.'' He turned to leave, hesitated, then turned around slowly and smiled. "Thanks, Commander. I needed that."

"It's all right, Colonel. In this case we're on the same side. Sergeant Becaude!"

Claude presented himself at attention in the doorway. *"Oui, Chef."*

"Escort Colonel Robinson out of the compound."

NINE

OCTOBER 21

HENDRICKS REGRETTED THE necessity of keeping Robinson uninformed as to the purpose of his mission, but that would change soon. Robinson didn't know it, but he was going with them—all the way. It had been left to Hendricks to make the final determination and it had been made. He liked the air commando. As for his spying on them, that didn't bother him at all. In fact he would have been disappointed if Robinson hadn't made some attempt to find out what they were doing. The last thing he wanted was a bloody robot in a position of responsibility who blindly obeyed every order. That was one of the factors that had helped to make up his mind. The other was that on his arrival he had seen, among Robinson's small portable library, a well-worn, obviously much-used copy of Sun Tsu's *The Art Of War*. When Robinson was out of the office Hendricks had opened the thin book and saw many notes made on the pages. Good notes. Good thinking. He knew then he would take Robinson with them.

"Duke!"

The large form presented itself in the doorway of his office. "Yes, Boss."

"Get Claude. I want to go over the training program, and bring the file on the men who speak Shanga. I'll want to interview them later today."

"Very good, sir."

While he was waiting he took his dog-eared copy of the two-thousand-year-old book out of his desk. Absently he opened it. It fell open to the part where the ancient sage made the comment that all war is based on deception.

That was what he needed to give him the edge. The Shanga-speaking men were to be more than interpreters. They were to be part of a deception he had in mind, if he could pull the ends together. If he couldn't do it, the basic plan and the rehearsal would still be necessary, but they would have to hardball it then. He would speak to Robinson about his idea tomorrow. That should make the tightly built officer quite pleased. He smiled and put the book away.

A knock on his door.

"Enter."

Duke and Becaude came in, standing at attention till Hendricks gave them permission to draw up chairs and be seated. To some it might have seemed strange that men who had worked together for as long as they had and were good friends as well should observe this form of military courtesy. But it was a habit they had silently adopted. Hendricks was the Boss, the *Chef*. When they were not operational the formality was dropped. But when they were working they knew that it had to be used.

"Claude, give me a rundown on your men, any trouble-makers or problems. Those are the ones I want to discuss at this time."

"*C'est bien, Chef.* I think that we have been very

fortunate in our selection. There are, as always, a few who may present problems later, but I think they can be controlled. I took these men only because of the time factor and did not have the opportunity to search for replacements. However, they have good fighting histories and you know several of them from the Congo days. The first is Doc Smyth-Wilson, our medic. Actually he was a doctor once, but he lost his license for botching an abortion while drunk. He's not a lush; it just happened that once. Since then he has never taken another drink, but I sometimes think he is trying to find a place to die. The other possible troublemaker is''—his voice dropped in register and in obvious distaste—''the Czech, Alfons Dubric. You recall him. He was with Schramme.''

A furrow deepened between Hendricks's eyes. He did recall Dubric. Very well he recalled the son of a bitch. As Becaude had stated, he was good as a fighter, but he was also a sadist. He had not only witnessed it but had the word from men he knew and trusted that Dubric had on many occasions killed for the pleasure of killing. And worse, it made no difference if they were women or children. That was something Hendricks had never tolerated.

He and Dubric had met before, right after the debacle at Stanleyville. Dubric had tried to push him then. They had both been younger and of the same rank, though with different commandos. Dubric had been disappointed that his efforts to bully the smaller Hendricks had failed. It was even more of a disappointment when the smaller man had broken his arm, laid the side of his face open to the bone, and ruptured him with a knee to the balls. He had never even spoken to Becaude about it.

''Yes, I recall him quite well. We will speak later of the good Alfons Dubric. He may serve a greater purpose than he suspects if I have him pegged properly.''

Both Duke and Becaude wondered what caused the slight upturn at the corner of Hendricks's mouth. It was almost a smile, but it was gone before they could be sure.

The other men Becaude talked about were of minor importance. All they needed was an example to be set and they'd settle down and do their jobs well enough. The more Hendricks thought about Dubric, the more difficult it was not to smile. When Becaude had finished they went over the same ground with Duke. Not much there to worry about. All the men had good records and history. As with the European contingent, some he had worked with before.

When that was finished Becaude went back outside, leaving Duke with the *chef*. It was time to go over the training program, and the days were growing short. They would have to move and move soon. His last communication from Anderson had bordered on the frantic. Mehendi was leaning on them bad and there had been a report that two of the women in the group were missing.

For the next three hours he and Duke went over the training program. Everything had been condensed. The men would have no problems with the weaponry. All arms would be familiar to them. Hendricks began to break it down into time elements and movements. There would be two parties, one under his command, the other under Becaude. Each would have their specific missions to accomplish within a fairly rigid time frame. Tighter than he would have liked it, but there was no other way. His mind kept going back to Sun Tsu. *All war is a matter of deception.* He would have to bring Robinson in on things faster than he thought. He needed his cooperation on a level that went beyond simply doing his duty.

"All right, Duke. I'm satisfied; but remember, we don't have the luxury of time to do something over and over again. They have to get it right and do it fast."

Standing up to leave, Duke gave Hendricks one of his big grins and said, "I'll see they cut it, Boss. Trust me."

When the large, muscular man moved out of his chair there was an ease to the move that made it look slow, almost lazy, and Duke was anything but that. Trust him? That went without saying. Duke would do what he was supposed to and more, and if any of the men gave him a problem he knew how to deal with that, too.

For the rest of the day Duke and Becaude put the men through their paces. They even put them through some close-order drills, which most of them did not like, thinking they were beyond that kind of thing.

Hendricks went over the maps and photos of Bokala, the airfield placements of bunkers, machine-gun nests, and the weather reports. The drone of the air conditioner was welcome to him. After the climate of Guatemala the desert air sucked the vitality out of one. And it was hard to concentrate when beads of sweat kept collecting on the tip of one's nose and dripped on the papers one was trying to study.

The sun was going down when he heard Becaude call the men into formation. It was time for retreat. He would be interested in how they looked after their first full day with his two gorillas: Duke the larger one, a big-smiling, friendly, semitame grizzly bear; and Becaude, short tree-stump legs, long, thick body, and arms almost the length of his legs. Yes, it would be interesting to see how their volunteers were holding up.

Settling his pistol around his waist and adjusting the soft billed cap, he left the cool comfort of his office to enter the dry blast furnace outside. Before he traveled the hundred meters to the formation his armpits were already sweating and his eyes had small wet pools in the hollows. Standing in front of the formation he looked the men over carefully. Duke and Becaude, standing in front of their re-spective sections, had put them through the paces.

All looked as if they'd had the dog shit kicked out of them. Faces were wan under fresh sunburns. Salt streaks ran down the front and back of their tunics. He could see that several had trouble keeping their legs from trembling. They had been run hard, but not to the point of complete exhaustion. Hendricks wanted them bent, not broke. A man who fell out because of heat stroke could do him no good.

Among the faces in the front rank he saw several he knew well. Among them was the sour, pale, sweaty face of Dubric. The years had not improved his looks. He still had the wary look of a hunted animal waiting to strike out. No. Not a hunted animal, a scavenger, and a dangerous one. Like the desert hyenas. His small, weak-looking legs supported a massive chest and shoulders. The head was small. There was a deep ragged scar on his face left over from a bad suturing job, and he had pale, washed-out eyes too wide for their sockets set over a nose that had seen the wrong end of too many knuckles. All that over thin bitter lips. His most prominent feature was a forward-jutting jaw that also reminded one of the hyena. Their eyes touched. Dubric remembered. But Hendricks looked at him with indifference as if the Czech was beneath his interest. He let his gaze continue to travel down the line. He knew that would infuriate Dubric.

Nodding to his section leaders, he waited. Duke stepped forward one pace and called out, " 'A' company all present and accounted for, sir. Two men in sick bay."

Becaude stepped forward next, gave the Legion salute, and the same response, except in French. He had one man in sick bay. He'd have to check on them later with their medic, Doc Smyth-Wilson.

"You may dismiss your sections, gentlemen, then report to me after mess. That's all, dismissed." Doing an about-face, he strode away from the formation, but not before he spotted the look on Dubric's face.

Yes, Dubric might serve a greater purpose. If he knew his man, sooner or later he would do exactly what he wished him to do.

Hendricks, Duke, and Becaude ate separately from the men at the long Air Force–issue gray metal tables. They prepared the food themselves. Those who had cooking talents volunteered and cooked in rotating shifts. The rations came from the Air Force and were surprisingly good: steaks, gravy, potatoes, and canned fruit for dessert, with coffee or tea. And all they wanted. There would be no complaints about insufficient rations.

After dinner Becaude and Duke came to Hendricks's office. The drone of the air conditioner was gone. With the setting of the sun the earth chilled in the desert. Where during the day the sun beat at one like a smith's hammer, at night, because there was no cloud cover to hold in the heat of the day, the temperature fell nearly to the freezing point. It was necessary to wear sweaters or heavy underclothing to keep out the chill.

Sitting them down, he poured coffee, and they talked over the day's activities. He was pleased things were going well. There had been only the normal amount of bitching from the men at what they thought were demeaning activities they had long since learned and—most of them—forgotten. Duke ran the weapons and demolitions classes while Becaude put them through team exercises at the squad level. The men had responded well enough, though a little slowly the first time or two. That was to be expected since they hadn't worked together before. Give them a few days to shake each other out and they would get better.

They had to. Their lives depended on it and he was going to make that startlingly clear to them. They would obey and do it instantly.

At that point they discussed the unlovely Dubric. When Hendricks finished there were grins on the faces of both of his subordinates. Especially after Hendricks repeated Dubric's dubious history. They had the same regard for child killers that Hendricks did.

After their meeting he instructed them to bring the Shanga speakers to his office for their interview. He wanted to see those men personally and study them. Their roles were too important not to attend to them himself.

The Shanga-speaking troops presented themselves at Hendricks's office. One by one they were shown in. First was Washington—Andrew Johnson Washington. Like many first-generation Americans, his family had gone overboard on making certain their children had names that sounded American. He and his brother Robert K., along with Jerome Whitehead and Randolf Bone, were vital to his plans.

Washington was large, strong, and cocky. Africa had not been diluted in his bloodstream. Take his western clothes off and exchange them for a loincloth, plaster his hair into a knot with cow dung and mud, stick some ostrich feathers in it, and he could have passed for a member of any one of half a dozen wandering tribes of desert-fringe nomads. Entering the office, he smiled broadly and looked at Becaude and Duke at their desks going over the day's activity reports.

"Say, what's happenin'? Hear I'm suppos' to see the main dude?"

Becaude beat Duke to the punch by making a small sign with his hand not to correct Washington's less-than-proper manner of speech. He indicated for Jerome, Bone, and the younger Washington to be seated.

Duke smiled wickedly. "That's right, Mr. Washington." Knocking on Hendricks's door, he entered briefly, then came back out. He held the door open, still smiling but this time somewhat more angelically. "You may go in, Mr. Washington."

Washington sauntered past him with the loose-limbed, knuckles-to-the-front, swinging gait so popular among young American blacks.

Pulling himself into a more or less erect position, he gave a three-movement sweep of his hand which didn't resemble the salute of any country Hendricks knew of. He frowned as he returned it. Outside the office, Duke gave Becaude a V-for-victory sign and settled back for the explosion. Bone, Jerome, and Robert K. saw the sign and looked a little uneasy. Duke just smiled pleasantly at them and went back to his paperwork.

Going over his record, Hendricks leaned back in his chair looking up at the large black man, who seemed to have a perpetual smile on his face as if he had control of every game in town.

"Mr. Washington, I wish to go over a few items with you. Please be seated." Washington settled his muscular frame into the straight-backed gray chair in front of Hendricks's desk and relaxed. Making himself at home, he lit up without asking permission. One thing old Washington had learned when dealing with honkies was to keep them off-balance. Keep pushing all the time and they hardly ever pushed back. Of course that only worked with dudes who weren't from the city. If that didn't work, why then you just had to break bad with them, but this square did not have that lower-Broadway look to him.

Hendricks went on as if he hadn't noticed Washington's lack of military courtesy, but a very small indentation presented itself between his eyes.

"Mr. Washington," he continued, "I see that you were born in northeastern Nigeria and lived there till you were ten years old, at which time your family emigrated to the United States where you lived with other family members for some time. Your father became a naturalized citizen and changed his name and the family's to your current appellations. Two years in the Army. One tour in Vietnam. Bronze star with V for valor. Purple heart with two clusters and half a dozen discipline actions taken against you. You do still have a fluent gift of the Shanga tongue, do you not, Mr. Washington?"

Washington smiled widely, showing strong, large teeth set between sensuous fleshy lips.

"Fuckin' A, man!"

Hendricks rose from his chair. He, too, had the beginnings of a smile on his thin compressed lips.

He began to speak softly.

"That is very, very good Mr. Washington." He came closer to Washington, moving slow and easy. Washington began to feel a bit wary.

"Because, Mr. Washington, your ability to speak that unspeakable tongue is the only reason that I do not at this time have one of those gentlemen out there come inside and teach you some manners by breaking at least one of your arms."

Washington straightened up in his chair. Who the fuck did this old dude think he was? The street lessons came back. If someone broke bad with you then you had to break even badder or they'd run over your shit.

Coming to his feet, he attempted the tried-and-tested form of glaring at Hendricks while his body went into hostile position number twenty-seven.

"Say, what, motherfucker?" That was the end of the conversation. Washington found his throat being held between thumb and forefinger. Just the two digits, and he was being propelled against the side of the office wall, unable to do anything. The strange grip had taken most of his strength away and his mind was already on the edge of darkness. Hendricks slammed him against the wall and stepped back, releasing his grip.

In the outer office Duke and Becaude nodded at each other in satisfaction, then grinned evilly at the blacks sitting with nervous expressions at the sounds coming from the office and the sudden shaking of the wall.

Washington came off the wall swinging, coming out from the shoulder with a bone-crushing blow to Hendricks's face. Hendricks wasn't there. He didn't step back, just moved his right arm in a half-circle catching Washington's forearm and rotating to the inside. He then extended his own arm with a butt hand straight to the face as his right leg hooked the back of Washington's knee. In slow motion it would have looked something like the movement of a shot putter when Hendricks's butt hand hit Washington flush in the face, at the same time sweeping his leg out. The young black went down with a *whump* that knocked the air out of his lungs.

The floor shook outside the office and the grunt of pain and expelled air spread the grin across Duke's and Becaude's faces even more. Jerome, Bone, and Robert K. did not look well at all.

Trying to get up, Washington found he didn't have the strength. The fall and the blow had taken his wind away. Blood was running freely from his smashed nose and split lips.

Standing over him, Hendricks never raised his voice. He spoke softly, as though he were patiently correcting a wayward child.

"Mr. Washington. Understand me quite clearly, for it

shall not be repeated. The only value you have to me is your language ability. However, I have others with the same ability. This is not the United States Army. You have no chaplain or civil rights officer to complain to. I do not care if you are black, white, or have polka dots so long as you do your job. And you will do it, and you will conduct yourself professionally—or I will kill you. Now get off the floor, you look ridiculous. Go to the washroom, clean yourself, and report back to me promptly in five minutes.''

Painfully, Washington got to his feet. Looking steadily into Hendricks's eyes for a moment, he saw nothing there. The pale eyes were unconcerned, as the man's voice was. He had no doubt that Hendricks meant every word. It caused chills to run through him. The man would kill him and do it without hesitation because of his actions, not his color.

Leaving the office he avoided the questioning eyes of Bone, Robert K., and Jerome. Becaude and Duke ignored him completely, as if they had heard nothing. Gathering what dignity he could, he entered the lavatory to wash the blood from his face. Outside they heard the sound of running water. He came back out in two minutes. The blood was gone from his face but the swelling had started. His face had the look of a boxer who'd taken one punch too many.

Returning to the office door he straightened his body, gave two short raps, and waited till the voice inside said quietly, ''Enter.'' He did so and closed the door behind him. He turned to step two paces away from the desk, body erect, shoulders squared. He snapped a sharp airborne-style salute and reported.

''Sir. Washington, Andrew J. Reporting as ordered.''

"Very good, Mr. Washington. Please be seated and we will continue the interview."

Washington was inside fifteen minutes. When he came out he had a different feel to him. Going over to Robert K. he said firmly, "Don't give the man no shit. He's straight up." That was all. Back still straight as a Swahili assegai, he left the building.

From the office a soft voice called through the door, "Next."

TEN

OCTOBER 22

AFTER A BIT of consultation with Becaude and Duke about Dubric they had come to a decision: whenever possible they were to lean on the man, not give him a break. When he farted one of them was to be there to note it and bring his mistakes to everyone's attention.

Knowing Dubric from the old days, Hendricks was certain that it wouldn't take but a few days to have him climbing the wall. Which was good since they only had a few days left.

Hendricks kept apart from the harassment of Dubric. He was careful to note that there was not anything that one could have put a finger on to indicate that Dubric was receiving treatment different from anyone else. No, his harassment was being handled quite subtly. If he knew his man, and he did, it wouldn't be too much longer before it took effect.

Robinson came in to visit at his office, bringing him some reports that Anderson had forwarded to him. His temper was much better, and now he took an active interest in what the mercs were doing, since Hendricks had filled him in on the operation and the part he was to play in it.

"I have been given permission to contact the agent in Mehendi's palace directly. As you requested, I have arranged a meet with him in three days. We'll take a private plane and fly down," Robinson informed Hendricks.

"Thank you, Robbie." They had gone to first names now that Robinson understood what the game plan was.

"I would like for you to come around this evening for retreat and again tomorrow morning at 0600 hours. We're going to be rehearsing the attack on the palace in the morning, then later in the afternoon we'll do the airfield. I would appreciate your advice and observations. But please make certain all of your people are reassigned away from the training area except, of course, those who will be involved in the airfield raid. I shall have the team that is not part of the exercise placed on guard duty there. An incident this late in the game would be most trying."

"Okay, Commander. I'll be good and keep my people away. How long will the exercise last?"

"Oh, I would say not more than four hours. We'll naturally run through it several times. But I think you will find it interesting. There might even be an unexpected entertainment for you, what?" Before letting Robinson go he added one more item.

"By the way. Prepare yourself and your men for a run-through day after tomorrow. Of course that will be entirely your show until my people get on the ground, but I shall of course go along as an observer so I can check their time myself."

"Okay, Hendricks. See you at formation this evening." Leaving Hendricks's office to return to his own, Robinson pondered the meaning of "an unexpected entertainment."

And he still couldn't decide if Hendricks was a Limey or an American. He spoke English like an American most of the time, but then he'd drop in those Brit nuances, saying things like "good show and bit of all right, what!" Most confusing!

Back in his office, Hendricks, Becaude, and Duke went over the plans and equipment to be used, and—of course—the men.

"How are they shaping up?" Hendricks had his own opinion but it was always best to get input from those working closest with the men. He hadn't had much time to become directly involved with them these last days, though he would of course take his part in the exercises. And while he did not go on the physical-training exercises with the men he did rise before dawn while the chill of the night was still on the desert to do his daily five miles.

Becaude spoke first. "*Chef*, the men are getting restless. There is some grumbling, which, if not stopped, may present us with problems later. They are becoming a bit surly at taking orders. I think it is Dubric who is causing most of the friction with the men."

Hendricks nodded his agreement. "Duke?"

"Same thing, sir. The men are getting short-tempered. I have had to stop a couple of fights in the last two days. They're getting edgy. They still don't know what the job is, and I think that's getting to them, too."

Leaning back in his chair, Hendricks placed his fingertips under his chin and thought a moment.

"Very well. Today is the day when they find out, and I think also when we settle our difficulties with Mr. Dubric. Now let's get on with the day's program. And I will speak to the men at formation this evening to, shall we say, set the stage properly?"

* * *

Robinson stood silently beside Hendricks as the hot dry
wind and the last of the distant dust devils danced and
whirled, rising and twisting and falling only to rise again.
Hendricks looked over his two sections. He could detect
the sullenness in them. Moving his eyes slowly, he didn't
speak at first and purposely let the tension build a bit
more. He took his time, allowing his gaze to linger for a
moment on one man after another. Coming to Washington,
he examined the big black man closely. He held back a
smile. Washington was looking good. Head held erect,
back ramrod straight. He'd do quite nicely. Then he came
to Dubric; he lingered a bit longer till he knew Dubric was
getting nervous, then he moved. At last he spoke, the wind
carrying his words clearly to all though he spoke softly.

"Gentlemen, it is time to reveal our mission to you.
Before I do remember what was said to you when you
signed on. From this day no man goes back until the
mission is over. Today we will conduct the first rehearsals
of the actual job that has been assigned to each section."

As he spoke Becaude provided a simultaneous transla-
tion for the French-speaking section.

"I will also repeat for the last time that you are under
the Articles of War and here we have but one punishment.
If you think that after you have heard what the mission is
you would like to leave us and go home, I remind you that
we have your passports. You are in the middle of a desert
and the nearest town is hundreds of miles away with only
one road out. Around you are trained soldiers who will kill
you on sight if you try to run away. If you did avoid them
then you would have a long and very dry trip across the
desert. I doubt very much if you could make it to any
frontier. Therefore you are here and here you shall remain
until we go on the job. Only those who are too sick to
fight will be detained at this place till it is over. However,

anything that even remotely appears as self-inflicted to avoid this mission will be treated the same as desertion.

"Next item. There has been some complaining, a percentage of which is natural. From this time on there will be no complaints permitted. No grumbling in the barracks, no loose talk, and especially no reluctance to follow the orders of the men I have placed over you. You will obey, and obey instantly. Failure to do so will result in the aforementioned punishment being implemented instantly."

He paused to give his words a chance to sink in, and once more watched the faces. Some had a look of worry about them, but not fear. Dubric wore his usual scowl, which twisted his face into an even uglier thing than it normally was. He didn't like what was said at all.

"Now as to the mission . . ."

At this their eyes lit up. He could almost feel them leaning forward to hear more clearly.

"We are going on a raid into the Republic of Bokala, which is currently in a state of civil war. Our job will be to rescue hostages being held at the Presidential Palace. We have two sections. The section under command of Sergeant Becaude has the job of securing the airfield from which we will evacuate the hostages and ourselves. Look closely at the men who will provide our transport. They are the only outsiders permitted.

"Now, the section under the command of Sergeant Falger will be with me, and we will have the responsibility to effect the release of the hostages from the palace. Everything must be done on time; every man must do his job. This will be no cake walk, so prepare yourselves. You have, in the last few days, shown your proficiency with the weapons given you. I have allowed enough time for you to become used to the climate and to get to know each other. We have no more time to waste. We will go in very soon, a matter of one week, give or take a day or two. The details of the mission will be explained to you by your section leaders later. For now they will move you out to the training area. The first exercises will be the taking of the airfield at Bokala. Sergeant Falger's group will act as area security.

"This afternoon we will rehearse their part and Becaude's section will do the same. To date we have had dry fire exercises. From here on only live ammunition will be used. So pay attention, or you could get killed by your own men. Be sharp and stay alive. Obey orders and stay alive."

His voice slowly rose in power to ride above the winds, and like the winds it was harsh, dry, and merciless. The men shivered. "Especially, listen and obey me and stay alive. From this moment on there is no backing out. *Everyone goes!*"

Robinson had stood hundreds of formations in his time but never one like that. The men in the sections were a hard crew, that he knew, and here the man beside him had told them that if any one of them did anything wrong he would kill them. Robinson shivered, too. He also believed him.

Hendricks turned the sections over to their leaders to release them from the formation.

"Come walk with me, Robbie, if you will. I'd like to talk to you for a few minutes. By the way, you will have the aircraft ready tomorrow, naturally?"

"Of course. It's sitting on the strip right now and the jeeps are already loaded inside."

Hendricks nodded. "Good. We're going to take part of a page from the Israelis' raid on Entebbe, but only a part. Tomorrow everything will be done in slow motion. After that things will pick up considerably. I want you to watch the exercise because you never know. There's always a possibility that we won't be able to get back off the ground, and if you end up being stuck on the deck with us, I think you should see how we work.''

Dubric wasn't bitching out loud, but inside he was fuming. Who did that son of a bitch think he was? When they'd been recruited they'd been told that if they didn't work out they'd just be detained at the forward base till the job was over and then sent home.

He'd already made up his mind that he wasn't going to go in with them. Not with Becaude or the one called Duke. And he was especially not going to serve under the command of a prick like Hendricks.

He'd had just about enough of them and their tough talk. They wouldn't dare pull the trigger. Hendricks had never had the guts for that kind of killing. He'd always been soft.

His scar gave him a twinge. It was sore and red from the sand and sun. By now, with the passage of time, Dubric was convinced that Hendricks had hit him while he wasn't looking. That was the only way the stuffed prick could have put him down.

The more he thought about it, the madder he got, and the more certain that Hendricks was just running a bluff. He wasn't stupid; he knew the man with Hendricks was a regular United States Air Force officer. The Americans would never permit a murder to take place on one of their bases.

No! Hendricks didn't have the balls for cold killing, but he did. It hadn't been too difficult to get hold of some live ammo when they'd been out with those idiots Becaude and Falger. Perhaps now was the time to put it to use.

The idea pleased him and gave him a warm glow that

spread down his stomach to his groin. The arms room wouldn't be very hard to get into. There was only one guard and he'd be easy. Then it was just a matter of taking one of the jeeps and getting out before an alert could be sounded. As for roadblocks, he'd bypassed or shot his way through those before. He could make it out. Maybe the rest of them couldn't, but he could, and before he left he wanted to leave them something to remember. He owed them all something for the way they had treated him. Like he was a fucking novice. Especially that Falger. The son of a bitch was always over his shoulder pushing and cursing, mocking him till he reached the point that he was fucking up and making mistakes that he would not have made normally. It was all their fault; he deserved better.

No! He demanded a bit of pleasure before he left the sand flea–ridden place.

As Dubric was ruminating over his revenge and plans for escape, Hendricks was holding another meeting with the objects of Dubric's wrath.

"How many rounds did he manage to steal?"

"He has ten rounds of 7.62 ball ammunition. It took the *cochon* three tries to get it. I finally had to just turn my back and walk away."

Lighting up, Hendricks offered a cigarette to Becaude, but not to Duke: he didn't smoke. "Well then. I think it is about time we put our Mr. Dubric under surveillance. After my talk today and the expression on his face, I think it is about time for him to try something. Now, let's go over his options. Put yourself in his place, realizing the man is a sadist, a coward, and he hates us all. If you were that man, what would you do? Duke?"

Stretching his arms to pull out some kinks, Falger scratched at his beard before answering.

"If I were him, which I'm not, thank God, I'd be looking for a way out of here. And if he's got the kind of rat mind you say he does, I think he's taken that ammo to use here. That means he has to go after something to shoot it in. Then he'll want some transportation to get out of here."

"Becaude, do you have anything to add or contest with Duke's interpretation of Mr. Dubric and his possible actions?"

Becaude shook his head from side to side, moving most of his body when he did it.

"*Non, Chef.* I think he is right."

"Good! Then we will put Mr. Dubric under watch beginning right now and take turns until he makes his move, which if I am correct could be in a matter of hours. Probably around three or four in the morning. Becaude, you take first watch and draw the special gear from the arms room.

"Duke will relieve you at 0300 hours and I'll take over at 0500 till reveille. Tell the man on the guard nothing. Knowing Dubric, and I do, I think that will be the first place he goes. Having a weapon will make him feel much more comfortable. So put your watch on the arms room and don't let him kill the sentry. If it looks like he has that in mind go ahead and terminate him right there."

Dubric couldn't sleep. The excitement! The thought of revenge, of bullets smashing into the bodies of those who had persecuted him kept his body warm, flushed. Sometimes when he squeezed his eyes as tightly shut as he could he could see the rounds entering their chests and heads, ripping and tearing and exploding organs inside their body cavities. Twice during those times he had had an erection. That was something else. He needed a woman, someone to push himself into. Thrust and hurt. That made him feel good.

It was time, 0300 hours. Listening to the breathing of the other men in the barracks, he knew they were in the deepest sleep of the night. Sliding out from under his covers he dressed quickly, leaving the barracks in stocking feet. He closed the door gently behind him and put his boots on outside. Overhead the night was clear, as always. The stars and planets were as brilliant as if he were on the top of a high mountain instead of in the desert of southern Egypt.

The air was crisp and his breath misted in front of him. Rubbing his hands together, he moved to where the shadows of the barracks gave him concealment. The arms room was two buildings over, a Quonset hut with just one entrance. The guard wasn't due to be relieved until 0400 hours. That would give him plenty of time. Stooping to the ground, he removed an empty sock from his pocket and filled it with sand. Slapping it against his left palm twice, he was satisfied with the weight. The improvised sap would do the job.

Crouched over, he jogged from the shadow of his barracks to the next and stopped, listening for any sign that would tell him someone else was outside. Nothing! Grinning to himself, he moved around the base of the building, his boots silent on the sand.

He could see the sentry clearly.

He was glad that it was one from the American contingent. He had never liked Americans very much anyway. If he'd had a knife he would have had more fun this night. There was something indescribably sensuous about sliding the edge of a finely honed piece of steel across the warm, paper-thin flesh covering the esophagus. Sidling back a bit, he made a wide circle, coming up on the Quonset hut from the rear: His back against the wall, he moved with smooth ease toward his target. He'd take the time to kill the American, too.

"I got him. Right at the edge of the hut now. Get ready."

Becaude focused his infrared glasses on the corner. There was the swine! He could almost see him smiling in the green phantom haze of the night-vision devices they had taken from the supply room earlier as Hendricks had ordered. Duke had just come to relieve him on watch and held the powerful hand lamp with the special infrared lens.

Earlier Becaude had prepared his stakeout, scooping a shallow trench in the sand. He was well concealed and could be at the door to the arms room in seconds. Now it was good that Duke was with him. Between them they would teach the dog a lesson for which he was long overdue. He wondered how Dubric would face his death.

Dubric peered around the corner. The guard had moved to the other side, idly waiting out the hours, not expecting any trouble. They were, after all, on a secure base with both air commandos and Egyptian regular army patrolling the perimeters. He had half turned when he heard a whisper of sand. The sap hit him on the left temple, stunning him, knocking him almost to his knees. Then it struck again and again, pounding him down to the ground. Dubric stood over him, his heavy arms drawing back for another strike, his breath beginning to come in short gasps as he settled into his work.

Grabbing the young man by the hair, he raised the sap over his head and prepared to bring it down and smash the man's face. There was no hesitation in him now. He was going to kill him. His arm began its downswing, all the strength of his heavy arm and body behind the blow. The blow was never completed. Dubric hit the ground rolling, coming up into a crouch, arms extended, fingers spread. Duke stood there with Becaude behind him.

"Come on, hero. Come to me," Duke invited him. "My back's not turned and I'm over five years old. Think you can handle it, chickenshit?"

Warily, Dubric eyed Becaude behind him and the rifle he was carrying.

Becaude hissed between his teeth: "You have no choice, but we'll give you one chance, and one chance only. Take Falger and I'll let you run. Maybe you'll make it. I will give you a ten-minute headstart. That is your only choice. Other than that I will shoot you right now."

Jerking his head from side to side like a trapped animal, Dubric knew he had no choice; Becaude, that fool, would do as he said. But there was the chance that in the fight with the young American he could get close enough to Becaude to get hold of the rifle.

A soft whine, which changed to a growl, started low in his gut and came bursting out of his mouth as he lunged forward, fingers spread, going for Duke's eyes, knowing that nine times out of ten even a trained man will react by blocking or making a move to protect the eyes. Dubric's nose was pushed up, the nostrils split to the bridge. Duke had not stepped back; he had moved in with a simple front snap kick. He split the Czech's face open.

Dubric went over on his back and kept rolling. Coming back up on his feet, he didn't hesitate. He came on again. He would break the spine of the American. He knew his strength, he had snapped backs before. He hit the ground in front of Duke in a roll and came up low under his guard, his arms wrapping around Duke's lower rib cage. His head tucked down, chin touching his chest, he tightened his grip and the ribs began to move.

By the cold light of the desert night Becaude watched

the two men struggle. He wanted to help but knew that he couldn't. This was Duke's fight, and if Dubric won he would live up to his word and give the animal his ten-minute lead. Then he would track him down and kill him.

There was no finesse. It had come down to a matter of brute strength. Duke pounded at Dubric's head, great heavy blows which should have knocked a normal man out. Duke felt his ribs going, then one cracked. Dubric could hear it. His fleshy lips grinned with pleasure. The heavy blows shook him but couldn't make him break his grip. He was going to snap Duke's spine, and if he didn't he would make sure he would never walk again. All his life he would be a basket case and that was almost as good as killing him.

Forcing his left arm down, ignoring the pain of a chest that threatened to cave in, Duke tried to fight off the heat building up in his head as his lungs labored to draw in a breath. Forcing his left hand between his body and Dubric's head, he twisted his hand out of the way when Dubric tried to bite him. But he managed to reach above the bridge of Dubric's bloody nose and dragged his fingers a millimeter at a time, digging in with his fingernails till he reached the eye socket. He accomplished this slowly, ever so slowly, trying to keep his mind alive knowing that if he fell Dubric would at the least cripple him. His nails dug trenches in Dubric's flesh and he was there. Softly at first, his thumb began to press the eye with constantly increasing force. Finally he punched all the way into Dubric's eye and it began to swell under the pressure of the thumb. Dubric screamed like a wounded beast but he wouldn't let loose. Duke dug in deeper and the eye burst, splattering out of its socket and spurting the lens out onto Duke's tunic. It stuck there, a clear plastic-looking thing covered with bloody jell.

Dubric could not hold on any longer; his grip weakened. Duke came down with his free arm and broke the grip, chopping at the bridge of Dubric's split nose. Then he angled his arm so it formed a cross-bar across Dubric's Adam's apple and locked on his other forearm, the thumb still in the eye socket, his fingers locking the grip by holding the back of Dubric's skull. He applied even more pressure, strangling Dubric, pushing him down to his knees, the muscles in his back swelling to the bursting point as he began to turn the Czech's head. He twisted it to an awkward angle where one more inch would have allowed him to hear the pleasing sound of Dubric's neck breaking.

"Stop!" Becaude moved in. "Stop!" he repeated. "The *chef* wants him alive. It will be better then."

The words sank in. Reluctantly Duke eased off, letting Dubric's hulking form slide to the sand. His mouth open, gasping for air the Czech sucked small grains of sand into his mouth as his lungs labored for oxygen.

Standing over him, Duke couldn't resist the temptation; he gave Dubric a great kick in the balls as he lay facedown. Dubric sucked in a mouthful of sand as he tried to breath in enough air to be able to scream again. He never noticed the crowd of faces that had gathered around him. Not even that of Hendricks, who stood to one side with a knowing smile on his face.

Yes, indeed. Dubric would serve a greater purpose in the morning.

ELEVEN

OCTOBER 23

Dubric was kept under guard by Duke and Becaude the rest of the night. Before leaving for reveille they turned him over to the man he'd sapped, knowing that he was probably the best suited temperamentally to make certain that the Czech didn't get away.

Electric tension ran among the men like a physical force. Hendricks ignored it. He made no reference to the previous night's disturbance, which bothered them even more. After releasing them to their section leaders for the day's training exercises, he and Robinson, who had come over for the formation, took his jeep over to the airstrip.

They arrived a few minutes before the men, who were double-timed over by Becaude and Duke. Hendricks drove all around the strip. The building that would simulate the terminal at Bokala was ready. Extra panels of plywood had been added at strategic points to give it the proper shape. Two C-130s were parked on the strip, one at the far end and the other in front of the terminal. Around the site were other simulated positions: machine-gun bunkers, mortar pits, pillboxes; man-sized silhouettes were placed at all of these objectives.

"I hear you had some kind of a problem with one of your men last night. Was it very serious?"

Hendricks nodded his head, "Yes, but nothing we can't deal with. All of that will be taken care of shortly."

"What are you going to do with him? Keep him in isolation till the mission is over?"

That same small half grin quickly touched the corners of Hendricks's mouth and then was gone.

"Oh, I think I can promise you that he won't give us any more trouble."

Turning across the strip to meet the arriving sections, Robinson suddenly had an uneasy feeling. He couldn't put his finger on it, but he knew that something was not being said.

Accepting the salutes of Becaude and Duke, Hendricks turned to face the soldiers. "Very good, gentlemen," he addressed the entire section, "this is the first exercise. On the strip you see a mockup of the terminal and enemy emplacements at Bokala. Sergeant Becaude will brief you on your duties and objectives. Then we will have a runthrough."

Turning to Duke, he said, "Take your men and place them on roving patrol, with special attention to anyplace where the strip could be put under observation. If you or your men come across anyone—I repeat, anyone—inside the restricted area, take them prisoner if it's not too much trouble. But don't hesitate to kill them if it appears they have any chance of getting away from you. That is all. Section leaders take over!"

Duke double-timed his men out of sight, leaving the strip to Becaude and his section. Becaude took over. Gathering his men around him, he unfolded a large map on the sand and began to explain the different objectives and the time element in which they would have to be taken. Robinson heard a couple of laughs at one point and wondered what they found so funny.

"What's going on over there? I wouldn't think this was a laughing matter," he said, turning to Hendricks.

Hendricks chuckled. "I think you might even find it a bit amusing when you see what I have planned."

Finishing his briefing, Becaude assigned his squad leaders, gave them their final instructions, and then trotted them onto the field and inside the transport aircraft.

Hendricks and Robinson walked to the center of the strip where they would be between the two detachments, the one at the far end of the strip and the other in front of the terminal. Checking his watch, Hendricks removed a police whistle from his breast pocket and held it ready between his teeth as he waited for the second hand to complete its sweep. When it touched zero he blew a single ear-piercing shrill. From the far end two jeeps trundled out with their crews moving slowly onto the sun-baked strip. They seemed unsure of where to go. Then men began filing out in a slow ragged formation from the transport in front of the terminal as commands were shouted at them by their new squad leaders.

Robinson shook his head in confusion. What were they trying to do? It looked as if they were going through a series of facing movements, but not with any great expertise. The whole thing, even if he didn't know what was going on, was incredibly sloppy looking, and some of them were laughing and obviously playing grab-ass. Hendricks watched for only a few seconds, then blew the whistle again, bringing a halt to their activities.

The whistle blew twice more, and Becaude responded by gathering both groups together and marching them to where Hendricks and Robinson waited. Wiping his brow with a handkerchief, Hendricks watched Robinson, knowing the man was totally confused. That was all right. He knew what he was doing.

Becaude called the formation to a halt and stood them to attention. Moving away from Robinson, Hendricks spoke to them in a kind and understanding voice.

"It appears that you have not fully understood your orders. Therefore Sergeant Becaude will go over them once more. Inform me when you have done so, Sergeant. That is all."

He turned away from them and went back to Robinson. The temperature was rising to incredible levels on the strip. Heat rose and danced in shimmering waves.

"Commander Hendricks. Just what the fuck are you doing? This looks like a cartoon operation. I thought you people were supposed to be professional. Shit, a troop of Boy Scouts could move better."

"Patience Colonel Robinson, patience. All will be well."

Robinson muttered to himself. The man was impossible. He began to have grave doubts about his mind and his capabilities and whether he really wanted to go on an operation with someone like him.

As they waited, he saw Becaude unfold his large map and once more begin to explain to the squad leaders their assignments and the purpose of their mission. He used a calm, quiet, patient voice as he went over the details. Robinson saw the squad leaders' heads bob up and down at points but there were still a few laughs coming from the troops. These were apparently not noticed by either Hendricks or Becaude. After a few more minutes Becaude put the men back into ranks and reported to Hendricks.

"Sir, as you have instructed, I have once more gone over the plans with my squad leaders and men."

"Thank you, Sergeant." Hendricks strode the few steps to where he could be in front of the assembly.

"Sergeant Becaude has assured me that he has given you a clear and concise picture of the operation." He locked eyes on the new squad leaders. "Did you gentlemen," he inquired gently, "understand Sergeant Becaude's instructions fully?"

They looked a bit nervous but all responded with a hesitant "Yes sir."

"Good, very good." He then addressed the whole assembly. "And do you men know what is required of you? Do you have any questions as to your orders?"

There was no response from the ranks.

"Very well, then I will have to assume that all of you present here know what is expected of you. Carry on, Sergeant."

Once more they were separated and placed into their respective aircraft. Robinson watched intently. Hendricks waited for the sweep hand on his watch and blew his whistle as he had before. Once more the men came out, sloppier than the first time in spite of the efforts of some of those who had served with Hendricks before to keep them in line. The jeeps trundled out, one each going to either side of the aircraft. The men with them were joking with the drivers, and the soldier manning the 106-mm recoilless rifle in the left-hand jeep was swinging the barrel, trying to hit the driver in the head with it. Those coming out of the terminal aircraft were even worse. This time the grab-ass was obviously spreading as the men jostled each other and laughed out loud, refusing to stay in step as the squad leaders halfheartedly called out orders.

As before, Hendricks did not let them complete the exercise before blowing his whistle. This time he blew it three times.

Robinson was getting mad. He was a professional soldier, and what he was watching was an abortion.

"My god, man! Don't these people have any control at all? Even if they don't know why they're doing this they could do better than that. How are you going to get any discipline into them?"

The smile came back to Hendricks's face in full this time as he looked over Robinson's shoulder.

"Oh, I think I will be able to manage that in just a few moments. Just remember your Sun Tsu."

Robinson shook his head. What the fuck did Sun Tsu have to do with any of this? He couldn't relate anything in *The Art of War* to what he was watching now.

Following Hendricks's gaze, he turned around to see Dubric, hands bound behind his back with baling wire, being brought across the field by the man he had sapped. Dubric's escort had a bayonet on the end of an FN assault rifle and looked as if he wanted to use it. At the same time Becaude had once more formed his section up and marched them to where they stood at attention waiting.

They, too, saw Dubric. The grab-ass came to an abrupt halt as a murmur spread among the troops. For the first time Becaude raised his voice, roaring so loud it was stunning, shocking the men into immediate silence.

"Silence, you pigs! The next man that speaks without permission will have an interview with me after the formation."

Dubric's escort had obviously been briefed. He placed the Czech three feet away from Hendricks's pistol side and waited slightly to the rear, his finger on the trigger of the FAL, his knuckles just barely white.

The heat was oppressive. Hendricks scanned the men slowly, taking his time.

"This man has been found guilty of several offenses.

First: attempted desertion. Second: assaulting one of his fellow soldiers with the intent to kill. Third: concealing ammunition and attempting to steal a firearm. He has been found guilty on all three counts.''

Robinson watched the scenario. As if in slow motion, Hendricks's hand went to his pistol holster. Opening the flap, he removed the 9-mm Browning, smoothly jacked a round into the chamber, and slowly raised the weapon to three inches from Dubric's temple. Then came the abrupt ear-slapping report from the sudden sharp explosion of a shot being fired into Dubric's head, half blowing it off. Brains and blood flew for twenty feet in a fine red spraying mist.

Robinson saw Dubric's head expand. It swelled up, then deflated as the hollow-pointed round entered his brain and splintered, transmitting kinetic energy into what was hundreds of pounds inside the skull. Dubric's remaining eye burst from its socket to hang limp and sticky on his cheek. All of this took what seemed like an eternity. Even when Dubric's body collapsed on the heated strip it went crumbling down ever so slowly, the legs quivering.

Then it was over. Everything was back in the real-time frame of reality and Hendricks was not even looking at the body. He was once more speaking to the men.

''I have told you that there is only one way out of here and Mr. Dubric has just found it. I will no longer tolerate any insubordination or slackness on anyone's part and for any failure there is only one punishment. You have just witnessed it.'' The assembled sections were holding their collective breaths, faces pale despite their sunburns. The older men grinned grimly. They knew Hendricks had made his point. It would go well now.

''Gentlemen''—his voice was no more excited or louder than it had been before—''if a group of soldiers have been given instructions to follow and the first time they fail to do them properly, it may be the fault of the commander. Perhaps he did not make his desires clear enough. Therefore he should give the instructions to his men again. If the men still fail to perform even after their squad leaders have repeated the instructions, then the fault is theirs.'' He put the pistol back in its holster and buttoned down the flap.

''The only things that I might hate more than a man who would attack his own comrades or try to desert his own command are those who are intentionally inept. I will not tolerate slackness any more than I have the actions of the recently deceased Mr. Dubric. The responsibility is yours, gentlemen. Make up your minds. Sergeant Becaude and I will be anxiously waiting to analyze your next performance, so that we may determine with whom the problem lies. Sergeant Becaude, carry on.''

Robinson's tongue couldn't work. During Hendricks's speech he had been dumbfounded and shocked. The man had just murdered one of his own men to make a point. After formation was dismissed and Becaude made them pass by, in single file, the draining body of Dubric, Robinson finally found his tongue.

''You crazy goddamned murderer. What the hell are you? Who the hell do you think you are? Judge, jury, and executioner! Do you know what you have just done? This is a United States Air Force installation and you have committed murder. I'll see that you're brought up on—'' Robinson never got out the word ''charges'' before he was looking down the suddenly incredibly large bore of Hendricks's pistol.

''Don't you ever speak to me like that until you know the facts, Colonel. Understand that I don't give a bloody shit whose base this is. I am not part of your armed forces and your rules do not apply to me or the men in my command. And yes, I *am* the judge, jury, and the executioner.''

Robinson found it impossible to pull his eyes away from the pistol bore, which was centered on his forehead right at the junction between the bridge of his nose and his eyes. He could almost feel the touch of the steel.

''The man I have just executed—not murdered, executed—attempted to desert. He tried to kill one of the other men in the process and steal weapons which I am sure he would have used to try to kill me or Becaude or Duke. Understand me clearly because I will not repeat myself. This is a military command, we are at war, and the rules and Articles of War apply. And I will enforce those rules. I have neither the time nor the luxury to put together a formal court-martial with attorney and ceremony. The man was guilty and he has been punished, as is my right. I am responsible for the lives of many others. His death has served to make as you say my 'Point' with the others, and because of that some of them may not die. They will obey and do their duty. They know Dubric was guilty, they know he deserved what he got. In a day or two the shock will go away and all that will be left is the sure and certain knowledge that I mean what I say. Go back, read your Sun Tsu, Colonel. Remember the basic laws of certain reward and certain punishment. They applied two thousand years ago and they apply today. And never, never speak to me that way again unless you're willing to pay the price!''

TWELVE

OCTOBER 23

IT WAS HARD not to look down at Dubric's body. The faint
metallic smell of copper hung on the air. The blood was
already thick and syrupy looking. From nowhere the flies
came gathering in several great black moving clots on the
corpse. Hendricks ignored the cadaver. Dubric had served
his purpose; he was no longer of any interest.

Robinson walked away from Hendricks fuming, frus-
trated, and a bit frightened, which angered him even more.
He had, in his time, killed men, but not like this. He knew
now what Hendricks had been talking about earlier. The
man had planned to kill Dubric even before he had done
anything. It was a cold, calculated move, designed to
inflict an element of fear on the other men. It worked.

Refusing to admit a personal defeat, he remained at the
field and observed the rest of the day's exercises. He still
had a job to do.

It was with a degree of chagrin that he saw that Hendricks's prediction and the philosophy of Sun Tsu were
both correct. The next time the men came out of the

transport aircraft they came out quick and smart. No grab-ass, no fucking around at all. The jeeps went into their positions quickly. The men behind the recoilless rifles were intent at their pieces. Those in front of the terminal went through their facing movements like a military school's marching team. Hendricks stood, back straight. Only the dark patch of sweat running the length of the back of his shirt gave any indication that the man was even human. He stood like stone with his stopwatch.

The rest of the day was the same. Three more times they went through the exercise. He did see what Hendricks had in mind for the marching team in front of the terminal, and wondered if it had any chance of working.

When Hendricks released the formation to return to their barracks the men had a strange look to them. Their faces were flushed not from the heat but from excitement. They had begun to pick up on their rhythm. As with all profes-sionals, they felt better about themselves when they worked as a team and knew instinctively when they were doing it right.

Even the men who went through the strange maneuvers in front of the terminal had the same excitement to them. Hendricks felt the death of Dubric was already receding in their minds. He saw their faces as they snuck glances as they passed him. The eyes did not show hate as he would have expected, or even fear. They held respect. Several of them nodded their heads as if for the first time acknowl-edging him as their leader.

Robinson left the field to return to the sanctuary of his headquarters where things were at least normal, familiar. He spent the rest of that evening trying to piece things together. Not just about Hendricks but about himself also. He did send a signal to General Forbes apprising him of the day's occurrence. That was procedure. He didn't think the general or any of his superiors would do anything about it. After all, what did they really care about whether a group of hired killers, as they considered them, did one of their own number in? It was no loss; neither was it a problem unless they recognized it as such.

It was nearly 2200 hours when he answered the knock on his door, stepping back to admit Hendricks.

"Come in." His greeting was short, his welcome curt. If Hendricks noticed it he didn't react.

Hendricks waited until years of habit and conditioning forced Robinson to offer his guest a chair. Only then did he sit, taking his cap off and setting it on Robinson's desk.

"Colonel Robinson. I think that we need to talk this thing out if we are to work together. We come from different worlds, and only the fact that we use weapons gives us any common ground. Our philosophies are obviously from different schools."

Robinson opened his desk drawer and took out a bottle of Jack Daniel's. He poured two glasses slowly, giving himself time to arrange his thoughts.

"All right, Commander, suppose you tell me the difference."

Hendricks took the glass of sour-mash whiskey, sniffed the sweetness of it, and took a small sip.

"Very well, I will. You are part of a great institution. Behind you and in front of you you have regulations and the support of one of the greatest powers in the world. You have, if I may say so, a great organization which is not unlike some of the major corporations in the world. You have security, hospitalization, retirement plans, the feeling of belonging to something that will last beyond even your years of service.

"In addition, if you have patriotic tendencies you have the satisfaction of serving your country or cause. Men like us, and I include myself in this analysis, have none of those things.

"We are outcasts, to whom other people only come as a last resort. And as a last resort the jobs we get are the ones no one else wants. If we have any advantage it is that we can pick with whom and where we wish to fight.

"As for the men, they are not necessarily all cut from the same cloth. They do these jobs for a variety of reasons. For some they once were as you are now, but when they were separated from the service they were unable to adjust to civilian life. They have a compulsion to soldier. Others, like Alfons Dubric, are no more than hired killers and worse, sadists. For them the chance to feed their passions is of more importance then the money they are paid. They are the worst. There are others who perhaps need the excitement. I have heard them called adrenaline junkies. Those who come for romantic reasons are soon disillusioned.

"And there is a difference between being a mercenary and a soldier of fortune. A mercenary is one who wears the uniform of his employer. He fights on the line for an established regime or a rebel party and signs on for a regular tour of service. He is a hired soldier. Others are those who take special jobs such as this one. We are not serving any country as soldiers on a battlefield. We go in, do the one thing, take our money and go home. That is a soldier of fortune.

"That is not to say that the line between the two descriptions are not frequently crossed. I have been a mercenary soldier and probably will be again. The men I have to deal with are hard men, harder than your best soldiers because they have to be. I don't say they are always the best trained but they have to have a hardness and coldness of the spirit to be able to continue. They do not have the security that gives you such confidence. A lost leg or arm and there is no pension, no veterans hospital. You are left just as you are, a cripple whom no country, not even his own, wants.

"You have to be hard. Showing a wounded enemy mercy could cause you to receive such a wound. Therefore you think carefully before exposing yourself to unnecessary risk.

"You must fight harder because if you're taken prisoner there is not a country to work for your release. Often, even after the war is over, you will never be permitted to go home. For the winner does not consider you to be a prisoner of war, only a hired killer, and they will treat you as such. If you are not put against the wall, the odds are you will be kept in a prison, which would make a Mexican chain gang seem like a vacation on the Riviera.

"I have seen the bodies of mercenaries who had been taken alive by Simbas in the Congo. They did not die easy. The blacks there sometimes had a hard time telling the difference between men and women. If you were young and white to be gang raped was to be expected. For others, sometimes it was no more than having three feet of a white-hot assegai spearhead slowly shoved up the rectum. Whatever they did it took many hours, sometimes days. That, too, is to be expected.

"At best perhaps you can expect to be placed in forced labor gangs and work till you die. No one will help. You are alone.

"The men I have under my command would be more than willing to fight against each other. They do try to avoid going into action against people they have served with before, but it is not a hard rule and sometimes you don't know who you're going to be fighting. In any case most make few real friends. It's rare that you have even one you may call a real friend. I am fortunate; I have two.

"Some of them out there have fought against each other on different sides of the conflict and now they are on the same side working together. The past wars do not count. When this is over some of them will trade names and numbers of other people like myself who might have need of their services. Perhaps they will work together again; perhaps they will fight each other again. It doesn't matter. If they survive they will meet somewhere, sit down, have a drink, toast the dead on both sides, and continue till they are stopped.

"The man I terminated today was a sadist, a rapist, and a child killer. I admit that I helped to set him up. I have no regrets. However, understand this about me. I am a professional soldier. I am not a butcher. And I will not tolerate anyone in my command who is. Dubric sentenced himself to death years ago. I have just carried out that sentence."

Robinson's eyes never moved from Hendricks's face as he spoke. He was trying to see behind the pale eyes. There was deep emotion there. Carefully controlled, but it was there. It showed in small things. The whiskey glass, which trembled ever so slightly when he spoke of the child killer. The emptiness around the eyes when he told of a life where your comrades one day would try to kill you the next. Robinson believed him. He was part of a world that Robinson knew nothing of, and he had no right to judge him without knowing that world.

"Colonel Robinson, I need your support. I don't want you just to obey orders. I need you to help because you wish to. This job is important to many people. If you do not like me, that I can understand and accept. Keep me out of it then, and think only of the job. As soon as it is over you will be rid of me and it is not likely that we will ever meet again. Though I think that I should regret that very much."

He paused to give Robinson time to think over what he had said.

Pouring another stiff shot of the sweet Tennessee whiskey, Robinson raised his glass to him.

"Oh, what the hell! Who knows, maybe after I get out I might be one of those who can't adjust and come to you for a job one day. Let's forget it and, as they say, get on with the job."

The two men drank, both thankful that a dangerous breach had been healed.

Duke kept to the far side of his barracks, giving the men time to talk things out. After the execution of Dubric and the termination of the day's training exercises, he had marched his men past the corpse, by this time swollen from the heat, its features puffed and blotched. The thick and blue-purple tongue was swollen from out of the jaws and held between yellow teeth stained with a film of dried black blood.

Several of them had turned pale, covering their mouths to hold out the smell of corruption, which was already claiming the body as the decay set in. After Duke had released them, he and Becaude had gone back. Wrapping the corpse in a poncho, they had taken it out to the desert and there, in an unnamed wadi, they had buried him. Neither of them said anything the other could recall. There was little to say.

Dubric had joined the hundreds of thousands whose bones had been left beneath the sands of the desert: Egyptians, Hittites, Persians, Romans, Germans, Italians, Greeks. The Sahara was one monstrous graveyard with room enough for a thousand empires to rest in.

The American contingent sat around their bunks in small groups, playing cards, talking, and smoking. Their voices were low but Duke knew what they were talking about. They were a tighter group than the Europeans. At least they all came from the same country; that gave them some common ground.

The deep voice of Washington overrode the others even though he was speaking in what he considered to be a very low tone.

"Shit man. I told you the boss was bad. You don't give the man no shit and you will walk away from this one." He pointed his finger at his brother.

"You listen to me, Robert K. Do as the man says and we'll come out okay with money in our pockets and the man back home off our backs."

Robert K. had a thin, sculptured face and didn't resemble his brother very much. He had a slighter build with long, sensitive fingers and an intensity to his eyes that made him always seem on the edge of saying or doing something of profound importance.

He did not look his elder brother in the eyes as he said with a higher, thinner voice, "But he just killed the man. There was no trial. Everybody's got rights."

Washington snorted, "Don't give me that human rights shit! What are you, some kind of a dumb nigger? You know about rights. And you know what a piece of trash that honky was. He was a baby killer. What the fuck you think this is, a kids' game? Man, this is for motherfucking real! Get that in your nappy-headed skull if you want to come out of this. What he did to that man is none of our business. Let's just do our job, not make waves, take the fucking money, and go home in one piece.

"I trust him. If he thought it was necessary to off the motherfucker, then it was fucking necessary."

Pissed at his younger brother's attitude, Washington stalked back to his own bunk. Lying on his back staring at the ceiling, he muttered, "Shit! I don't know what to do about the little son of a bitch. I had to wipe his nose all his fucking life. On the street, in school, even in the fucking Army. Now we're here because the overeducated little fuck was caught holding on to eight ounces of coke."

He didn't know who to blame, himself or too much schooling. All his life Robert K. had been a dreamer. Civil liberty. Black Power. Return to Africa. All that so-called relevant jive shit. Washington knew better; he'd been born in Africa. He remembered what it had been like then, and it didn't look any fucking better now. The memories of another tribe attacking his were all too clear: smoking, burning huts, men lying with dusty black skins slit open by pangas, red blood on black skin. That's why his family finally went to the States. They had been taken there by a missionary organization who had made their family their yearly "good works" project. Even now when he let himself recall those days he felt a hate for the Luda tribe that was almost totally consuming. And his brother thought he could help bring all blacks together. Shit, since the whites were pushed out of Rhodesia, now Zim-fucking-babwe, there hadn't been a day without tribal warfare.

Robert K., born in the States, didn't have those memories. To him it was all romantic dreams. He wanted to go back to the Motherland and bring knowledge and wealth, to be a part of the grand union of all the tribes, to throw out the white man once and for all and institute a truly universal black culture.

Washington sincerely worried about his younger brother. He had refused to listen to anything. The boy didn't know when he was well off. As far as Washington was concerned, the States were his home and that was that. He had no desire to return to a life of disease and poverty, of fifty and sixty percent infant mortality and fear. Constant fear. But he was responsible for Robert K.

Jerking his body up off his bunk, he went over to Duke's bunk set apart at the rear door.

"Say, can I talk to you for a moment, Sergeant?"

Duke indicated for him to take the other end of his bunk, putting away the K-bar knife he'd been working on.

"Sure, Washington, what is it?"

Uncomfortable, he tried to find the words. "Well, it's like this. Me and Robert K. ain't exactly the same kind of people. I mean he is a good kid and all that and smart. Lots smarter than me. He's had three years of college. But to tell the truth, I don't think he ought to go on this job. He just don't have enough experience."

"I thought he was in 'Nam?"

"Yeah, sure he was. But he wasn't really in any bad shit and I was there to . . ." He hesitated. ". . . you know, to take some of the heat off him. But that was different over there and I think this job has a good chance of breaking really fucking bad. You see, he is the sensitive type. I'm just not sure he can cut any real killing. Maybe you can speak to the man for me about it. If you do, I'll owe you a big one."

Duke shook his large head from side to side. "You heard the boss. Everyone goes. But I'll pass on what you said to him. He'll let you know real soon. That's one thing the boss does is make up his mind without wasting time. But I wouldn't hold my breath on your brother being let off. We are going to need everybody we have to do this thing."

Standing up, Washington looked down on the bearded white man. He had never liked to ask anything from whitey, but this was for his brother.

"Okay, Sarge. But I want you to know that whatever happens I appreciate it and I promise you this, that if I'm around I'll see that Robert K. does right. I promise you that."

He left Duke to return to the methodical sharpening of his combat knife on an oilstone. The whishing of the good carbon-steel blade as it passed back and forth over the stones was soothing. Not glancing up, Duke knew when Washington was back at his bunk. He felt that Washington meant what he said. And he would speak to the boss about it in the morning. It might be best if Robert were placed where he couldn't do much damage if he fucked up.

At mess the next morning, Duke brought up the subject of Washington's brother to Hendricks. They talked about it for a few minutes. Duke made a suggestion and Hendricks nodded his head in agreement.

Leaving the table, he passed by Washington and motioned with his head for him to follow Duke outside.

Standing by the side of the mess hall he shivered from the early contact with the rising sun.

"Okay Washington, this is what the boss agreed to. We don't want anyone in our section to have the chance to go to pieces. It's too touchy. We're going to reassign him to the European section."

Washington started to protest but Duke cut him off with an upraised hand. "Wait a minute. Let me finish. What we're going to do is assign him to Doc Smyth-Wilson. And it may be handy for them to have a Shanga-speaking man with them, too. Don't worry about the language thing. Doc is Limey and Becaude and probably half of the others speak some English.

"If he's as sensitive as you say he'd probably prefer to be working with the doc, taking care of the wounded. And when the hostages come in there are certain to be some in need of care and understanding. This might be just the thing for him."

Washington didn't have to think about it. He knew this was the best offer he was going to get. "Right. Thanks,

Sarge. But say, will Robert K. have to move to the other barracks? I don't think he'd be very happy with a bunch of people he can't understand.''

Pushing off the side of the building, Duke looked up at the sky. A flock of Egyptian vultures was circling something to the south beyond a serried range of dunes.

"No. The boss said all he has to do is report to Doc in the mornings at the dispensary so he can learn some first aid while he's here. He's off the rest of the duty roster except for the regular training exercises, which everyone has to participate in.''

Washington took the big man's hand and shook it. "Thanks, Sarge, and like I said, I'll see that Robert K. does right by everybody.''

Hendricks knew the reason for Duke coming to him with the unusual request and he knew the reason why he honored it. Duke had a brother he'd lost in 'Nam on a heliborne operation. And if Washington was right about his brother, then he certainly did not want him on a job where stealth and steel nerves were required. One moment of panic on anyone's part could get them all killed or captured. With Doc Smyth-Wilson he'd at least be of some use, and going in with the Becaude section there was no way he'd blow anything if he got rattled. All in all it would probably prove to be the best course of action for everyone concerned.

After mess, for the first time, all hands were issued live ammo and weapons assigned to each man. These were to be kept with them at all times. Any man who did not have his weapons within arm's reach twenty-four hours a day, and this included going to the toilet, was to be fined one hundred dollars with the amount doubling for each offense. The only exception was the shower and they would be placed in the rack provided for them outside the shower stalls.

Hendricks redoubled their time on the mock-ups. From that day all training was done with live ammo, including the recoilless rifles.

Since Dubric's execution the men's morale had surprised Robinson by actually improving, and their speed and efficiency in the practice runs was obvious. It even seemed that the separation of the two groups into European and American had served a purpose. The two sections were competing against the other on the firing ranges and in every way they could.

This Hendricks encouraged. He took his part in all exercises and long after the men had crashed face-down, exhausted, into their bunks, he was up working on the operational plans, searching for mistakes and calculating risks. He needed to speak with the agent in Mehendi's palace.

If the man could do two or three things they would, he figured, have a better than seventy percent chance of pulling the operation off with minimal casualties not to exceed twenty percent of his total force. If he couldn't come through for them, then he would have to drop both odds to fifty and fifty.

On the morning of the third day of dry runs was the first time that Robbie and his men came into the game. They loaded the airfield attack force into the bellies of the aircraft and made practice landings and takeoffs, then came back and reloaded with the palace section and took them up for practice jumps with full gear and drop bags. He was as hard on his men as Hendricks was on his.

Time was critical, the placement of the aircraft critical. Everything was critical, and now they had gone into night-time training, using every piece of gear in their inventory. The new shipment of ammo had come in along with several other shipments of Hendricks's toys, but Robinson was more concerned with getting his two C-130s repainted with the proper markings.

Finally this morning Robinson had been sent the name of their contact, Captain Jalingo Kelo. The agent would be their ticket into Bokala. Even if the man on Mehendi's staff called Kelo was not able to do the things Hendricks requested, they would still go ahead and take their chances on just confusing the enemy. They would know that very soon. He'd just that morning received a telex that the meet was on and Robinson was to take Hendricks to rendezvous eye to eye with the man.

When he told Hendricks that the meet with Kelo was set, the expression of relief on the man's face was obvious. "Thank God. At last. Now maybe I can get some answers to a few questions without having to go through that asshole Anderson."

Taking Robinson's arm, he escorted him to the door, saying, "By the way, do you have any of that sour-mash whiskey left? I think it's time you and I went over this whole thing from A to bleedin' Z, don't you? Maybe you can see something I missed. If not then we'll have a good solid drink to the whole bloody show, what?"

THIRTEEN

OCTOBER 27

FROM BÎR MISÂHA they headed south into the Sudan over Laqiya Arba'in where they took up a heading of 213 degrees, a straight course to al Junayna. Touching down, the light plane left a streamer of dust behind it as it taxied to a stop at the single metal hangar that served as terminal and repair center for the strip. Robinson had been here several times before when he had arranged for health workers to be brought in. He had made a friend of the commanding senior officer, a tall dust-black Sudanese with a gap between his front teeth that threatened to split his face in two when he saw Robinson. On his chest he wore the oversize version of a pilot's wings on a thin khaki shirt.

"*Rrobbinnsson.*" He added extra everythings to his speech. It took some time for Hendricks to be able to follow his version of English but Robinson apparently had no problem.

After Hendricks was introduced as a health consultant for AID on his first tour of Egypt and the Sudan, Keikei shook hands with him. His hand was as hard as the sun-baked earth.

Keikei gave him a long slow once-over, then grinned at Robinson. "Right. Very good. Most proper. Welcome, welcome. You will stay for dinner?"

Robinson restrained a grimace. Cuisine in the Sudan often left much to be desired.

"I'm sorry, Keikei, but we're on a tight schedule. I just want to fuel up, take a leak, then get on with it. But we'll see you on the way back."

Keikei laughed a deep stomach-rumbling laugh. "Ahh, yes. Spooky business again I see. Very good. Very fine. Most proper. Gas by all means the very best. Most good."

He yelled orders at two men in threadbare, patched, once-gray coveralls. From the hangar they rolled out two fifty-gallon drums on a dolly and also a hand pump.

"Ahh, yes. Most good. Spooky business. Very interesting!"

Robinson looked a bit embarrassed. "C'mon, Keikei, knock it off, you can never tell who's listening."

Keikei's eyes narrowed as he turned around in a 360-degree circle. "You see someone else listening? Show me!"

His rock-hard hand came up with a Smith and Wesson .357 Magnum, the hammer cocked back. "Where is the dog? Who would listen to private talks of you and me?"

"Relax. There's no one there. I just said there could be."

Keikei stuck a finger, with a nail on it that could have peeled a coconut, to the side of his nose. "Ahh yes, loose lips sink ships." He laughed again with that great bellowing sound.

"But I have no ships."

The .357 Magnum disappeared into a custom Bianchi back holster at his spine.

Groaning inwardly, Hendricks moved to the hangar to get out of the sun. The flight had been long and mostly boring, though there were a few more riverbeds and the ground had a bit more vegetation. It was nothing like the Congo. One day the desert would take it all. From Casablanca to the Cape of Good Hope, Africa would be just one great desert with pockets of green that everyone would fight over till they burned them out, too.

Robinson visited with Keikei till their plane was ready to go. Hendricks kept to himself, enjoying the opportunity to stretch his legs and work out the kinks that he always got when he had to sit in one place too long.

A whistle from the hangar summoned him back. Shaking the rock-hard hand of Major Keikei once more, he climbed back in and strapped down. As soon as they were airborne he asked Robinson, ''Where did you run into that character?''

''Oh, I first met him at Keesler Air Force Base in the sixties. He was there going through the air traffic controllers' school and I was teaching a course for intercept control technicians. We shared a few at the officers' club from time to time and I drop in on him now and then when we're in Egypt. It's always good to know someone on the deck in a different country. But don't let his act throw you. He's got a mind like a Philadelphia lawyer. That's why they keep him out here. If he ever decided he wanted to he could probably take over the country.''

From al Junayna, Robinson took up another heading of 193 degrees. Keeping the plane at around ten thousand feet they made the flight to Marza-Mangueigne in southwestern Chad. ETA was 2200 hours. Jalingo Kelo would meet them there. Landing permits for Chad had been no problem. The troubles with Libya, to the north, had made her very receptive and aware of the importance of good relations with the Western powers.

With the coming of night the land, viewed from the sky, appeared very desolate and lonely. Only scattered glows on the earth could be seen as they passed over villages and small towns. Robinson's face was steady in the luminescence of the instrument panel.

Contented, thought Hendricks. At last he's getting into the thing.

There are few things more boring than a long flight in a small aircraft. All you can do is sit, and with the night there is even less sense of movement, of making any progress to your destination. But finally Robinson spoke into his mouthpiece, using that strange manner of speech all pilots seemed to be intimate with and no one else could understand. Even with a certain amount of static crackling and hissing the men in the air and those on the ground seemed to understand each other perfectly.

Pointing with a finger to the right of the nose of the aircraft, Robinson said, "There it is. Marza-Mangueigne. We're on the glide path and we'll be down in ten minutes."

He was exactly right. They came in low over a row of flat-roofed houses much like those in most of North Africa. There were a few streets with electric lights glowing, lonely pillars of the modern age. Then the strip appeared, lit on both sides. Robinson touched down so easily Hendricks wasn't sure they were on the deck till he throttled back on the engine and began breaking.

Hendricks thought, the man is one hell of a pilot and handles this thing better than I do a car.

Taxiing to the far end of the runway, they were met by another of the handcarts with gas drums and hand pump. With the drums was a World War II–vintage weapons carrier, which looked as though it still had what was left of the original paint on it.

Hendricks climbed out of the plane, taking his leather case with him. He almost stumbled, his left leg had gone to sleep on him. Thumping the limb on the side to get the circulation going again, he saw the driver had given Robinson the keys to the truck before he walked away across the field to where a number of lighted buildings stood in a cluster.

Grinning at Hendricks's discomfort, Robinson called sharply, "Climb in and let's go."

"All right. No need to get so bloody testy about it. You're used to being cooped up in those things for days on end; I'm not."

After climbing in the driver's seat, Robinson started the motor, let out the clutch, and pulled off the runway, taking them over to a section of the fence with a manned gate. The guards who were normally there had pulled back about fifty feet. He could see them just at the limit of the headlights. They looked as if they were carrying Mats-49 submachine guns. A good solid piece of weaponry. Probably the best thing the French had made since the end of World War II and the seventies.

Robinson faced the truck directly into an open gate and stopped. He cut the motor, blinked the lights three times, and got out. "C'mon if you want to meet the man."

He led the way to the edge of the headlights, walking without any excess speed, Hendricks a step behind him moving in the same manner. Stopping at the edge of the light beams, where the shadows gained in strength, Robinson spoke to the darkness. "We're here. This is the man you're to talk to. I'll leave you to each other."

Turning, he went back to the truck and sat in the cab. Hendricks stood alone in the dark at the lights' rim.

"Mr. Smith, I presume?" Hendricks asked.

From the shadows a man came slowly forward, a Russian Tokarev automatic in his hand.

"Welcome to Africa, Mr. Jones. I hope you will excuse my caution, but I assure you it is a good policy for survival."

Hendricks had no arguments with that.

"If you will come with me, please."

The figure waved at the truck, the lights went out. Hendricks's eyes blanked out at the sudden change. It would take a few minutes for them to adjust again to the dark.

The shadow, now darker than the night, stayed in front of him as they walked another twenty feet away to stand by the trunk of a baobab tree.

There was an awkward moment as the men waited for the opening remarks, which would set the tone.

Hendricks waited patiently for Jalingo Kelo to speak, first letting his body relax, not wanting to show by his body language any anxiety or unease.

Jalingo Kelo opened with, "I do not have much time. I must be back in Bokala by tomorrow night, and the bus service here leaves much to be desired."

"Fine. Let's get on with it. What do you have for me?"

By the fleshy trunk of the baobab Jalingo Kelo bent over, coming up with a battered beige vinyl suitcase.

"In here are the latest schedules for the guard changes and the number of men on duty in the palace. Also, I went by the airport yesterday and visited a while with some of my comrades. You will find the report of that visit also along with the normal disposition of the security forces. You do know that even with the best of luck many are going to die. The Askaris of Mehendi will not go down easy."

His eyes were beginning to adjust. He could make out the form of Jalingo Kelo better. The night was crystal clear and even without a moon the stars gave him enough light to see the speaker was a tall wiry man, the kind whose muscles gave him a strength beyond his thin surface appearance. His hair was cut short to his head in tight curls. From what he could see the face had lost weight from the first photos Anderson had given him in Guatemala. The strain was beginning to show. How much longer could he hold up?

"When are you going to come? So far the captives have not been hurt. They are tired, hungry, and fearful, and with good reason. Okediji is very near the capital now. I believe that when the first shots are fired inside the city the prisoners will die. There is not much time left."

"Soon. Very soon. I need to ask a few questions. First, am I correct to assume you still have access to the communications center in the palace?"

Kelo nodded. "Yes, I have my normal shift in addition to other duties."

"Good. Now, you said you had friends at the airport. Have you ever talked to them over the palace commo lines?"

Kelo moved to rest his shoulder against the trunk of the tree. "Yes. I have spoken to them and given instructions to the tower several times."

Hendricks moved closer. "Did any of these have to do with aircraft movements?"

"Yes, several times when we had shipments coming in from Libya. The times of the arrival of the arms planes are not made known even to us, till only minutes before they are due to arrive. This is done in order to reduce the possibility of sabotage."

"How do they contact you?"

Both heads jerked around! The pistol in Kelo's hand came up quickly, then dropped back to his side. The yapping of a hunting pack of desert jackals sounded as though it were only a few feet from them.

"We have a set series of different frequencies, which are monitored at specific times. If we receive the signal at 0300 hours, for example, then we know the aircraft will be coming down within the next hour, and I or whoever is on duty will communicate with the control tower and the aircraft will be brought straight in with the fields clear and security on alert."

He didn't like the sound of "security on alert" but it was only natural.

"What language is used by the Libyan pilots coming in, and do they have any specific call letters to ID them?"

The jackals yapped again. There was a different tone to them. Jalingo Kelo nodded his head in their general direction. "They have made a kill this night and will feed." Then he answered Hendricks's question. "They speak English, as most of our controllers were trained in England, and yes there is a code given to the control tower. However that clearance code comes from the palace after we receive the Libyan approach signal. It is a prearranged code, which is based on the date of their signal and the time. Always it is a six-digit numerical sequence."

Hendricks thought about that for a moment. This was critical. "If you were manning the center you could then give them any number series you wished and they would accept it?"

"Of course."

"Good, bloody fucking good. That gives us our key to the lock at the airport."

Hendricks moved closer to Jalingo Kelo. He wanted to watch his face when he said his next words.

"We are coming within the next ten days. There is something which you must do to give us a chance of pulling it off."

Even in the dark he could see the muscles work under Kelo's dark skin as he told him his plan. When he had finished he pulled back a step.

"Can you do it?"

"Yes. It will be done."

"All right. Wait here, I have something for you."

Returning to the truck, he leaned into the window. Robinson looked at him, curiosity stamped all over his face, but he held his tongue.

Hendricks shook his head. "That is one tough man over there. If this thing goes down right it'll be because of him. Give me the case."

Handing it over, Robinson never had the chance to say anything before Hendricks had turned and walked back to the baobab tree.

He handed the case to Kelo. "In here you'll find something you need, which might make your job a bit easier."

For the next ten minutes Hendricks went over the basic plan with Kelo, telling him nothing more than was necessary. But what he did tell him was still more than he would have liked. Yet there was no other choice. Without Kelo, the job would fail anyway. He had to be trusted and, according to his files, he had good reason to get that trust, the kind Hendricks liked best. He had blood reasons to hate Mehendi and still not want to give his country over to Okediji.

Going over the contents of the case with him, Hendricks explained the fine points of some of the equipment. Kelo was a quick study. It took only once for him to get it down right.

It was done. The two men stood for a moment in the African night looking at each other, each making his mind up. Then they shook hands and again Kelo repeated, "Come soon or there will be nothing to come for."

Turning quickly, he disappeared into the night, taking the leather case with him. Hendricks picked up the suitcase Kelo had brought for him and walked back to the truck.

Robinson drove them back across the flightline as the guards took up their positions again at the gate. Hendricks had one good look at them as they passed.

Airborne once again, they headed back to Egypt over the dark land below. Hendricks thought about what it would be like the next time he came this way, the men who would be with him and which of them would not return. He thought he knew the names of some of them already. He couldn't always tell but sometimes there was something you couldn't put your finger on with certain men. They had the feel of death to them. He knew it didn't make any sense, but he always felt it; and over the years he had been proven right too many times to ignore it completely. Sometimes he thought he would not let a particular man go on a job, but then if he didn't he knew there would be someone else taking his place who would have the same feel to him. And that man would die, too.

Robinson broke into his thoughts. "What did you think of him?"

"Kelo?"

"Yeah."

"I think that there is one hell of a man. It doesn't matter what reason is driving him. I wouldn't want to trade places with him. He has the toughest job of us all. I don't know if I could do it. To be with men you work with all day and night, to fight alongside of them, eat with them, know their families and personal lives. *No!* That's too tough for me. I'll take it the way I have in the past. I don't want to know them.''

Looking out the window at the dark below, he said softly, almost inaudibly, "*Bonne chance, mon ami. Bonne chance.*"

FOURTEEN

OCTOBER 27

FOR LEOPOLDO OKENDIJI, leader of the Bokalan Freedom Alliance, the report he had just received was most welcome. It appeared his time was finally at hand. Soon he would have all that he deserved, payment in full for a lifetime of abuse, fear, and poverty at the hands of the carrion-eating Shangas. Now the cycle had turned. It had not been easy but it had been very, very satisfying.

The Shanga were the largest ethnic group in Bokala, but when all of the minority tribes were counted they were in essence the majority. That was why he had thanked the powers of creation for putting a jackal such as Mehendi in power.

It was a natural progression for one such as the jackal who feeds on offal. One by one he had alienated every tribe but his own by killing, by wholesale burning of villages, by forcing thousands to flee across neighboring borders to live worse than the beasts of the night. They stayed in death camps, which the whites referred to as refugee centers.

He had worked in Bokala when the president-general was only a colonel. He had sat in his chair off the Rue Pasteur and Okediji had placed his razor at the beast's throat. It had taken great willpower not to give him a shave closer than any would have dreamed possible. The temptation often made his hand tremble with the desire to let the cold German steel slice deep into the carotid artery and let flow the life blood of the one who had killed and tormented so many of his people.

But it had not been the time, and the bodyguards had always been close to their master. Suspicious, their eyes red from the smoking of ganja, they watched his every move with automatic weapons in their hands. To kill the beast he would have had to give up his life instantly. That was a price he was not then ready to pay, for he knew that destiny had marked him for a greater cause.

Hate was his god. It directed his every movement. It gave fire to his words, which fanned the flames of hope in the breasts of all who heard him. A great hate. Enough to go around for all who had caused his people such pain, especially the whites, who kept the beast in power, supplying him with guns and money. He hated them almost as much as he did the Shanga.

The struggle had honed him to his own razor's edge. His body was lean, ribs clearly seen through his khaki shirt. His face was worn, the eyes and cheeks sunken. But the eyes blazed with the hot coals of passion.

In spite of all the difficulties, those long years of going from one refugee camp to another, and speaking, cajoling, begging, arguing—one by one, then by twos and tens, and at last by the hundreds—they had come to him; and when they came, so did others. The little yellow men with their smiles and cold brown eyes. They wanted their share of Africa, also. They needed the raw resources: bauxite, gold, uranium, and industrial diamonds. And if they could in the process interfere with the expansion of their enemies' spheres of influence, then it was so much the better.

He had accepted them and a few advisors to aid in the training of his warriors. They had smiled when the aircraft came in from Zimbabwe loaded with the first shipment of the tools of war. He had shaken their hands and also smiled when they called him a comrade in the struggle against world imperialism. But he knew they had their own empire and wanted to loot what would one day be his. He had no use, either, for these hard-smiling men. When the day came they, too, would go.

It was clear that they wished to give him more than he asked for. They wanted to send doctors and teachers, help raise and educate his young, build up his security and intelligence forces to protect him from the capitalists and their insidious schemes. Ahh, yes! They wished to give him all of these things—and much, much more. He would take what he wanted and leave the rest. As with all outsiders, they thought because he had tribal scars on his face he was a fool.

He knew those doctors and teachers would be used to steal his people from him, to put different ideas in their minds and make them discontent. The intelligence and security forces they trained would be led by officers who had been to their schools away from their homelands where they would be indoctrinated. And when they returned they would be the creatures of the smiling polite men from the East. That would not happen. He would dance at the end of no other nation's string. He would use them as they were trying to use him.

He needed only the weapons of the outside world; nothing else would he tolerate. In the future any who came to

Bokala would do so only as hired labor. None would be permitted to settle or own property.

When it was finally done, the land would be purged and his tribe would be supreme, leading the others to a grand alliance. He would bind them together with blood.

Blood! He could smell it now. The blood of the thousands who had already died by his order and his hand. He closed his eyes, his thin face taking on the look of one approaching ecstasy. He felt again the pain he had given those he hated.

Nowhere had a white face come into his hands that he had left alive. They were part of the blood payment he gave to his allies and his tribe. He gave them the whites for their own, and they paid them back in their own coin: in pain and humiliation and finally death. It was a great binder of souls, the blood of the exploiters.

He would sit apart from his people while they played, watching over them as a loving father would his children. Only when they called for him would he join in the games, and they always called. Taking his Soligen steel straight razor he would delight and awe them with his sensitivity and skill as he made the cuts, thin red streaks which opened up to an inch wide. Then, with swift deft strokes, he would demonstrate how to peel the flesh from a man or woman's face. Making the first cuts under the jawline, with great craft he would undercut and pull the surface skin back over the skull, leaving only raw red screaming meat and exposed nerves while he held a bleeding mask in his hands. It warmed him, the appreciative applause and chanting of his warriors and women. It was a good and great thing.

In exchange for their love he gave them everything. No one was spared, not miners or merchants, not teachers or priests, nuns or children. He gave them all to his own beloved children.

And soon he would give them the capital of Bokala. Many of his successes came from a man he had never met. But through his information he had been able to prevent the Askaris from winning many battles. Time and again this man had proven his value to the revolution. At great personal risk he stayed by the side of the jackal. Now this man had sent word that a great opportunity was at hand. The hostages taken by Mehendi were to be rescued by a raiding party of mercenaries. The airfield was to be taken by another.

This man had also promised that on that night Mehendi would die. Okediji could barely contain his water, he was so excited at the prospects it offered. Even if the jackal was not killed, the loss of his palace and the airfield would destroy the confidence of his forces.

The attack on the palace would come soon. When it came he would be ready, waiting. His men would move at night, and like the animals of the plains who sought shelter from the sun in their burrows, they would dig in and wait during the day. And they would wait patiently, not moving save at dark when they would leave their holes. When the moment came he would give the order and they would rise from the earth and sweep into the outskirts of Bokala, spreading fear and confusion in the streets.

They would burn and kill all they came across. Some would have the honor of attacking the Askaris from the rear, creating confusion and panic. He would save what petrol he had for his commandeered trucks and cars. When his moles came out of their burrows, his main force would be brought up rapidly, bypassing strong points to burst through the demoralized lines of the Askaris and enter the city as conquerors.

There would be a great bleeding that night, and not all of the blood would be black. He had his own plans for the white captives. They must not be taken away from him. Nor could he tolerate white mercenaries in his land. This was a magnificent opportunity to demonstrate to the world that no more would Bokala tolerate interference—by anyone. He would strike such terror into them that never again would a mercenary force ever dream of coming to this land.

It was difficult to restrain himself, though he knew that a hasty move now could cost him dearly. It would not lose the war but it could prolong it, and he wished an end to it immediately. Many of his men were becoming weary. If he had not taken the city of Tarangara many of them would have left him.

He gave them the city and all that was in it. He gave only this order. "You may have everything you wish but destroy no machinery or buildings. Do not burn cars or trucks. These things are now ours, and are we children to destroy that which belongs to us?"

They obeyed him. The killing and raping was rampant. Though he had ordered no fires, some did start, and his men ravaged the streets by the lights of the flames. The screams of the Shanga women were sweet to his ears as they were dragged from their houses and his men took them, forcing their husbands and sons to watch when they were passed screaming and bleeding from one of his men to another. Then they were given death in the old way with the panga.

He did not know how many had died in the four days since he had given the city over to his warriors. Perhaps four thousand, perhaps ten. There was no way to count, but the stench of death and threat of disease made him put an end to it, which was just as well. His men were exhausted from the efforts of their triumph. After the flush of lust was drained he had issued a more orderly program to cleanse the city.

Block by block the hated Shanga were dragged from their holes, their clothes and property taken from them. They were herded together and whipped naked through the streets. Kibokos, the rhinoceros-hide whips, lashed their backs to the bone as they were driven from the city into the bush. No food, no water, no shoes, no clothes. All they were permitted to take were their lives and many of them died before they reached the outer limits of Tarangara.

For himself he took nothing, contenting himself with the interrogation of captive soldiers and the few whites who had been foolish enough to remain in the city. They gave him great pleasure, especially the men when he took their women from them. He demonstrated for them how a single shining blade could almost instantly turn a woman's breast into a tobacco pouch for one of his officers.

They were fools. Somehow they thought their god or government would help them. And how they screamed, both the men and the women, hour after hour till their throats were too raw to scream again, and all they could do was whimper and beg for death, which he gave them but in his own time. His own very long time. Their children died more quickly, a cut throat or a shot to the head. If they were very young then it was a simple matter of grabbing them by their ankles and swinging their heads against a rock or the wall of a building.

For two weeks the lines of people streamed from the city. He had not thought it would take so long to move them all out. When it was finally done he had taken his car, a new Mercedes with air conditioning, into the countryside escorted by his best men. They drove toward the border of Zaire. Even at the edge of the city the dying had begun. In the fields along the road were dark masses where entire families had stopped and died. Many of them bore the marks of pangas on their bodies, deep gashes which reached the bone and sometimes deeper. The Shanga had many who hated them.

When at last the smell of decay was so strong that it overpowered the Mercedes's air conditioner, he ordered his driver and escort back to Tarangara.

It had been a great triumph, and now he knew his men lusted after Bokala and its women and riches. Even though a large number of the population was moving out of the city, trying to escape, there would be sufficient people and riches left behind to amuse his men. He didn't care about them. He wanted the city and he wanted the palace. He wanted to seat himself in the big black chair of power from where Mehendi had lorded over the land. Now it was to be his turn. He would have the palace and all that was in it as his just reward. The rest he would leave to his men.

Now all they had to do was wait for a message from the man called Kelo. He had waited long and could do it for a time more. But when he finally did hear from this man he would reward him greatly.

Now he had many things to attend to. Plans had to be drawn up and meetings with his commanders and the smiling little men had to be held. He would demand more aid: food, petrol, ammunition.

Returning to his office, he didn't see the ruin made of it, the fact that the toilets no longer worked and it had taken a week to get the electricity back on. The little men had sent for engineers. There were none among his people who could deal with the machines.

Trash and rubble littered the streets and pariah dogs searched among it for more food. It all had amused him, especially the little men's concern at how long the dead had been left lying in the streets. Only when they had delicately explained the matter of disease and the effect it could have upon his men did he give the order to clean up and burn the remaining bodies in a mass grave outside of Tarangara.

That alone had taken another week. By then he, too, admitted the atmosphere was getting a little ripe. He wondered how long it would take to clear the dead from Bokala, and hoped it would take a month or more.

FIFTEEN

OCTOBER 28

As soon as they touched down at Bîr Misâha Hendricks went into conference with Duke and Becaude.

"We have a chance! I met with our contact in the palace, one Jalingo Kelo, a captain on Mehendi's personal staff. I gave him the outline of the plan and some gear. He says he can do what we ask. On the night we take off a signal will be sent over Radio Cairo, which he says is popular with the Askaris. So there won't be any suspicion if he has it tuned in. When he receives the signal he'll know that we are airborne and on our way."

Reaching into the bottom drawer of his desk, he pulled out a full bottle of Johnnie Walker Black and cracked the seal. Pouring each of them a full three fingers in a water glass, he raised his own glass to each of them. They stood, eyes on each other.

"Gentlemen, it's a go. We have three days!"

Together as one voice they gave the toast as they had countless times before at moments such as these.

"*Vive la mort. Vive la guerre. Vive le mercenaire!*"

The glasses were drained.

From that moment on the tempo of everything increased threefold. Hendricks kept an eye on Robert K., but Washington's brother seemed to have settled down and even appeared to be contented to be working with Doc Smyth-Wilson.

The men were getting their edge now. They moved smoother, quicker. Their confidence was high as they gained respect for each other, and now there was no grumbling. They didn't know the exact time they would move out, but when Hendricks had returned they had sensed the difference in him and knew it was a go. Soon they would be moving out.

If a man didn't carry his weight or slacked off, they took care of it themselves. A carefully chosen word or two about the hazards of their business and the recalcitrant party soon saw the error of his ways and got his shit together fast.

Robinson was putting the pressure on his crews, too. The new paint job was soon finished. When the European section saw the huge transports with their new markings, Libyan rondels in place of the United States Air Force stars, and they were given their new uniforms, which were of a different pattern than those they had originally been issued, the rest of Hendricks's plan became obvious. Smiles and grins spread across faces as they nodded knowingly at one another. They knew now the reason for the strange parade-ground exercises they'd been made to do.

Among everyone the energy level was incredibly high, and they worked twice as hard as they had before. The talk of women and drink lessened. Their minds were on one thing.

The night when they finished their training all the groups were brought together. Robinson stood slightly to the rear.

Hendricks had invited him to this occasion; few other outsiders would have been permitted to attend. Under the cold stars of the Sahara the men stood in silent ranks, their weapons slung, feet spread apart shoulder width at parade rest. The faces were good, steady. The intensity level behind the eyes was incredible. Robinson could feel it from where he stood.

The two sections were ready. The parade ground was lit by the lights of four trucks.

This was the good time. It came all too seldom for Hendricks. There was something that could never be put properly or accurately into the spoken word. Such as how he felt when he looked at these men and men like them. Soon they would go to fight and some would die. But this night there was to be no sorrow. This was *la nuit des baïonnettes*, "the night of the bayonets" when the final edge was to be put on each man's weapon. For on the morrow they would go into battle.

Standing before them with the lights of one truck on him, he raised his fist, an FAL 7.62-mm assault rifle in it.

"*Mes amis*, my friends and comrades." He spoke in English and French, alternating the words with ease.

"This is the last night. This may be the last time we drink together or stand as one again. It is a good night, this *nuit des baïonnettes*. Look to the faces next to you, for they are your family, your brothers and your fathers. The future is not for such as we. We have only this night, this time, this place. Our ranks grow less each time we gather. You know the names. Hoare, Warbel, Schramme. Hundreds of others. They are not with us in body but they are a part of us.

"We have a guest this night: Colonel Robinson. Let us show him what we are. Food and drink is ready. We toast no nation, no cause but that of ourselves. We are perhaps the last of our kind.

"Tomorrow let us make certain that not one man here fails himself or his comrades, and let those we meet in battle speak our names in whispers for years to come."

Robinson could feel a physical swelling among the gathered men. Knuckles turned white on the pistol grips of their weapons. Faces grew stronger. Eyes blazed with new lights of fire.

"This is our night, *mes amis. La nuit des baïonnettes! Vive la mort! Vive la guerre! Vive le mercenaire!*"

The gathered men answered him as one, repeating his words as they drew their own bayonets and held shining steel points raised above their heads as if they could attack the very night skies of Egypt. They cried, answering him as one voice in the dark:

"Vive le mercenaire!"

Over their cry Hendricks made himself heard. "Break ranks and greet your brothers, for they may not come this way again."

Robinson had never seen anything like it. These hard men turned to one another: Americans, British, French, Belgians, Germans. All of them came together and embraced each other. Hard fighting men put arms around one another's shoulders and kissed each other full on the mouth. There was nothing feminine about it. These were warriors who belonged to another time, another era. The kiss they gave was one of respect and remembrance. From many eyes tears welled up as those who were not there were recalled.

Then it was time to eat and drink. Firearms were stacked. Only those on guard were permitted weapons, and they would have to wait only one hour before they were relieved. Each man would have his turn to be with comrades this night, for they knew it would be the last time for some of them. This was a moment that all had the right to share in.

The barriers were down. The men drank, but none to excess. They didn't need it. Around campfires, songs floated up into the dark night sky in half a dozen languages. From one fire in the hollow of a dune the flames cast an amber glow on the faces of the men as an incredibly clear, youthful voice reached over the tops of the others in its crystalline purity. Robinson thought it must have come from a very young man indeed. It had the ethereal quality of one who had perhaps sung in the Vienna Boys' Choir at one time.

The rest of the men fell silent as the German lyrics reached out to them. Then, slowly at first, one by one other voices joined in, each in a different language; but the song remained the same. The strains of "Lili Marlene," perhaps the most famous of all the soldiers' songs, drifted over the desert to lose themselves in harmony with the weeping of the rustling night winds blowing across the Sahara to the distant sea.

Robinson moved closer to the campfire where the bell-like notes still dominated the other voices with incredible gentleness and sorrow. Hendricks walked up behind him. He saw the singer, his face broken by a hundred fights, thick shoulders and knotted hands that could snap the neck of a man with ease. His age was hard to tell, but the years of his life were written in the scars on his face and soul.

Instinctively, Robinson knew this man had fought on the frozen steppes of Russia. He was old in a thousand different ways; he had killed and seen killing as few ever would, but the song coming from him was like that of a child: innocent and pure.

Speaking softly so as not to break the moment, Hendricks whispered, "That's old Rudy. He was with the Gross Deutschland Division."

Robinson couldn't take his gaze away from the man's face; it was ageless, and the song was timeless in its loneliness and sorrow for every soldier who had ever marched away and left the one he loved behind to await his return.

Old Rudy's face was turned up to the heavens as he held the last notes, stretching them out as if reluctant to let them go. Around the fire Robinson saw tears running freely from the men's eyes as one by one they dropped out of the singing and left it to the old soldier. Then it was gone. The night was empty and with the dying of the song the men began to return one by one to their barracks. The rest of this night would be a time alone for each man.

One man presented himself to Hendricks.

"*Chef?*"

"Yes."

"*Chef*, with no disrespect intended, I wish to ask why"—he indicated Robinson with his head—"this man is here tonight? He is not one of us."

Looking over the man's shoulder to the dying embers of the campfires, Hendricks turned his pale eyes to him.

"You are wrong, *mon vieux*. He has the right. Tomorrow he goes in with us, and it may be that he will die with us. For that alone he has the right."

The man looked Robinson straight in the face as if weighing his soul. Robinson returned the gaze steadily without aggression. He let the man peer deep into his eyes.

"*Oui, Chef*. As you say. He has the right."

Then he was gone. Robinson felt as if something had been pulled out of him.

The men had all dispersed. Becaude and Duke had started to come over to Hendricks and Robinson but something made them pull back, and they, too, returned to their barracks and their men.

Taking Robinson by the elbow, Hendricks led him to the fire where old Rudy had sung his song. He leaned over and picked up a half-full bottle of rum. Raising it to the fire he looked at the amber fluid as the lights danced and wavered in it.

"Come, Colonel, drink with me."

When he stepped forward the heat of the campfire washed across the front of Robinson's body, flushing his face even as the chill of the night turned his back cold in contrast. But this night everything was a contrast: the men, their songs, their faces.

Hendricks put the bottle to his lips and swallowed deeply, letting the burning liquor slide unrestricted to his stomach. Lowering the bottle, he looked at Robinson. "Well? You have something in your face that needs to be answered. What is it?"

He handed the bottle to Robinson, who held it without taking a drink.

"I don't know. I still don't understand you or the men with you."

Hendricks squatted by the fire, his sharp features accented even more strongly by the glowing of the flames.

"I tried to explain it to you that day after Dubric. But there is no way to put it into words. The men you saw tonight as good comrades ready to fight and die for one another, which they will do, are still strangers to you, but maybe that is because they are strangers to themselves. If they had enough time together, they would grow close, but they don't. The closeness and the loyalty they have right now is to themselves and to the unit, but when the unit is no more, that closeness and loyalty will also pass."

He shook his head, groping for the words Robinson

needed to hear. At last he just shook his head slowly from side to side.

"There is no way to express it. We are an association of men who have to do this thing of ours. Maybe I can explain it like this: it's like one who becomes a priest. You either have the calling or you don't. And it *is* a calling."

Robinson felt that what Hendricks had just said was as close as one could ever come to the truth. It was a calling and a priesthood, a priesthood where men saluted death freely without fear or sorrow. If sadness was felt for a fallen comrade it was because he had gone on and they were left behind.

Tonight when that man had looked into his eyes, he felt something tug at him for which he had no words.

"What is this *'nuit des baïonnettes*?' "

A terrible sadness came and went from Hendricks' face. It remained only in the set of his mouth and the slight stooping of his shoulders, but he quickly corrected that by straightening his back to stand as if on parade ready to make a report.

Hendricks kept his eyes on the fire and Robinson knew he was looking back, using the flames to fuel his memories. When the words finally came, at first he wasn't sure they were coming from the mercenary.

"It wasn't so long ago, and yet for some it was a lifetime and more. In the Ebola Valley of what is called Zaire today a band of men found themselves surrounded by the enemy. For four days they held a small village on a rise by the river but were unable to get to the water. Those that tried died. Those the Simbas took died horribly. Four days and nights and every day the ring of the living on that rise grew smaller. Men's lips cracked open to expose the red tender flesh beneath, then that also cracked and dried.

"By dawn of the fourth day there were eleven wounded,

sixteen able men, and one officer alive out of one hundred and seventeen who had come to the valley. Scattered about in the yellow grass and thorn brush were over three hundred of the enemy that would not return to their kraals. It was a good killing time. All fought hard on both sides. The outnumbered defenders were running low on ammunition, but the Simbas had to attack across open ground with little or no cover.

"Before dawn the last shot was fired from the defenders. It was fired by the officer who pointed his pistol straight in the air. Neither he nor his men would kill any more of the enemy that day. They did not wish to. Before that last round was fired the survivors had talked among themselves and had come to a decision. While it was still dark they paired off into eight doubles, each standing by the one he liked, or in some cases perhaps by the one he disliked, the most. The officer was the odd man and stood alone. The ones who were wounded and had to be helped were given that by the medic. A quick injection of air into the vein and they were gone quickly.

"Eight pairs and one officer waited for the first light. They didn't want to die in the dark. When the sun began to rise, as it only can in Africa, huge, red and angry, each man embraced his partner and kissed him farewell. Even those who did not like each other did this. Then, as one, they drew their bayonets once more. They clung together, holding themselves against their partners. Then at the command of the officer they drove those long sharp blades into each other's heart.

"All died within seconds of each other, leaving only the officer alive, for as I said there were eight couples and the officer. He had no one to help him. Not that it couldn't have been arranged in some manner, but there was one thing he wished to do first before joining his men.

"From across the dry field the Simbas began to come forward. They have an instinct, you know. Somehow they knew the last shot had been fired and there was no one in the village to do them any more harm. They came across slowly, weapons hanging limply. They walked, taking no cover, dusty ebony faces shining where the sweat had cut through to the skin.

"The officer waited, standing in the circle of his dead men where they now embraced each other in death. He continued to wait. The Simbas were no more than thirty feet away when they halted, a living circle around the dead. Not a word was spoken; there was only the sound of soft breathing as the sun finally cleared the rim of the world.

"And the officer waited. Not moving, his own bayonet held to his side, he waited until the commander of the Simbas made himself known. God, he was a powerful-looking devil. He had a high-arched nose, wide nostrils, the neck of a bull, and arms which could lift the world. He came out of his ranks to twenty, then to ten feet, and stopped. He, too, was waiting for something.

"Now that he was there, the officer tried to smile but it was very difficult. His lips broke and bled. He licked the blood with his tongue and spread it around his mouth, then swallowed some so that he was able to speak.

"To the Simba leader he said, 'Welcome. We have waited for you all of our lives.'

"The Simba's eyes grew narrow. They were very dark with yellow rims.

"The officer swung around in a slow—oh, so slow—circle, the tip of his bayonet showing the Simba leader his men. When the circle was completed he raised the blade up to chest level, nodded his head at the Simba, and said, 'We win!'

"Then he plunged the blade into his own chest and fell upon the bodies of his men who had gone before him."

Eyes blinking, Robinson pulled himself back. He had lost himself in the story. Hendricks hadn't moved; he was still looking into the coals. Somehow Robinson knew the tale wasn't over. His throat rasped suddenly very dry. "What then?"

Hendricks turned to him, smiling gently. "Why, the officer didn't die. He missed his own death. The blade passed the heart. Perhaps he was too weak to judge properly or too frightened to be accurate. Whatever the reason, he lived. And while the Simbas stripped the bodies of his men and cut them into pieces, their leader would not let them have the body of the officer. The Simba pulled the blade from the officer's chest and sat beside him in the dust of that dead village all that day until it grew dark.

"He gave him neither water nor help in any manner. He just sat and waited. Sometime in the night the officer's eyes opened to see the strong chiseled black face watching him. There was no emotion in it. It was hard as granite. The Simba spoke, saying only, 'It is not for me to kill you. That I leave to you and the gods. If it is your fate to die, then you will. I have waited this long only to say this to you.'

"His voice stumbled over the next words, which were not natural to him. '*Vive le mercenaire!*' "

"Then he was gone, he and his men leaving the officer where he had fallen. The officer did not die. Somehow he survived and to his last day he will always know that at that last great moment he failed."

Robinson didn't want to ask the next question but he couldn't stop it. The words tumbled out. "Who—?"

Hendricks laughed bitterly. With his right hand he split

open his tunic. The pale scar on his chest gave Robinson the answer he already knew.

"That was my first command."

"Did you ever see the Simba leader again?"

Bitterness filled every syllable as Hendricks replied, "Yes, I did. One year later I killed him at a village called Meklate."

Raising the almost-forgotten rum bottle to his own lips Robinson did as Hendricks had and opened his throat to the burning fluid. Dropping the empty bottle to the sand, he said quietly, "*Vive le mercenaire.*"

Hendricks rose from the fire to stand in front of him. He put his arms around Robinson's shoulders and embraced him strongly. Robinson could feel the man's body through his tunic. It was warm from the heat of the campfire. Then Hendricks took Robinson's head between his hands and kissed him full on the mouth. It was a steady, deep kiss, sexless, but the feelings transmitted to Robinson were as strong as any he'd ever had. Hendricks had accepted him.

Stepping back, the mercenary leader looked Robinson deeply in the eyes, as the other man had.

"Welcome to the brotherhood of the damned. For now you are as surely cursed as any of us." Without another word, he left Robinson beside the dying fire.

Robinson stayed there till the last coal was covered by a fine thin gray ash. Then he, too, turned away. There was a feeling in him now of having become something more than he was and of having lost part of himself in the process. He, like Hendricks, could find no words to describe it. But there was no more time to think about it. He had work to do, too. His men and equipment had to be ready. When he reached the strip he looked at the silhouetted shapes of his planes standing on the runway cold and impersonal. To-morrow they would come alive. Turning back to where the campfires were he saw only dim glows as they died out one by one. He didn't know how long he had stood there. Lifting his eyes he saw Orion the Hunter overhead. To the distant constellation he whispered softly, ''Ave, Caesar, morituri te salutamus.'' Hail, Caesar, we who are about to die salute thee.

For the first time he thought he knew, if not the meaning, at least the feeling of the words spoken by the ancient gladiators of Rome when they fought to the death for the pleasure of the mobs and the kings.

It suddenly grew very cold. The night wind whipped about, touching and tugging at him. Then it was gone and for the first time in his life he felt truly alone.

Terribly, terribly alone.

SIXTEEN

NOVEMBER 1
0100 HOURS

INSIDE THE TRANSPORT each man made his own final equipment check. Straps were loosened or tightened, weapons and drop bags examined. Some touched good luck tokens and mumbled nervously under their breath. Most were just silent, waiting, expectant. In some the adrenaline rush made the tiny muscles at the sides of their temples jerk spasmodically or turned the corner of a rigid mouth up into a half grin that they weren't aware of.

Hendricks sat at the tail end of the starboard stick. They'd tailgate this one, go out the rear end when the jump master ordered the doors open, two sticks going out side by side. It would take less than fifteen seconds for all of them to exit the aircraft. Then they'd be on their own, hanging helpless for endless seconds in a night sky.

On his lap Hendricks went over a map showing the drop zone, a large open field where some English planters had once tried to raise peanuts. It was abandoned now. The fields lay fallow. The native workers had long since returned to their home villages or had just wandered off to put some distance between them and war.

Hendricks thought about Kelo. This would be his first test. Would the transport be there? Robinson had confirmed that the trucks had crossed the frontier, but were they where they were supposed to be?

From the front of the plane the jump master hit the ten-minute warning bell. Hendricks rose up and signaled with his right hand. "Number one stick, on your feet." They rose. Number two stood. Hook up. Twenty-five men slipped the metal clasps of their static lines onto the steel cable running overhead on each side of the aircraft.

"Sound off equipment check." From down each line came the response. One okay, two okay, three okay, till all had checked in. The tailgate opened, exposing the men inside to the clear cold night air of Africa. The aircraft was slowing down, dropping to the jump altitude.

Another ring of the warning bell. Five minutes. Soon the yellow light went on over the open tailgate. When it turned red they would go. No one would be permitted to back out of this jump. The jump master had moved to stand by the open gate, keeping his eyes on the front and on the men. At his side, holster flap open, he had a .45 with a round in the chamber ready to use if anyone should think about calling it quits at this stage of the game. That would not be permitted. Hendricks needed every body he had.

Night wind rushed in the open tailgate, bringing cold tears to his eyes. He wiped them clear with the back of his hand. Moving to the edge of the gate he looked out. He saw dim glows on the ground as if they were stars whose light had traveled thousands of years to reach them. They were cooking fires from the villages they passed over. To the east there were distant flashes that rippled through the dark and were gone. Heat lightning over the mountains.

Yellow light. The jump master yelled over the roar of the engines and wind, "One minute to go!"

Hendricks felt his stomach tighten as his scrotum tried to draw up higher. He had never gotten to where he really liked jumping, especially at night.

He was ready. Red light. He didn't know when his feet moved to place his body outside the aircraft. Suddenly he was just there, a tremendous roaring in his ears from the engines, his body falling, then the welcome, body-snatching jerk that said his chute had pulled out of its bag and was opening. As always there was the sense of relief and the feeling that one had cheated the odds again. Running his hands up his risers to check that they were straight, he looked over his shoulders right and left. The rest of the stick was there, their chutes blossoming dark in the night, the camouflage patterns rendering them nearly invisible. He could barely make out the darker bodies swaying back and forth, slowly oscillating as the men tried to gain control of the swing so they would hit the deck more or less upright.

Pulling down the risers to his front till his knuckles were against the center of his chest, he watched for the darker shadow of the tree line to give him a way to estimate the distance to the earth. He suddenly saw the trees, not many but enough to separate them from the horizon. At what he thought was the level where his feet would be even with the treetops, he released the risers held to his chest, letting them snap back up to break his downward fall when the canopy caught a bit more air. He hit ground. Going into a sloppy PLF, he rolled over, hitting the quick release on his chest which broke him free from the chute. He quickly released his weapon and looked around. He couldn't see shit. Others were beginning to hit the deck. From his kit bag he took his set of infrared goggles and put them on, turning the switch in the center to power up the lenses. From the bag he also removed a small but powerful hand

lamp with an infrared glass. Casting its invisible glow
around and up, he saw his men coming down now in twos
and threes. Those with night-vision glasses did as he had
and put them on to guide the others and scope out the area.
No one was to be seen. Good! Now, if Kelo was right,
there would be a barn at the south end of the barren field
behind the line of trees. He could pick out the trees but not
the barn. The range of his hand lamp wasn't strong enough
to see beyond the tree line.

His men were all down and there were no injuries that
would slow them up. Duke was already hustling them into
a defensive perimeter, spreading them out, mixing the men
with the night glasses among those that didn't have them.
Belly down, they formed a circle, weapons pointing out,
rounds in the chambers, ready.

Duke ran over to Hendricks and knelt on one knee, his
Uzi with the extended integral suppressor aiming into the
dark.

"Should I check it out now, boss?"

"Yes, go ahead, I'll hold things down here."

Duke headed out into the dark to the southern tree line
and disappeared, a green phantom that wove and dodged,
taking advantage of all cover—even in the dark.

Overhead the second drop was coming in. Hendricks
aimed his light into the night sky, knowing that it would
be seen by the cargo master who, like him, had on a pair
of the Israeli-made glasses. Only he would see the thin
beam of green radiance reaching up to the sky. Parachutes
began to open as the heavier supplies were shoved out the
tailgate. Hendricks, speaking in a normal voice, told the
men, "Don't get under the drop. Pass it on." They did,
knowing that if one of the containers came down on top of
them, it could kill them or injure them so badly they would
have little chance of surviving the operation.

Dull clumping sounds said the containers were hitting the deck. Hendricks had ordered everyone to stay clear of them till they were all down. When that happened he waved his arm, signaling them to go after them. Several of the chutes had to be dragged down to collapse them. The containers and their contents were hauled to the edge of the perimeter. Only one was opened from which three RPGs and half a dozen rockets were taken, just to be on the safe side.

A ghost with an Uzi came running back across the field. No one fired or spoke to him. Duke dropped back to his knee by Hendricks. "They're there, and the area seems to be clear."

Hendricks nodded. "Good. But let's go in at the ready." Standing, he jerked his arm up and down, the signal for ten men to break away from their comrades and join him.

"All right. Go in and spread out. Duke will take you. Bring the trucks out to us here. No lights!"

The men spread out, moving warily across the black open ground but did not lose any speed. It was done at a half run.

The rest of Hendricks's team waited. From behind the tree line came the distinct whine of a truck starter trying to engage. It missed a cough then settled into a throb. Then the second one kicked in. The trucks were coming. In less than two minutes the larger elephantine shapes of the trucks painted in the splinter desert-camo pattern of the Bokalan army bumped over the field coming to rest at the edge of the team's defensive perimeter. Four men jumped to the front of each truck attaching on adhesive plastic rims with black red thick glass centers eight inches in diameter.

"All right. Get the gear loaded. Washington, you and Jerome take the drivers' seats. The rest of you get in the back and get your equipment ready for use. Remember, use only silencers if we run into anything on the road. Those of you with the night glasses are the eyes for the others. You men without them do as your teammates say, without hesitation. Now let's go. Move easy and no talking.''

He climbed in the rear of the first truck. Duke took the tail, the men divided evenly between them. Flaps were dropped and the empty crates Kelo had promised were piled up at the rear, making the trucks look as if they carried a full load. He and Duke both moved to the front behind the cab and cut holes on either side for a gunner to take up watch.

Washington was in the lead truck, Randolph Bone beside him.

"Well, bro. It be time to start earning our money." Taking his cap off, Washington placed the IRG on his head, adjusted the straps, and turned on the headlights. "Right on, mother. This is fan-fuckin'-tastic. You know they say you can even land a plane wearing these suckers."

From behind his cab a short terse voice jerked him into action. "Cut the bullshit, Washington, and let's get moving!"

Washington laughed softly. "Yessuh, Cap'n, this boy is movn' now, suh." Easing off the clutch, he let the truck's tires grab easily, smoothly picking up traction as he pulled toward the edge of the field.

Leaving the barren field behind them they pulled onto the dirt road that would take them into the capital city of Bokala.

Washington was enjoying the experience of driving in the dark with no lights. He was trying to figure out how to take a set of the IRGs when he got paid off for the job. He laughed at himself for being so stupid. Shit man, I just steal 'em. What else.

Heat had already started to build up. Wearing double uniforms didn't help much. The open window provided some relief but the air was heavy, oppressive. The storm front was coming in. Going back the way the truck had come, Washington turned on his headlights, then hit the dirt road leading to the highway that went to Bokala. Fifteen miles to go.

There were two checkpoints to get through, one of them at the bridge crossing the M'pini River, which was almost dry now. But an hour after rains came it would be a raging torrent. Hitting the road, Washington checked the odometer. He had to have his distances down perfectly.

In the truck behind him, Jerome drummed rhythm patterns on his steering wheel; his partner was silent. Turning to look at his shotgun rider, Jerome could see, even in the haze of the goggles, that his rider's eyes seemed wide and frightened.

"Be cool, bro. This turkey is going down fine. Jest fine. Jest don' you tense up on me. If there's any shit to take care of I'll do it."

They passed no one on the road. The only village they went through was silent and dark. Only the weak yapping of a pariah dog left behind by its masters gave any indication of life. In fact just behind the village in a drainage ditch white sticks lay scattered about amid round milky stones. That was where most of the villagers had ended up when Mehendi's troops had taken them out to the ditch. He had lined them up and hacked them to pieces with pangas after first raping the women as their men and children watched.

Thin beams of green light cut through the dark, showing no signs of life. Even the animals had left. Empty kraals of beehive-shaped wattle and thatch appeared, then passed quickly out of the lights.

Washington watched the road carefully, driving relaxed but ready to respond if anything unexpected presented itself. All they needed was to break an axle or throw a driveshaft. Do as the boss said, keep it at thirty and steady. All was cool. No rush. Just make it easy on yourself.

Checking the odometer, he saw that there was just over a click to go. Raising his hand he rapped on the rear of his cab.

"We're just about there, Boss."

Hendricks's muffled voice came to him from the rear. "All right. Remember your orders."

"You got it, Boss."

Pulling the truck over to the side of the dirt road, he cut the motor and turned off the lights. The trailing truck stopped twenty meters behind him. All the men jumped off and spread out into the brush, taking cover.

Hendricks checked his watch against Washington's.

"Give us fifteen minutes, then come on through. Just be natural."

"Got it, Boss. You take care, hear?"

"Duke! Move 'em out."

Taking point, Duke led the way off the side of the road about a hundred and fifty meters out, then straightened out to run parallel to the road. Hendricks stayed to the center of the column. If things went right they'd bypass the guardpost and Washington and Jerome's trucks would come on through to pick them up on the other side. If he could, he wanted to avoid any killing before he had to. Premature action could blow their element of surprise or put the city on a stronger alert profile.

Dry brush gave them plenty of cover as Duke led them in and out of gullies and washes, taking one direction and then another but always coming back on course. He followed the line of least resistance, moving with the land. After ten minutes he halted, raised his arm, and pointed to the right. The guardpost. Four men. Sandbagged position one, what looked like an American .30-caliber light machine gun. Looking up he saw a strand of wire coming down from a pole. Landline communications. Duke signaled to Hendricks.

Hendricks nodded, moved up to the front, slapped Duke on the shoulder. Duke took three men with him and cut across the road to the side where the sandbagged position was. He'd be there to cover the trucks in case anything went wrong. Hendricks took the rest of the group on past, swinging out in a semicircle that brought him up to a curve in the road well out of sight of the guardpost. He signaled his men to settle down, and they took up positions covering the road to their flanks. Now it was Washington's turn. Fifteen minutes had passed.

Washington, Jerome, and their shotgun riders had taken off the infrared shields from their headlights, then stripped off their first layer of clothing, exposing the uniforms of the Bokalan army. Washington had promoted himself to senior sergeant.

It was time to go straight in. Climbing in the cabs, they cranked up the trucks, pulled back out on the dirt road, and headed for the guardpost doing forty miles an hour. It was a good solid speed, not too slow and not so fast it would convey any sense of urgency. A good solid speed.

It took him only three minutes to reach where he could see the guardpost illuminated in his headlights. Two men stood in the roadway, waving their arms. To the right he saw the light machine gun traverse, and it was looking down their throats. Bone made a gurgling sound.

"Don't tense up on me, motherfucker. If you do you won't have to worry about those dudes. I'll do you myself."

Bone choked back his fear, forcing his eyes straight ahead. He was frozen.

Washington began breaking, nice and normal. He took a quick look at Bone's face. Ahh, shit, man! That fool's gonna get me killed. The feel of the Browning 9-mm between his thighs was a bit comforting, but not much. He hoped that Duke and his men were where they were supposed to be.

Breaking to a halt, he lit up a Nigerian cigarette as the guards checked them over from a distance. Then, one on each side, they moved forward to his truck. Washington was just preparing to give them a normal greeting when Bone broke. His body started to shake as tears ran in streams down his face. He opened his mouth, his throat muscles quivering. Washington knew that he was going to howl.

Ahh, shit, man!

The two guards stared in wonder at Bone. As so many did in Africa, they had a superstitious fear of the mad. While their eyes were on Bone, whose howl had just begun at the back of his throat, Washington came up with the Browning, whipped it over his left arm, and shot the guard on his side of the truck just above his left eyebrow. Not waiting to see the effect of his shot, he leaned across Bone and took out the other guard with two quick rounds, first in the cheek, the second in his right eye. As he did, he whispered out loud, "C'mon Dukey-Doo!"

The remaining two guards behind the LMG felt dull thuds against their backs, then a coldness in their chests where the front of their bodies suddenly exploded to let in the night air.

Bone's howl had reached deafening proportions. His eyes bugged out of their sockets, his jaw opened to the point of cracking, and the scream kept coming. Washington shot him in the temple.

"I tol' you, nigger. Be cool! You jes' wouldn't listen."

Checking over the bodies, seeing that there was no need for a brain shot on either of them, Duke and his three men, their weapons giving off thin wisps of oil smoke from the silenced barrels, went over to Washington. Duke told them to get in the rear truck, then looked into Washington's cab at the slumped figure of Bone.

"Flipped on you, didn't he?"

Washington looked a bit embarrassed but forced a big white grin. "Well, Boss, this is jes' one of those rare times when black wasn't beautiful. Probably had a honky in the woodpile somewhere."

Duke leaned back to look at the second truck. Jerome was still sitting behind the wheel. He waved an okay at Duke.

"Okay, put the IFRs on your trucks while I take care of something."

They did as he said while he went back to the sand-bagged bunker. Throwing over one of the bodies, he found what he was looking for, the field telephone. Quickly he made a couple of minor adjustments to it with his pen-knife. If anyone rang, the phone wouldn't be dead. They'd just get static back on their end. Line problems.

When he finished he gave orders for all the dead to be dragged over and dumped in the brush. That included Bone's body, too.

Moving to the front of the truck he took Bone's place in the front seat.

"Well what are you waiting for? We still got some work to do tonight."

SEVENTEEN

NOVEMBER 1
0430 HOURS

WASHINGTON GRINNED AGAIN, settled his spaceman goggles on his head, started the motor, and pulled out, followed by Jerome.

"You know, Dukey-Doo, this is going to be one hell of a night."

"Call me Dukey-Doo one more time and you won't see morning."

Washington took a look at Duke through his goggles. Even with the haze the set of the bearded man's mouth said quite clearly, "Shut the fuck up and drive." Washington nodded his head in agreement. That was just what he was going to do. No more Dukey-Doos, no sir!

When the trucks reached Hendricks's position, he stepped out on the road. Washington stopped. Going to the passenger side, Hendricks looked in. "Problems?"

"We had to take out the roadblock, Boss. We had one casualty—Bone!"

Hendricks saw the blood on the back of the seat but only said, "Clean that up."

Duke wiped down the seat with a rag; when he had finished, Hendricks asked, ''Are the phone lines taken care of?''

''Yes, sir. I fixed them so if anyone calls it'll just sound like the phones have a problem and aren't ringing through.''

''Very good.'' Hendricks went to the rear and waved to the rest of his men to come out and get loaded back up. They still had miles to go before the sun rose. As soon as they were all on board they moved out. They were on schedule but not with much leeway.

Through the haze of the IFRs the sides of the road showed stark limbs of trees standing twisted and angry, as though trying to reach to the distant heavens for the waters that came only often enough to sustain life, never enough to stave off the thirst of the land and that which lived upon it. Between the isolated baobab and the trees called elephant tusk, the grass was still dry and yellow.

Only the rising dust thrown up by their heavy tires marked their passage. The men in the trucks were ready. More than ready. For most it would be a relief when they finally moved into action. It was the waiting that fed the cold spots of fear lying at the bottom of the gut. With action the cold would turn hot, as hot as human blood.

Washington kept an eye on the odometer. ''We're coming up on the next checkpoint, Boss,'' he called back in his deep voice.

''All right. Give me the mark when we reach it.'' Peering through his peephole, Hendricks wiped away tears brought by the harsh, dry wind rushing against his face. The check couldn't be seen but in the distance were lights. Too many to be a village and spread out too far. Bokala was only minutes away.

The truck began slowing down again, easing to a halt. The process at the first checkpoint was repeated. This time

Washington had no trouble getting through. The guards figured that if they had passed through the first one then there was little need for another check. And the insignia of the Presidential Askaris on the sides of the doors made their decision easy for them. They waved the two trucks through.

Washington picked up his cargo again a kilometer past the checkpoint. He had to wait a few extra minutes till Duke returned from another job.

Hendricks spoke to him quickly before he climbed back into the truck. "All the charges set for 0520 hours?"

"Yes sir. At 0520 the lights go out all over Bokala."

"Good. Let's go. The door's open."

In the next kilometer they began to pass a few individuals and family groups on the road heading out of the city. At a small bridge the refugees turned off the road to go into the bush, reluctant to pass the military checkpoints. As the trucks passed, Washington saw that the refugees avoided looking at him. Their bodies took on a tenseness around the shoulders and back. They were dirt poor; all they had they carried with them. Men with tumplines around the forehead bent over under their loads. Women carried bundles balanced on their heads and had small, round, softer-looking bundles wrapped in long scarves hanging from their backs. Babies! The children who could walk, small, black stick figures with distended abdomens, stayed close to the larger, dark figures of their parents. Even in the IFR lights of the trucks their eyes were incredibly large, stark and glowing against the dark dusty faces. If they wondered how or why the passing trucks with the insignia of the Askaris on them had no visible headlights they didn't show it. They wanted no part of the men with guns in the trucks.

Washington kept his mind off of them. It gave him an

uneasy feeling. His blood came from those sad, thin figures seeking safety in a land that was only slightly less hostile than their own people. He knew that most of them would die in the next days or weeks. There weren't too many of them, perhaps twenty different groups. Most who could had already left the capital.

He was glad his brother wasn't here to see this. He had too much social conscience. One of these days it'd get his ass killed. Too sensitive. No, he was better off coming in with the second unit. He wouldn't like the shit that was going to go down this morning.

Hendricks had him pull over once they passed the last group of refugees. It was time to take off the IFR headlamps. Trucks driving blind in the city would attract too much attention. From here on they would move as if all were normal.

Taking off their goggles, Washington and Jerome rubbed their eyes. The white lights of the headlamps didn't look natural anymore. Everything was too bright. But it took only a few moments for them to adjust to this new condition.

As they continued, Washington came to a large sign in English and French welcoming travelers and tourists to the "Great Capital City of Bokala."

Hendricks snapped his fingers. The men in his truck tensed. He knew they would be feeling the same thing in Jerome's truck. They were coming into the city. Weapons were held a little tighter, fingers caressing triggers. Their weapons were now the only security they had and their only way out.

The boxes in the rear of the trucks, which hid them from outside eyes, were pushed out of the way. The flaps were still down but the ties could be released with the pull of a cord. From the openings in the flaps eyes looked out at the rows of clapboard shacks on either side of them.

It could have been any of a half dozen towns in the West Indies or on the Mosquito Coast of Honduras. With one exception: the silence. The city was heavy with silence. The thousands of unnoticed sounds that said a city or village was alive were gone. There was nothing.

Washington followed the road as if he'd been driving it all his life. He knew exactly where they were. He had memorized landmarks as well as the streets from the photos. They didn't have far to go. The Presidential Palace was on the outskirts away from the town's center.

A motorized patrol passed them. Four men in a jeep, the two in the rear facing backwards, fingers on the triggers of their AK-47s. The shotgun rider kept his concentration on the front, an RPD light machine gun pointing its ugly nozzle ahead of him. Washington lifted a hand in seemingly uninterested greeting and passed them by. When he put his hand to his face he was surprised to find it covered with sweat.

As the jeep went on about its patrol of the empty streets, automatic weapons followed their progress from the backs of the trucks until Washington turned off to the left on the Rue Liberté. They were almost there.

Now they saw thin glows coming from a few buildings near the heart of power where the streets were patrolled. People still lived here, some of them officials and members of Mehendi's tribe. They had nowhere to go. If he fell so did they. They were committed.

Three more patrols passed them in jeeps and on several corners walking slowly were two-man teams. Security police. One started to raise his hand to flag down the lead truck. Washington ignored him, shaking his fist as if he were in a hurry, on important business with no time to play games. Dropping his half-raised hand, the security man lit a cigarette, the glow clearly showing tribal scars on his face. He turned back to his companion to take up once more their lonely and mostly boring foot tour of three square blocks. They weren't too concerned. Okediji and his savages were still far away to the south and there hadn't been many cases of terrorism in the city for the last two weeks.

Tapping on the rear, Washington got Hendricks's attention. They were there. Peering through his peephole, Hendricks saw the front of a large tin building with locked double doors. Cutting the lights, Washington walked casually up to the doors and opened the unlocked warehouse, swinging the doors wide. He climbed back into the truck, pulled inside, and turned off his lights after entering. As soon as Jerome's vehicle was inside he went back and closed the doors.

From the backs of the two trucks, stiff, tense men piled out taking up positions around the warehouse, two men each covering the two windows at the east and west sides. To the south there was only the rear wall. Inside the building were crates, boxes, paper, and refuse to show this once had been a place of business. Now it, like most of the city, was abandoned.

"Squad leaders, here!" Duke and the squad leaders presented themselves to Hendricks at the doors to the warehouse.

"Gentlemen, it's time to move. Use your goggles; make sure your men are silent. No talking, no gear rattling. Give each of your men a personal check over. If he isn't right then it's our ass. Remember, if possible, avoid any confrontations with enemy patrols or sentries. We want the palace, not a general firefight. If it is absolutely necessary to take out someone en route, use the silencers. I'll personally shoot any man who fires without permission."

Looking at every man's face, Hendricks tried to see

behind the eyes. Their eyes were good, steady. There was
a fire in them with the knowledge of impending action, but
that was as it should be. It would put them on the edge.
They'd be sharp, ready to cut when the time was right.

"Give me a time check. In six seconds, five, four,
three, two, one. It is now exactly 0418 and thirty seconds.

"Form your teams, the designated men to remain with
the trucks. Remind them of their time schedule. If they're
not on time, then no one's going home. Now, let's take a
look at the target."

Duke took point, taking them out of the south window
to where they'd have the protection of the shadows. The
air held a slightly acrid smell of wood smoke mingled with
the denser, cloying aroma of decaying trash. With his
goggles on, Duke led the way, Hendricks staying to the
center of the Indian file of camouflaged and heavily armed
men. Foam-rubber-soled boots whispered beneath dark-
ened windows. They crossed the first block, weaving in
and out of the shadows, weapons at the ready. But in each
man's mind was the warning from Hendricks.

At the next block they had to wait until a motor patrol
moved on, then by twos they sprinted across the wide
thoroughfare that was the Avenue des Marches. It was
lined with modern office buildings built by the French
before the country was granted independence. Now they,
like most of the city, were empty and desolate.

Duke raised his hand, signaling a halt. The mercenaries
hunkered down, watching to the front and rear. There, in
front of them, was the national park. Tall trees lined untended lanes where lovers once walked or hid themselves
in groves of flowers to make love on warm nights. And
across from the park was the palace. Lights glowed at all
corners, illuminating the figures of the men who patrolled
the edifice.

Casting the beam of his IFR handlamp, Duke saw a couple of two-man teams moving among the untended growth of the park, using conventional flashlights to probe the dark.

Hendricks saw them, too. His mouth close to Duke's ear, he whispered, "We have no choice. Take Washington, Jerome, and Johnson with you and take them out!"

Duke's back was turned, but Hendricks felt his smile as he nodded his head. Jerome, Washington, and Johnson held a quick hushed conference. They all grinned.

Waiting till the Askaris moved away into a thick grove of trees, the four men sprinted on silent feet across the littered pavement where windblown debris and trash collected in patches and clumps against curbs and buildings. They disappeared into the cover of the trees. Hendricks and the rest of the team waited, half-expecting to hear shots at any moment.

Slinging their assault rifles on their backs, they tracked the Askaris. Washington and Jerome took the ones on the left, Duke and Johnson the ones to the right. They had their laser-sighted pistols out, silencers extending their muzzles.

Once they spotted their targets, Duke and Johnson crawled on their bellies closing the gap with their quarry. The Askaris halted. One of them turned around looking through the dark in the direction of the two stalkers. He had felt rather than heard something. It was animal instinct.

The Askaris moved, coming toward the mercs lying hidden in the bushes. Cold beams from the flashlights probed the dark. They came closer: thirty feet, then twenty. When the beam of the flashlights swung to the right, Duke and Johnson rose to their knees. Each fired two shots, going for the head. The laser sights made a miss impossible. Johnson's target had a quizzical expression on his face a half second before his right eye was blown out the back of his skull. He had seen the tiny dot of red that touched on the temple of his partner's head. The second shots were superfluous. Through the goggles the heads of the Askaris looked as if two large green grapes had been held between monstrous fingers and suddenly popped. Subsonic exploding rounds have that effect. The bodies dropped, empty sacks that crumbled to the grassy floor of the park.

Washington and Jerome went about it in a more direct manner. They were wearing their Askari uniforms. Shouldering their assault rifles, they simply walked up to the two unwary patrollers. Washington gave them a low-voiced greeting, then put on a startled look and pointed to the Askaris' rear. When they turned to look, he and Jerome shot them in the backs of their heads using their laser-sighted suppressed .45s.

Within seconds the bodies of the four Askaris had been dragged back and hidden in a flowerbed.

Stepping to the edge of the park, Duke gave an up-and-down movement with a clenched fist.

Hendricks slapped the man in front of him on the back. "Let's go!"

EIGHTEEN

NOVEMBER 1
0515 HOURS

THEY WERE ACROSS and under cover in a matter of seconds. Hendricks motioned for the radio transmitter operator to stay close to him. Communication was going to be very important in the next minutes. It was almost time!

Carefully they kept out of any possible visible range of sight from the palace walls, concealing themselves in bushes and shadows and lying close to the earth. Each man knew that the slightest sound or movement could mean death or even worse, capture. They were lucky that Mehendi had sent all available forces to fight against Okediji.

There was a drizzle now and it was increasing to a gentle steady rain. It wasn't much more than a heavy mist but it helped conceal them.

There were only two armored cars; they looked like British Saladins. They stood, one at each corner of the palace facing the park and giving cover to the broad avenue. Those would be the biggest threat, but if things went as planned they'd be taken care of from their weak side. The rest of the security consisted of no more than the troops of Mehendi's bodyguard manning the walls and a few military police units patrolling the city streets to inforce the curfew.

Traffic around the park was almost nonexistent. Even the majority of homes for two or three blocks around the park were vacant. The residents, smelling trouble, had moved away, putting as much distance as possible between them and the soldiers of Mehendi. Those soldiers at the palace were well known to be a bit trigger happy.

In the deserted streets one could feel only the night wind and see only the fleeting flickers of dark swift birds as they fed on insects. Searchlights from the two corner towers facing the main street occasionally swept over the grounds of the park. Inside the palace, lights in two offices on the upper floor glowed. Several times Hendricks saw shadows move across them. Someone was working late. He knew that one of the windows was that of the communications center. The wall blocked any view of the ground-floor windows, though he knew there were lights on in the ballroom from the glow cast up to outline the top of the wall. A streetlight at each end of the block was the only other illumination.

It was getting close now. Everything had to be on schedule. One bit of wrong timing and they'd all be dead men, or worse. He wished he'd been able to talk face-to-face with Kelo one more time. If he didn't do his job then they were all goners. Three minutes to go.

A single truck loaded with drunken troops trundled past, the truck sounding as if it was badly in need of a new carburetor.

From a distance Hendricks thought he heard a woman's scream but it was cut off too quickly for him to be sure. It could have just been hysterical laughter, but somehow he doubted it. One minute to go. He clicked the send button on his radio transmitter and was answered. He snapped his fingers once softly, signaling the designated men to put the Israeli infrared goggles on and adjust the head bands till they fit snug. The powerful hand lamps were turned on, casting their invisible beams. Only those with the night-vision devices could see where the beams went.

Thirty seconds. He snapped again. The two-man teams got ready. Fifteen seconds. Hendricks's mouth was dry, sticky, and foul tasting, as it always was just before he moved into action.

He gave a single quick click on his hand radio transmitter and was answered immediately. On the other side Duke was ready to move.

Five seconds. God! I hope Kelo is on the ball. The streets went dark.

Kelo stepped into the palace commo room at the moment the streets went dark. He had been waiting for it. His face showed nothing of the tension that had been eating at him for the last weeks. This was the time. If it went down right he might even have a chance to put a bullet or two inside Mehendi's brain.

The emergency lights kicked on, powered by the palace generator. Walabahji Djbouk set the pistol in his hand back down on the desk by the radio transmitter. Kelo nodded his head at him. Djbouk turned back to his radio desk, working on a coded message.

Kelo moved up behind the communications officer, his hand trembling slightly with anticipation. He stared at the man's back. There was a pimple right at the collar, the head of it picked off where Djbouk had scratched at it. Kelo's eyes focused on the small swelling. He smiled. For the first time in years he gave an honest truthful grin, his wide lips splitting to show large strong white teeth.

The silenced Ruger with the suppressor built by Stroesser came to a stop one inch from the pimple. Kelo saw a shiver run up Djbouk's spine as goose bumps rose around the pimple. He knew the man felt something, that sixth sense. Gently, without rushing it, he squeezed the trigger. The .22 hollowpoint long rifle bullet entered the pimple— severing the spinal cord. Firing twice more he placed each round an inch higher than the other. It was unnecessary; Lieutenant Djbouk was dead. The only sound from the .22 was a very slight hiss, like that of a man taking a breath, and the tiny clatter of three small empty cartridge casings hitting the wooden floor of the commo room.

Easing the body from its chair, Kelo sat down at the radio and made his call to the airfield, informing them they were going to have company in a few minutes. He gave them the call signs and code which would permit the incoming aircraft to land in safety. He deftly avoided the control officer's attempt to draw him into idle chatter, claiming much work and messages waiting to be decoded.

Satisfied, he rose from the chair. He took up the silenced pistol and put three more rounds into the radio set, then two more into the backup unit across the room. There would be no more calls made from the palace this night. Taking his time, he changed clips, slapping in a fresh one. He still had one more job to do—the palace generator. A quick glance at his watch; he was on time. Locking the door behind him, he headed for the basement and the generator.

Hendricks's space-goggled men moved out, circling to avoid the eyes of the armored-car crew. Only one of them was on watch and he was more concerned with the four days of discomfort that he and his crew had endured. They had not been permitted to leave their vehicle except to relieve themselves, but then they had to return at once. Even their meals were brought to them. And now to make things even worse their discomfort was compounded by the first drops of rain. He was about to take a look around but it was too much effort and he was too weary and miserable to concern himself with what was nothing more than the shuffling of leaves going past him in the dark.

They made it past the Saladins to the far corners. Hendricks sent two men for each corner. They had only seconds in which to do the job. Through his goggles he saw the green-hazed bodies move across the sullen street, their bodies pushing up against the wall. Lightning crackled across the sky for a second, splitting the heavens with earth-shaking rumbles. The ghost forms moved a step away and he saw their hands raise and sparks of phosphorescent light rapidly spit out of the hands of the number-one man as number two threw a rubber-lined grappling hook up onto the lip of the wall and began to climb. Good, he thought, they're going to do it. Glancing back to the left he saw the same progression taking place. The suppressed Uzis had done their job. Silently they had killed the two sentries at each of the corner towers and his men were already climbing up over the wall to take their places. The crews of the armored cars heard nothing. Whatever sound might have been made by the silenced Uzis or the crumpling of bodies shot through the face and head were covered by the continuous rumbles in the sky.

From around the palace came cries of confusion and laughter. Power outages were not uncommon. Hendricks heard the diesel generator in the rear of the palace cough, miss, cough again, and begin to kick over. Lights were coming on again on the palace grounds though the rest of the city was in darkness.

Hendricks wondered if Duke and his men had made it.

Two quick clicks over his radio transmitter, which were repeated once, reassured him. They were there.

Their section of the wall cleared of enemy troops, Duke and his team dropped into the rear courtyard to take cover in the sculptured bushes and gardens. To his right he saw the dark shape of the palace garage and three two-and-a-half-ton Chevy trucks parked side by side in front of it. Good! He'd tend to them later.

He took advantage of the coming storm and the cover it gave and had his men make a run for it to their assigned targets. Within thirty seconds ten satchel charges of fifteen pounds each of C4 explosive had been attached to the wall around the guards' quarters and the rear offices. They were connected together by a strand of primer cord attached to one charger. When Duke twisted the handle one third of the palace walls would crumble and those inside the blast area, if they survived the multiple explosions, would probably have headaches and a loss of hearing for the rest of their lives.

Satisfied with his handiwork, Duke signaled his men to pull back to the cover of the gardens and conceal themselves. It wasn't yet time. He fed out the wire spool that would connect the primer cord to the charger when he was in position. The satchel charges were well placed, each concealed from casual view either by parts of a hedge or in shadows under window lips.

Lying in a bush, dripping with tropical flowers bouncing gently up and down under the weight of raindrops, a chill ran over his body caused by the same rain soaking into his battle dress and onto his skin. It felt good. The thing was going down better than planned; no casualties taken on his part. The only dead were the limp bodies of the Askaris he had left behind when they'd taken the walls. Satisfied, he communicated his status to Hendricks. He was ready for the next act to begin.

Hendricks had the four corners in his possession. And Duke was in place, his charges set. Now for the next stage. So far Kelo had been on the money about everything. Time check. Give the troops on the parapets time to settle down. Don't be in a rush. With the streetlights out only the searchlights presented any problem and they swept by in fairly regular patterns.

He waited till he established their routine again. Tapping the soldier next to him on the shoulder, he gave him a slight shove signaling it was time. The merc did the same to the man next to him. They slid out on their bellies to where they were still in the shadows. When the light swept by, they raced hunched over to the east guard tower. The rope and grappling hook had been moved so they could climb directly into the guardpost itself. Both men were up and inside in less than forty-five seconds, by which time the searchlight was making another sweep.

Now for the left. He sent Washington and Jerome. The process was repeated. He was in good shape now if the lid would only stay on a few more minutes.

On the west tower the men with the night glasses ducked down out of sight leaving the tower to Washington and Jerome. For now it was up to the two soul brothers to handle things. They'd have other work to do in a few minutes. Washington pushed the bodies of the dead palace guards to where they'd be out of the way and checked the belt on the light machine gun. Jerome stood facing out toward the park, his back to the inner grounds. Washington was waved at by the roving patrol from the ground. From the dim glow coming from the windows of the palace only his shit-colored uniform was visible, so he casually returned the wave to them and they passed on.

Sweating profusely, Washington shook his head. How in the hell did he let that honky mother talk him into this shit? He checked his watch. Soon it would be time to take out the roving patrol. He knew there was another on the other side of the palace. The six men of the patrol should be no problem. The two men lying in the bottom of the tower had the goodies to do their shit for them. Then they'd have to set the charges on the gate.

Franklin, lying on the bottom of the tower, raised his head up over the concrete lip and looked toward the park. Hendricks turned his infrared light off and on twice. The signal. Franklin whispered to Jerome and Washington, "Do it!" Washington moved the LMG over slightly where he'd be able to cover the gate tower if Jerome got into any trouble.

His partner was to move out of the tower and head down the walkway, killing the men spaced out between him and the gates. He'd have to provide Jerome with cover till that job was done. With one hand on the LMG and the other on the handle of the searchlight, he swept the light back and forth, careful not to break the pattern that had been established by the previous tenants. Once Jerome had done his shit they would then have to provide cover for the courtyard between them and the goggled men. That's when the two lying down in the tower would have to kill the guards on roving patrol in the courtyard.

Hissing under his breath, Washington gave his watch one more look. "You ready to do this mother, Jerome?"

His partner grinned, his startling white teeth glowing in the dark. "Bet your ass."

Jerome began his walk down the parapet, taking his

time. He didn't want to call any attention to himself. The model 1911 .45 with the laser sight and extended silencer snout hung limply by his side. The rifle he had taken from one of the dead men was slung casually over his shoulder. He came to the first man. This one was too easy. The man never even heard him coming. His eyes were following the magnetic sweep of the searchlight. Raising the pistol, Jerome placed the red dot of the laser sight behind his ear and shot him, blowing three-fourths of his skull out the front of his head. With one hand he caught the body by the shoulder and eased it to the floor of the walkway. One down.

He kept on moving. At the next position there were two men. One hailed him pleasantly by what Jerome assumed was the name of the man he'd just killed. He waved his empty left hand in greeting.

"*Jambo, M'pelek na swathil!*" He asked how they were doing. The nearest man turned to face him and again came the *thuuu* of the silenced .45. Jerome knew what he was doing. This round took the man just below his nose, erupting out of the back of his head, throwing blood and brains over the back of the next man who never really had time to register what was happening before another of the heavy, slow slugs from the .45 hit him in the temple.

Jerome changed clips. Best to have a full load in. He had a clear path now to the tower guarding the gate. That would have to be timed close, but there was enough light to see whether or not the team on the other tower had made it there. If not, he was to kill the men, take over their gun, and start blowing away the men in the opposite gate tower. Then Hendricks and his men would come over the wall and go for the palace itself. They'd hit from the front and Duke and his team would come in from the rear

and seal off the guards' quarters, keeping any who survived tied up till they could be dealt with.

Keeping ten feet between him and the tower, he waited,
facing out to the park and glancing repeatedly to his left
till he saw what he had been waiting for. His counterpart
on the other side of the wall was ready. They looked
across at each other and gave a short mutual nod, raised
their laser-sighted pistols, placed the red dots, and began
firing. One shot for each guard, again in the head. None of
the rounds missed; all four men went down. Jerome thought
to himself, Motherfucker! If we'd had these cocksuckers
in 'Nam the shit would have been different. These are
definitely no-miss, sure-hit motherfuckers. He turned to
face the palace taking a small penlight from his side
pocket. He aimed it at a window on the second floor, third
window from the left, and blinked it twice. The signal was
answered. Two minutes to go. Turning back to face the
tower, he gave a thumbs-up sign to Washington. The two
men lying doggo in the bottom of the tower got ready to
head down the stairs to the courtyard. Facing back to the
park, he knew that Hendricks was watching him. Raising
his right arm, he brought it up and down twice, quickly.

Rising to his feet, Hendricks hissed, "Let's get to it! On
to the wall." His team moved out in a ragged line as they
broke out of bushes and from behind trees. The first men
hit the wall with grappling hooks and were clambering up
as the next group came behind them. Hendricks was the
second man up. As soon as he got to his feet on the
rampart the palace went dark. Kelo had gotten the generator. The two men in the tower with Washington headed for
the courtyard. The infrared lights attached to the barrels of
their weapons guided them. They were going hunting.

As soon as all of Hendricks's team were on top of the
rampart he spread them out. Scoping out the courtyard at

the north side, he saw bright flashes reach out again and again. With sweat running down his back and from his armpits, he waited for the sound of any return fire. There was none. The roving patrol had been taken care of.

Washington and Jerome were given the assignment of taking out the Saladins when the shit went down. Each had one of the fifteen-pound satchel charges with a five-second fuse. Washington took the north corner tower and Jerome the south. From there all they had to do was lean out, pull the striker, and drop the charges on the Saladins. Even if they were five or ten feet off, the explosive would damage the thin-skinned vehicles enough that they could be taken out easily by an RPG.

Hendricks led the way into the courtyard. He jumped from the wall, going into a roll, coming up with his FN at the ready. Followed by the rest of his team, they spread out across the tailored lawn and moved in on the palace, one man each to every downstairs window in the front. Five were assigned to the windows of the ballroom. Running hunched over, expecting to hear the flat staccato crack of a machine gun ripping at him at any moment, Hendricks stepped over the two dead sentries at the entrance. Behind him those not assigned to windows spread out on either side. The dark was their friend. In the green glow of the infrared the door stood flat and immovable.

A satchel charge was hung on the door. The demo man holding the striker in hand was ready to pull at the signal. Stopping, Hendricks looked right and left, raising his arm. The men at the windows responded in kind. They were ready. Only the men at the windows of the ballroom had the flash-and-stun grenades. The rest of them had two-pound satchel charges of C4 plastique. The only thing they had in common was that all of them had three-second fuses, including the charge on the door.

His arm came down and simultaneously strikers were pulled on the igniters. Through every window, so close together it was impossible to distinguish any difference between them, the explosives were thrown, crashing through the glass. Only two flash-stun grenades were heaved into the ballroom windows, the throwers trying to angle them so they would land at the far ends of the ballroom away from the main body of prisoners.

Backs against the wall, the men only had time to draw a quick breath before the explosions went off. There wasn't time enough for screams as Hendricks's men hit each of the windows and climbed inside. They found only mangled dead bodies lying smashed against the walls. The main door had been blown thirty feet inside the hallway, killing both guards inside. Hendricks went in followed by three of his men. There was chaos in the ballroom. The stun grenades had done their work. The guards inside weren't able to do anything; they were frozen or slumped against the walls, eyes open, eardrums ruptured, fingers unable to pull the triggers on their weapons.

In the guards' quarters, sleeping men didn't have time to register the cause of the explosions to the front of the palace before their world erupted. Duke grinned nakedly in the dark, the patterns of his camouflage face paint turning the smile into something unworldly. He twisted the handle of the charger. The rear wall of the palace crumbled inward, bringing down a section of the second floor onto the first, burying bodies alive. Duke and his team sprinted for the openings they created in the walls, leaping inside, their weapons firing. Anything that moved died and anything that looked dead was shot again, for safety.

It was nearly impossible to focus on anything in the dust and smoke. The only clear sounds were the screams of the wounded and dying, and they were being silenced. So far so good. They were at the door leading to the palace interior and the hallway connecting to the front reception area. Calling two men over to him, Duke detached them from the clearing party and sent them off to the palace garages. Both had previously served time as professional car thieves. They could get anything made in Detroit, Tokyo, or Bavaria open and running within one minute.

The rescue element was inside. People were stumbling in the dark, many of them on the floors, their mouths open, unable even to scream. That would change in seconds. Quickly the team lashed out. Flashes appeared as small bursts of manmade lightning reached out and hit their targets. Askari guards died everywhere. One hostage, a man wearing only a white shirt and pants, went down when he somehow came off the floor at the moment a burst of automatic fire was on its way to the chest of an Askari. Both died. There was no time to worry about mistakes.

The front entrance to the ballroom burst open. Hendricks was inside, his men spreading out. Grabbing the bodies on the floors, they hauled them to their feet, shuffling them to the doors and windows. Women began to scream as they regained the ability to utter sounds. But several of the hostages could not even scream or hear because of ruptured eardrums.

Then it was over. And inside the ballroom eight Askaris were dead, plus one hostage. He would be left behind. There was no time to carry dead weight.

Several hysterical women and two men who seemed unable to control their mouths or their bowels sobbed or screamed. Hendricks silenced this with a burst of machine-gun fire into the ceiling.

"Silence!" he yelled. "We have come to take you out. Obey my men's orders and you will get home. Give me any shit and I'll leave you behind. Now shut your fucking mouths and do as I say. File out of here quickly into the front courtyard. You'll be loaded into trucks and moved out. No talking, no hesitation. If you give me trouble I'll either leave you behind or kill you myself. Now get your asses moving and take nothing with you but your bodies. Now go. We don't have much time."

NINETEEN

NOVEMBER 1
0531 HOURS

ROBINSON HAD JUST picked up his signal from Hendricks that all was a go. The signal had come in just as the rain had begun to fall. He called down to the tower using the information and the clearances provided by Kelo. He was in essence being welcomed with open arms. The runways were clear for his approach.

Hitting the buzzer, he gave the warning bell for his passengers in the rear.

Becaude stood and yelled above the roar of the engines, "We are going in. As soon as we have touched down get ready to exit. You know your targets. Let nothing stop you. In this job, if one man fails so could the mission. Remember, no prisoners. We have no time for such niceties, so kill them all."

The whine of the hydraulics letting down the landing gear interrupted him.

"It is time. Check your weapons, rounds in the chambers, safeties on till you exit the aircraft. Wait for the order, then go and kill everything you see. This is a free-fire zone and no one out there is on our side.''

With a shudder, the transport began to drop, lining up on the string of lights below. Robinson was on the glide path coming in smooth and easy.

His palms were slick with sweat as they held the controls. He began to cut back on the throttle, lowering the flaps, trying to keep his mind on the job at hand. He ignored the possibility that he might be bringing them into a trap. If Kelo had not done his job or if the mission had been blown by Hendricks and his group, then there would be guns waiting for them as soon as they touched the tarmac. But he forced his mind to focus on the present task. His body knew otherwise, giving out all kinds of signals: the sweating of his palms, a tremor in one knee, a sudden tiny tic at the corner of his mouth, which was suddenly very dry and foul tasting. The wheels hit. One slight bounce and he was down. Reversing his props, he rolled to the far end of the runway knowing that the second aircraft would be hitting the deck fifteen seconds behind him. There was no gunfire, only the normal radio transmitter chatter from the tower welcoming them to Bokala International Airport.

Becaude said, ''Into your vehicles and make ready. Safeties off when you hit the strip. Move easily, say nothing, look friendly. Remember we are coming in to bring aid to the government and act as advisors to assist Mehendi's armed forces. Don't forget the rehearsal back at the base. You are now Libyan soldiers, so try to look as much like fanatics as possible. If you believe it, they'll believe it. For most of you that should present no difficulty.''

There was a short burst of nervous laughter that died quickly. The tailgate was swinging open. Outside the fine mist was being swept into small cyclones by the prop-blast.

Through the open tailgate Becaude could see the next plane setting down. They passed the tower and terminal. The second aircraft would take the terminal; his men had other work to do.

Wheeling around to face the way it had come, the transport came to a stop. Robinson kept the motors running slowly, not wanting to shut down completely till he knew what the situation was.

In the lead jeep, Becaude led the way down the ramp followed by the other three. There were four men to a jeep, the long tube of the 106-mm recoilless rifles angled over the windshields. They split up, two jeeps on each flank of the aircraft, and waited.

As the trailing aircraft taxied over in front of the terminal, Becaude moved out to meet it. He stepped out of the jeep wearing the uniform of a major in the Libyan army.

The C-130 came to a halt and its cargo offloaded, marching out in neat ranks, ignoring the drizzle and steam rising from the tarmac. They looked good: khaki trousers bloused in desert boots, a camouflage jacket and desert-sand steel helmets. Their AK-47s were slung over the right shoulder, the pistol grip in their hands, fingers by the trigger, barrels horizontal.

With sharp steps, they quickly responded to the commands given by Becaude in Arabic. Behind the infantry came twenty more men with the long tubes of RPGs held across their chests, a rocket in each of the bores. Around their bodies each carried eight more of the rockets in sand-colored pouches, as well as their own AK-47s slung across their backs. They also looked good. Obeying Becaude's commands, they formed into two ranks facing the airport. Another command and they began to perform drill movements. Right face. Oblique, rear march, weaving back and forth inside their own ranks in a choreographed series of movements that brought the attention of the terminal guards fully on them.

Coming out of the terminal most of the guards watched in open admiration as the maneuvers were executed. They nodded to each other in satisfaction. Their good friend Colonel Muammar Qadhafi had certainly sent them some of his very best men. They looked good and were obviously quite professional. The RPG men split up, five to each side of the infantry, and knelt on one knee, faces rigid, showing nothing. The Bokalans were too far away and it was too dark for them to see how many of the so-called Libyan's had blue eyes and fair hair.

Becaude moved his jeeps out to their positions, each of them taking up a place on the compass facing to north, south, east, and west. The barrels of the long rifles glistened with the misting rain. The two-man security teams came off the jeeps standing to the sides away from the rear of the recoilless rifles. The exhaust blast from one could kill a man if he was within twenty or thirty feet of it.

Becaude checked the radium dial of his watch. He could see figures watching their movements from the tower. Keep looking, *cochons*, and very soon you will see something quite special.

Over the radio Robinson had to answer a query.

"Yes, of course. The colonel has sent you his very best men to assist you in your hour of need. They are performing for you now as an act of solidarity. Yes! That is right. His very best. All of your troubles are over."

Becaude gave the word to fire. His jeep's weapons were fired as the signal for the others to join in. Four recoilless rifles vomited out their projectiles, high-explosive rounds that left a trail of fire behind them in the dark as they leapt out of the tubes toward their targets. The jeep Becaude had been in took the tower with its first round of high explosive.

The men in the tower barely had time to register that something was not quite right before the first round hit the window. Bodies erupted and bloody ribbons of intestines mingled with the wreckage of the communications equipment. The other three jeeps hit their targets: guard towers and machine-gun nests. Two of the jeeps combined to exterminate the barracks on the west side of the field where the airport guards were quartered. Between them they threw ten rounds into the barracks as the two side men from each jeep stayed on the ground advancing with them, spraying the few who made it out of the burning buildings with automatic fire from RPK-74s. They used the new Soviet 5.45-mm cartridges.

The barracks began to burn from the inside. The screams of the men were masked by the continuous roar from the explosions taking place around the field.

At the first whooshing sound of the recoilless rifle the mercs in front of the terminal went into action. There were over twenty Askaris watching their performance from the terminal. Several stood inside behind the windows. Most of them were in front of the main entrance under a metal awning.

As if they were forming the old British square the first rank of riflemen knelt on their left knees, raising their rifles to their shoulders. The second rank remained standing. Then all opened fired, within seconds, sending several thousand rounds into the close-huddled bodies of the Askaris. Half of the RPG men launched their rockets into the interior of the terminal. The remainder turned to destroy machine-gun emplacements, two armored cars, and a halftrack parked on the side of the tarmac. They they reloaded and fired again, taking up new targets. The front rank of the detachment of riflemen assaulted the terminal as the rear spread out, moving against the surviving Askaris in mortar pits and on perimeter patrol.

Becaude jumped back into his jeep and moved out, his recoilless rifle teams taking out the buildings as they went by. They blew up hangars and supply depots. Frantic Askaris looked for someone, anyone, to tell them what to do. Why were they being attacked by their friends the Libyans? All senior officers were already dead. A single sergeant rallied six men to him and began to return effective fire. Two mercs went down; one was dead and the other had his left leg hanging by strips of tendon where his kneecap had been blown off. One other lost two fingers on his left hand when a single bullet clipped them neatly off. The Askari sergeant and his men finally went down in a hail of automatic fire, punctuated by the blasts from three RPG-7 rockets.

The mercs quickly cleared the field taking over the mortar and machine-gun positions. They turned the Askaris' own weapons on them. Becaude reached the terminal and ran inside, his AK at his hip. The first line of mercs who had hit the terminal had cleared the ground floor. Two of them were dead. The rest were now working on clearing the upper floor but were meeting stiff resistance in the confining area. The Askaris were able to pour heavy fire on the single flight of stairs leading to the second floor.

To a merc standing in the open where he was exposed to fire from the doorway, Becaude roared, "What are you doing, fool? Don't get any more men killed. Wait here and take cover."

Racing back outside, he caught a movement out of the corner of his eye. An Askari stumbled out of the dark, his uniform smoking. All the hair on the left side of his head had been burned off. He was just stumbling around, hands outstretched as if pleading for someone to help him. Becaude blew his chest out without hesitating. He yelled to the gunner in his jeep, "The upstairs! Take it out. Three rounds high explosives, then quit."

"*Mais oui*, Sergeant!" came the happy response. As fast as they could be loaded the high-explosive rounds were shoved into the ass of the tube and launched at the upstairs windows of the terminal.

The mercs downstairs ducked their heads as plaster and chunks of the ceiling rained down on them. Becaude was back inside before the third round was fired. When it was, he screamed at them, "Follow me!"

Racing up the stairs he fired from the hip. He could hear whimpers and cries but at first saw nothing. The room was filled with dust and smoke. Then through the setting fog he saw a few figures staggering to their feet as though drunk. Their black faces were covered with a thin layer of chalky pale dust from the whitewashed walls. Hands reached out blindly as rivulets of blood cut channels through the white dust. Darker blotches changed the camouflage pattern of their uniforms where tears in the fabric showed leaking red gouges of flesh.

Moving into the room, Becaude placed short bursts into everything that moved. Then there were no more standing figures. He was followed by the others. They fanned out, putting single shots into the heads of all they found whether they looked dead or not. Becaude had said everyone died and they were following his orders. No prisoners were taken.

There was nothing more for him there. Running back down the stairs, he scanned the area. Already it looked like just a mopping-up operation. They had effective control of the field and his men were taking over the gun placements. Checking the time, he saw it was very good. The men had done quite well. They were ahead of schedule. A group of ten men, two with RPGs ran in front of him heading across the field to the flaming barracks. Several Askaris had gotten out alive and taken cover in a drainage ditch.

Becaude yelled after them, "No heroes. We can't afford losses. This night is not over yet."

Walking briskly, he headed for the control tower. One of his men was at the metal-faced door. Once inside he climbed the stairs leading up to the control room. Twice he had to step over bodies lying sprawled head-down on the stairs. Inside the control room it looked like a butcher shop from the diseased mind of a Hollywood horror-film writer. The heavy shells of the 106-mm recoilless rifle had destroyed everything. There was nothing in the room that even vaguely resembled a complete human being. An arm still holding a telephone rested on the top of a metal desk. Other pieces of anatomy were strewn about in careless fashion. One look. It was enough. No one would make any calls from this room.

Back down stairs, he told the man at the door, "Tell my driver to take his recoilless rifle off the jeep and put it in the tower." He didn't worry about the back blast. Half the ceiling was gone and there were no windows. From there he'd have an increased range of fire for the 106-mm recoilless rifle. They might need it.

Taking his radio from its clip on his web harness, he opened the channel to Robinson.

"We got it. Keep your eyes open, though, and I'll send some men back for your security." He checked his watch again. If it was going right for Hendricks, he and his crew would be there within fifteen minutes.

Robinson turned the controls of the plane over to his copilot and climbed out of the seat. Picking up the Uzi he kept by the side of his seat, he jacked the cocking lever back to the open position, then walked back through the rear of his plane. He went down the ramp and out onto the strip. It was incredible that in less than ten minutes the place had been taken and everything but the terminal and tower was in flames. He could see dark huddled shapes on the tarmac with darker shadows around them where blood had spilled out.

A merc in his Libyan khaki and camouflage was walking toward him when his arm suddenly came up. The AK in his hands spit out flashes of fire. For a second Robinson thought the man was trying to kill him, but he heard the dull thump of bullets striking flesh behind him! Dropping, he went to his belly, but not before he saw the merc go down, his face a dark red bloody mask in the light of the burning strip.

Two Askaris were already down, killed by the merc. Robinson took out two more with short controlled bursts. In the half dark of the flames their faces looked insane, sweaty, black contorted features with wild white places with tiny black dots where their eyes should have been.

They went down and, as Becaude had ordered, he went over to each and put a single shot into the brain, then turned back to the merc. There was nothing to be done for him. There wasn't enough left of his face for Robinson to know if he'd ever seen him up close before.

Picking up the merc's weapon, he went back to the Askaris and did the same, collecting their weapons. It was not good policy to leave things that went bang lying around.

His crew chief stuck his head tentatively out of the open

gate. Seeing the dead merc, then stepping out gingerly, he saw the crumpled bodies of the Askaris and the weapons Robinson was holding.

"Think I could have one of those as a souvenir, sir?"

Robinson spat back at him, venom dripping from his words, "Certainly you may, Sergeant Fields. All you have to do is go and kill one of the men carrying them." He turned his back on the sergeant, who quickly disappeared back into the relative safety of the aircraft hull.

The field was secure, at least for a time. How much time he couldn't tell. The mercs were clearing debris away, setting up new positions for the jeep-mounted recoilless rifles. Others were on perimeter defense by the wire barrier on the far side of the field. They were spread thin. But of the 120 Askaris assigned to the defense of the airport, less than 15 had escaped by clambering over their own barbed wire and fleeing into the night. That was regretful. But they all had known it would be unlikely that they could take out everybody. There was always a rat or two who escaped the trap.

Walking down the center of the strip, Robinson saw a group of mercs running from one of the parked aircraft. Mehendi had half a dozen old Mig-15s and a few surplus French helicopters. They looked like Alouettes and were at least fifteen years old. Parked at the other end of the strip, in front of a burning hanger, was an old C-47 or Dakota, whichever one preferred. It looked pristine and obviously very well cared for. The mercs were setting charges on the aircraft and choppers. One of them headed for the gooney bird. Robinson stopped him.

"Place the charge but don't blow it yet. There's a chance we might need a backup." The merc stopped, his face sweating through soot and grease, eyes wild with the killing. His breath came in short harsh gasps.

Robinson tightened the grip on his Uzi. He watched the merc closely as his head bobbed up and down, the wildness in the eyes fading. Robinson eased off the trigger pressure of his weapon. Then the look was gone. The man snapped to with a quick French salute.

"*Oui m'sieu*." He did a sharp about-face and ran to the C-47, placing the satchel charge under the nose wheel and wrapping it securely with a piece of elastic black tape. He pointed to it for Robinson to see, then raced off into the night.

In the east came the faint beginning of the false dawn. The real one would come soon enough. By then he wanted to be off this piece of ground and back in the cleaner air of the sky heading toward Egypt.

Turning back to his aircraft, he could see the mercs separating their dead and placing them in neat rows as Becaude went over each man searching the bodies for anything that could identify them later. Men were such sentimental creatures. In spite of orders, there would always be one or two who kept a girl's picture or a letter on their persons. If things went well the dead would leave with them. If not, then there must be nothing on them that could be incriminating.

There was another small figure moving among the wounded mercs. Doc Smyth-Wilson. After the killing was done it was his turn to use his gentle hands to treat the wounded. Robert K., with eyes wide in his dark face, followed after the small medic with the healer's touch. Men would live this night because of him.

He lit up a smoke, ignoring the whooshing of flames by the POL dump as a fuel tank went off, sending a gout of oily flames two hundred feet into the air.

C'mon, Hendricks! We don't have all day.

Robinson laughed. That was exactly fucking right. They did not have all day. Soon there would be more black faces with automatic weapons coming to the field to kill. They had to be gone. He checked his watch. By Hendricks's schedule they had twenty more minutes, max. If they had not made it to the airport by then, he was to load up the men on the strip and take off. Hendricks and his team were to be abandoned.

C'mon, Hendricks, don't force me to make a decision about this. For god's sake, don't be late. Don't be late. Don't be late.

Robinson's thoughts were making him sweaty.

TWENTY

NOVEMBER 1
0548 HOURS

HENDRICKS'S MEN HAD the center covered and he knew Duke was holding the rear. It was time to buy them a little leeway. He knew that by now the barracks at the edge of town would have been notified and troops would be there within minutes. Taking the whistle again, he blew four times quickly, then repeated it. From the rear Duke heard and obeyed. He called to his men, "Pull it out! And use the white phosphorus and thermites. Let's burn this turkey."

Ignoring the hostages' outcries and pleadings, his men passed them through the windows and down the front hallway to the waiting trucks. Hendricks went back into the interior of the palace. When the last of the captives was out of the building, Hendricks pulled the pin on a WP grenade and tossed it down the hallway. The gray beercan-sized bomb hit, rolled, and came to a rest at the doorway, which Hendricks knew led to the private quarters of Mehendi.

From the reports Kelo had given him, he knew that Mehendi's quarters were really a large reinforced bunker inside the palace. The doors and walls beneath their paneling of carved mahogany were two inches of homogeneous steel and the sides of the walls were reinforced concrete. If he had gotten in, he knew that Mehendi's personal guards would have been ready for them. He wished to take no casualties if it could be avoided. The captives were his prime responsibility. It was with regret that he didn't feel he had the time to spare on blasting it open and killing the son of a bitch. Maybe Kelo would have better luck after they'd gone.

Exiting down the steps past the bodies of the dead, he stepped to the right as the grenade went off. The hallway behind him filled with acrid white smoke as the building began to burn wherever the thousands of specks of phosphorus touched wood, cloth or paint. From inside he heard screams where the shining, burning bits had touched the flesh of men not yet dead. He wasn't concerned.

Duke came trotting up from the back as Washington and Jerome left their places on the walls and ran up to Hendricks.

"Take off those Askari uniforms. I don't want you to get shot by our men."

Hastily they obeyed. The gates were open; a captured two-and-a-half-ton truck moved outside. His two trucks from the warehouse pulled up in front, joining them. The lead driver leaned out the window.

"Get 'em moving boss. There's a load of shit coming our way. We could hear the explosions clear over in the warehouse and on the way here we passed a lot of excited people with guns. In a minute they'll figure out what to do with them."

Hendricks nodded his response. "Very good. Just keep cool and we'll be gone in a minute.

"Washington, take the second truck. Duke, put the captives in the center ones and I want you to take point in the first truck. Place some men with each of the center trucks to keep the captives quiet. Now let's get them on and moving. We are on schedule and we wouldn't want to keep our friends at the airfield waiting any longer than necessary, now would we?''

To the rest of Duke's element he commanded, ''Get out to the front with the RPG men, send them to me and you remain there to give cover. Be ready to get aboard the last truck as soon as it begins to pull out, but not until then.''

The RPG men who had been left in the park ran over to him, their tubes clutched between white-knuckled fists. So far all they'd done was sit in the fucking bushes. They'd missed the action.

''Take your tubes and start burning me some buildings across the park and down this street. Let's create some more confusion for our soon-to-arrive angry guests.''

Grinning widely, the RPG men split up, each taking a sack of rockets with white tips from the back of the rear truck that they'd left behind at the warehouse. Incendiaries!

Loading the tubes with ease, they picked their targets. Hendricks looked to the skies. The rain had almost stopped.

The first rockets were launched from their tubes and streaked through storefront windows. Each man fired five rockets. Some went into residences adjoining the palace. Nodding with satisfaction at their progress, Hendricks saw several fires begin to burn inside the buildings. From one, great gouts of smoke and flame erupted where a rocket had ignited several drums of fuel oil that had been hoarded.

Mehendi cowered in his apartments. Who was attacking him. Okediji? The Americans, the British? He wanted to run, to use the tunnel he'd built from his bedroom to an adjoining house. Only he and his most-trusted men knew of its existence. The work crews of Luda tribesmen who had dug the tunnel had all been executed.

He looked with longing at the panel behind his bed. Through the thick walls he felt the explosions and heard the machine-gun fire, and the muted screams from dying men. Now through the ventilators came the first acrid wisps of smoke. His palace was being put to the torch. Still he waited.

Outside his bedroom door, six of his personal guards waited, their weapons loaded, facing toward the steel-plated door. He had no doubt that they would fight to the death for him, which was just what he needed. It would buy him some time.

Heat began to be transmitted to his room; the smell of smoke was heavier. It was almost time to make a move, but not yet. At his desk he touched switches. His quarters had their own power source and ventilation system. He pushed the switch that totally closed off his apartments from the rest of the palace. The air began to clear as filtering systems went to work recycling the air in his apartments. But the heat was increasing. Putting his hands on the walls, he could almost feel the flames outside. But he had to wait. To move too soon could be disastrous.

From the south corner of the palace a group of six men came out of the dark, their hands clasped above their heads, fingers interlaced. Behind them was Calvin, probably the youngest of the mercs. His combat record had been good during his tours with the 173rd Airborne Brigade in Vietnam. He was prodding them on.

Moving them against the wall, he reported to Hendricks. "I found them trying to get out of the window, sir. What do you want me to do with them?"

Feeling the blood rise to his face in anger, Hendricks roared at him, "*Kill the sons of bitches and do it now, you bloody little shit!*"

Martin Hendricks accented his orders by swinging around the bore of his 7.62-mm FAL assault rifle, his finger steadily taking up the trigger slack, the bore lined up on the sweaty wide-eyed face of the object of his wrath who suddenly recalled the fate of the last man who had disobeyed orders.

Flames from the windows of the burning palace rose up behind the prisoners, turning their green camos into a mixture of bloody patterns that were in sharp contrast to their black, terrified faces.

Calvin swallowed. This wasn't what he had thought he would be doing when he'd been recruited. Hendricks's finger eased up off the trigger slack as the boy took up his own weapon. The FAL shuddered against his side. The blacks went down. Two had to be put out with another burst to their heads.

Hendricks cursed to himself, Fucking amateurs, can't do a bleeding thing right. Out loud, he said, "All right, get them on board and get out of here while we still can. We can't hold them off forever!"

From around him came orders. They were eagerly obeyed. His mercs wanted to be gone. They had been lucky for too long. His men pushed, tugged, and carried the hostages into the backs of the commandeered trucks. Men, women, children, all were piled on top of each other.

Two of his mercs squatted in the back of each truck to give cover to the rear. One each stood on the running boards, hanging on as well as they could, one hand inside the windows, the other hand holding their weapons, fingers on the triggers. Explosions coming from inside the burning palace gave impetus to his orders; ammo stored in the guards' quarters had caught fire.

To the left across the park an Indian fabric shop exploded. Then there was another explosion in the center of the park and another hit the curb of the street moving toward the palace. Each was only a few seconds behind the other.

"Mortars!" Hendricks cried. "They're ranging us! Take off when you've got a load. I'll hold them up here as long as I can."

Two of his men went down, shrapnel splinters tearing holes in their uniforms. He thought one of them was a Special Forces demo man but he couldn't be sure. The man had lost most of his face.

Clouds of smoke rolled over the streets, masking the broad avenue as his trucks pulled away with their cargos of terrified humanity.

Ignoring the next barrage of incoming mortar rounds, Hendricks strode to the end of the street. Two blocks away he could see them coming. Dodging and darting shadows leaped from doorway to doorway as they advanced.

Behind them other sections of the city were in flames. He wondered who had set the fires. Maybe they had some help he didn't know about. Whoever or whatever, it was to his advantage. Confusion was his ally.

Duke knocked out the windshield on his side of the truck, laying a light machine gun with its bipod extended out of the opening. Slapping the driver on the shoulder, he said, "Let's get gone."

The lead truck took off. Grinding gears, it moved away from the palace gates. Washington wished the women and some of the men in the back of his truck would shut the fuck up. Their constant whimpering and whining were getting on his nerves. This job was hard enough on him as it was.

The small convoy pulled out, leaving the ranging mortars behind as they turned a corner. They had the protection of office buildings to shield them from shell fire. Suddenly a squad of Askaris came from out of nowhere to stand in the center of the road. The squad leader's right hand raised imperiously for the trucks to halt. Before the lead truck was close enough for the Askari corporal to see the machine gun on its hood, Duke cut loose a long hosing burst that ripped the man from his crotch to his throat. Then the bullets, every fifth one a tracer, went after the rest of the squad. He got three, leaving the survivors to the trucks behind him. They rumbled past. By the time the last truck went by, all eight Askaris were dead.

Hendricks had taken the shotgun seat in the second truck with Washington. Like Duke, he had broken out the front windshield, as had all of the other mercs riding shotgun. During the firing up front, he was sure he had heard Duke break out into laughter that kept time with the chatter of the LMG.

Glancing quickly out the side of his eye at Hendricks, Washington asked, "You think we gonna pull this off, Boss?"

Keeping his eyes to the front, Hendricks responded acidly, "We will know that in a very short time now, won't we?"

Several long bursts of automatic fire from his rear made him question it himself. On his radio he was given the report.

"We got company. Looks like a weapons carrier full of Askaris is on our ass."

Holding the transmitter close to his lips, he spoke to Duke in the front truck.

"We have company coming up fast behind us. Push it, but don't get reckless."

Headlights coming from the opposite direction closed with them.

To Duke, he transmitted, "Take it easy, maybe they'll turn off."

Wishful thinking! From the pursuing weapons carrier there came another long burst of automatic fire. Tracers streaked overhead. The lights in front swerved. They were trying to block the road. Three vehicles, two trucks and a jeep, formed a barrier across the road, and troops were offloading fast.

The lead truck swung off the road and onto the sidewalk on the left. Washington did the same to the right and the two trailing trucks also split up. Hendricks was out of the cab before the truck came to a stop, yelling to his men, "Spread out! Get those RPGs out and put them to work. It's time you earned your pay, gentlemen. This has been a milk run so far. Let's see if you're worth your hire. You have five minutes to kill me those sons of bitches and do it right, or we're all dead men!"

The mercs didn't have to be told where to go. Light machine guns were set up where they would have control of the streets. Riflemen took cover behind abandoned cars and trucks. Others were lying in the rubble of a looted storefront. They waited for the word from Hendricks.

The hostages were hustled into the lobby of an office building after the door had been shot open. They were protected by five mercs who had orders to stay with them no matter what.

The RPGs went to work just as two rockets headed their way from the vehicle barricade to their front.

Calmly, Hendricks stepped out into the road. He needed to get a better look at the situation. There was no way around. They were cut off in the center of block. They had to go on through. A stream of machine-gun bullets passed over his head by a few inches. They were ignored. Carefully he looked the situation over. He turned to his men.

"RPGs, you're going to be my artillery. Keep fire on those in front. Duke, take care of the weapons carrier behind us."

Rallying the rest of his men, he gave them their orders. "Stay close to the buildings. Don't expose yourself until we're ready, then I want you to move faster than you've ever moved before. Go after them. Don't give them time to think. With every barrage from the RPGs you'll have a few seconds to get closer. Wait for that time, then when I give the word, hit them, and hit them hard. Don't worry about saving ammo. We've got to break through."

RPG rockets took off, giving out a burst of sparks as the main charge ignited after they'd left the tubes. They streaked for the barricade. Askaris leaped for cover when they saw the rockets launched. That was what Hendricks was waiting for now.

"Hit them now! Move it out." He led the way, weaving and firing short bursts from his FAL. Not looking behind him, he could feel the men with him. From somewhere there came a cry, low at first. Then it rose to a skin-chilling crescendo as more voices joined with it. For a moment Hendricks wondered who it was that started it. Then with a shock he realized it was he. He and the assault group were screaming like the berserkers of old as they rushed at the Askaris, each man's weapon firing. The RPG men had to be careful not to shoot into their own men, but they managed to get off three rounds into the trucks and one of the jeeps, all exploding with a satisfactory result.

The Askaris taking cover from the first rockets raised their heads in time to catch part of the blast from the second barrage. They raised their heads again in time to see Hendricks and the mercs were on them, weapons firing. When magazines went empty, boot and combat knives were drawn and used with wicked effectiveness.

The tension in the mercs was released. They wanted to fight, wanted to kill; it was good. It was very good. The burning enemy vehicles turned the mercs' camouflaged painted faces into those of demons. The Askaris broke, scrambling away, leaving their weapons behind. Hendricks stood between the burning jeep and the truck. An Askari sergeant on his knees held his hands out in front of his face, eyes turned away as if this would ward off that which he was certain would come. It did. Hendricks literally blew his head off, half a magazine hitting the sergeant in the throat from a range of four feet left little.

One jeep was unharmed. Hendricks spoke to Calvin, who was standing beside him, a bloody Gerber combat knife in his hand hanging loose.

"Snap out of it. You did well. Now get in that jeep and move it out of the way and stay in it. You'll drive for me." Calvin tried to find the words "yes sir," but his throat was too dry and aching. His legs and arms were weak, trembling. This was the first time he'd ever killed a man with a blade. It was totally different from using a rifle. It was—personal. That was it. With a blade you felt the man's death transmitted to you through the steel.

"Stop daydreaming and get the jeep out of the way!"

Calvin snapped to. The jeep was moved.

Hendricks felt a presence behind him. Turning, he saw Duke standing in the road. Looking further back, he saw the weapons carrier was gone.

"What happened to the weapons carrier?"

"I think that we're not the only ones in town." Duke pointed his head to the horizon. A red shimmering glow

rose over the tops of the buildings. It was like driving
across the New Mexico desert at night and seeing the
lights of a city behind a hill in the distance.

A good portion of Bokala was burning and they hadn't
done it. It was on the other side of the palace.

Duke nodded. He knew what Hendricks was thinking.

"I think Okediji has come to town. That's why the
Askaris broke off and ran."

"Duke."

A calm, seemingly unconcerned voice responded. "Yes,
Boss?"

"Is our own transport ready?"

"Yes, sir. All ready."

"Good. I think we're going to need it shortly."

Duke said nothing, only quietly watched the face of his
boss. Hendricks showed nothing on the outside. The flames
gave his features a hot flush, accenting the sharp angles of
his cheekbones, giving him a slightly satanic look. But
Duke knew his mind was cool. Martin Hendricks was one
of the last of the old ones.

Splinters from a near-miss, which had struck the corner
of the building where he was standing, had peppered his
face. Blood ran down in thin streams mixed with sweat
and ash.

Hendricks thought to himself, this is not going down
right. If Okediji is hitting the city, that means he'll probably be going after the airport too. He looked at the flaming
glow over the buildings. It was to the northwest. The
airport was almost due north. He had no doubt that Okediji
would move on the airport. The helicopters and equipment
there were too valuable a prize not to go after as soon as
possible.

He kept those thoughts to himself. His men had enough

to worry about. Right now he was giving even odds that they'd even be able to make it to the airport.

Shots snapped close by, close enough that he could hear the sonic cracks. Not all of Mehendi's men were on the run. No time to search out the sniper. But he didn't have to. Duke had already spotted him in the second-story window of a hardware store. Borrowing one of the RPGs, he put a round into the window. There was no further response from the sniper.

Hendricks had no more time. There was still a good chance that Mehendi's troops could catch up to them. And he hadn't planned on Okediji showing up. The odds were just too high against it. Now, instead of just having Mehendi and his Askaris to deal with, they'd walked in the middle of a raging firefight between two tribal factions and were more than likely to catch shit from both ends.

Automatically he swung his rifle in a smooth, practiced move and pulled off three rounds on full auto, blowing the spine out of a black huddled shadow lying near the corner of a building. One of the Askaris hadn't been killed. He'd been playing dead but a tremor in his leg had given him away.

Calmly he went over to the jeep where Calvin waited for him with the motor running.

To Duke he said, "Get them loaded. We still have a little ways to go."

TWENTY-ONE

NOVEMBER 1
0550 HOURS

KELO WAS IN the basement where he'd cut off the palace's main generator. He sat in the darkness beside the dead body with blood running from its nostrils and listened to the sounds of the fight going on overhead. The darkness of the generator room was close about him, but he didn't mind. He knew he was about to repay a debt of long standing.

In the dark he could see in his mind's eye the bodies of his wife and his six-month-old child in their village. He had been away. By the time he had returned they had been dead for three days. Three days, during which time the animals and insects came to feed on their swollen, bloated forms.

The only reason they hadn't been fully consumed was because of the abundance of dead bodies available to the scavengers. The entire village had been exterminated. One hundred and twenty-three men, women, and children. Even the dogs had been killed. All about him was the thick, sweet cloying smell of death. And the flies. They always came when there was dying, hovering over the dead to drink up any remaining moisture the bodies might have. He hated flies. For the rest of his life they would bring to him the image of his wife and child lying in the dry dust.

He knew how she died and how long it had taken. He was an African. His child was perhaps more fortunate; its skull had been smashed open by a boot.

Mehendi had commanded the company of Askaris who had eliminated his kraal. Perhaps it had been he who had raped his wife and killed his child. But whether he had done it or not didn't matter; he was still the one responsible. The butcher! Now, after all these years, he was able to pay him back. He could have killed Mehendi many times over the years, but that would have been too easy. Mehendi had to suffer. Kelo would take away from him the one thing he loved most—his power, thus his pride. Then, when he had done that, he would kill him, kill him in a way that he and Mehendi knew. They were Africans and a thousand generations of savage life under the brutal laws of nature lay close to the surface. All of the polish and refinement of western schools could never take it away. It was part of their soul and spirit.

Automatic fire rattling overheard made him smile. Good, some more Askaris were dying. He touched the tribal scars on his face. Two lines running vertically, wide scars left open to heal, they marked him as a member of Mehendi's own tribe. Long years ago he had taken the razor blade and cut them in himself and then had begun to plan his revenge.

He had joined Mehendi's own regiment before he took power. He had known Mehendi would rise to heights and he helped him achieve it. They had fought side by side and Kelo had killed for him, stood with him in rivers of blood. That didn't matter; they were only Ludas. He had no more use for them than he did Mehendi's tribe. That was another thing that one never overcame. The tribe, the family. It was all. His own people had been a small tribe in Bokala, small because of artificial boundaries that had cut them off from their main tribe to the south and had left them very limited and weak in a land filled with enemies. If it was to advance and have peace all of Africa would have to be redefined along tribal boundaries. Till then there would be no end to the killing.

But for now he was content with the killing that was going on upstairs. He was pleased that he had been able to make white people do his dirty work for him as his people had done so often in the past for the whites.

He cared nothing for them either, but at least he felt he understood the mercenary leader, Hendricks. He might even owe him something for his services. At least Hendricks was honest about what he was and what he did. No apologies, no social justifications were necessary. He was a warrior, or would have been in another time and place. He, like Kelo, knew about himself. What he did was not something he had control of. It was ordained, something that was passed down through the ages. They both had it. Kelo, the barely contained violence of Africa, and Hendricks, the need to fulfill himself and knowing he never would. Both were condemned to dissatisfaction with all that came their way no matter how well or hard they tried.

Overhead a dull thump shook the building slightly. It was much lighter than the first explosion when the walls had been blown around the Askaris' quarters. Grenades, maybe? Yes, if all went well this night, he would owe the white mercenary leader something. How he would pay didn't concern him at this time. It was enough for him to know the debt was there. It was now a thing of honor between them.

Dust drifted down and then smoke. Good! The building was burning. He wanted it to burn as his village had. He would give the mercenaries five more minutes, then they would be gone. It would have been too dangerous for him to show himself while they were in the building. His uniform would have gotten him shot before he could get out any explanation to Hendricks's men.

The five minutes passed. The smoke was getting thicker. Covering his mouth and nose with a sleeve, he came up out of the cellar into the hallway leading to the rear gardens. Running out of the palace, he passed by bodies whose uniforms were just about to reach flashpoint. The smell of cooking flesh was sweet in his nostrils; it was good to see the dead. Now, if the gods were with him, he would soon stand before the monster he hated and teach him the meaning of pain.

As his palace burned beyond his reinforced apartment doors, Mehendi was preparing for the worst. He was finishing his packing, taking from his safe the files and documents he would need if he were forced to flee and live in exile. Among them were bearer notes totaling over ten million U.S. dollars.

The drone of his filters changed, as did the sound of the generator. The burning palace was overheating the wiring system. He had no choice; he had to go. Resisting the temptation to put on his dress uniform, with a deep sigh of regret he put on instead a gray Savile Row suit of English worsted, with fine thin pinstripes. The tailor in London had said it gave him a slim, debonair look.

He prided himself on his foresight in building the passageway leading to the house across the street. The house had been owned by a rich Hindu merchant who, along with his family, had long since gone to meet his ancestors. He had been found guilty of the crimes of treason and profiteering against the state and person of President-General Mehendi. But Mehendi had not permitted the property to be sold; as far as anyone knew, it was still vacant. From there he would make his way through a carefully plotted course that would take him out of the city to a small airstrip where a plane waits always kept under guard, fueled and ready to fly. His pilot was in the outer rooms with his personal guard.

He called to him over the intercom. "Major Bagega, will you come in please."

Bagega obeyed with a degree of alacrity, alarmed as he was by the current turn of events. To the commander of Mehendi's personal guard he ordered, "Remain here. I will confer with the president. It may be that he wishes for us to depart the palace. If so, I shall inform you of the necessary preparations."

The Askari captain saluted in the British style, stomping his booted right foot down on the plush carpet to acknowledge his orders. He, too, was relieved that a decision was being made. It was getting very hot and the air was becoming thin. His men were beginning to sweat as they waited, staring at the doors. The best course of action would be to leave this place. He knew that the president had an escape route. There was no doubt in the captain's mind that the president's most trusted men would escape with him, for he had been assured of this by Mehendi himself several times over the last months.

Locking the door behind him at Mehendi's command, Major Antoine Bagega stood at attention.

"Don't just stand there, you fool. Help me with these."

Mehendi indicated his bags and valises, four of them. Inside were the things he would need to live a graceful life outside of his country. Or perhaps he would need their contents to start a counterrevolution. He had gotten used to being the sole and absolute master of his own country.

Stepping to the side of his bed, he removed a small sliver of silver from his pocket and inserted it into an almost invisible hole in the wall. When the silver needle penetrated to its maximum depth, he could hear the locks open. Swinging the panel back, he waved impatiently for Bagega to enter first. At this point he would trust no man behind him. Bagega's arms and hands loaded, did not fail to notice the menacing bulge in Mehendi's right pocket. He led the way.

Carefully, Mehendi locked the door behind him and bolted it shut with a heavy steel bar. The interior of the passageway was lit by battery-powered lamps on the walls. There was a definite incline as they went forward. The tunnel would take them to the adjoining house across a narrow byway, under the house's surrounding wall, beneath its garden, and into a basement that had been dug for just such an emergency.

Mehendi felt that if nothing else, he was a realist; the current turn of events had not been entirely unexpected. Once he was in the secret hideaway he would be better able to make an analysis. In essence, the Indian's former home had been turned into a small headquarters, with communications equipment, cabinets stacked with arms, containers of food and water, and the same kind of homogeneous steel door that secured his own quarters in the palace. From there he could monitor broadcasts and view the surrounding streets of his city to determine just what caused the day's disturbances. The upper floors of the house had been allowed to deteriorate; indeed they had been helped along in the matter. They were in such bad shape that even thieves knew there was nothing of value to be had, and the house had been left alone.

They came to the end of the tunnel, and another steel door. Using the same silver key, Mehendi operated the locking mechanism and pushed the door open. As he did the lights inside came on automatically, illuminating the interior. The safe house was well appointed. It had rich mahogany and ironwood furniture, plush sofas, and Persian carpets. There were weapons racks on the walls, communications equipment in a small adjoining room, and his own desk, the top inlaid with carved ivory from elephants he had killed himself. But there was something else.

Captain Kelo! He was sitting behind the desk. Mehendi was relieved to see that one of his most trusted officers had escaped the destruction of his palace and had come to him in his hour of need. Kelo had served him well over the years and was one of only three living men who knew the secret of this refuge. Indeed, it had been Kelo who had suggested the possible need for it in the first place. He had supervised the construction and the subsequent execution of the Luda workers. Yes, he was a most reliable and valuable man, a man who loved him well. But why was he sitting at his desk?

"Captain Kelo!" he began, his voice stern but friendly. "It is good that you have come. Tell me, what is the cause of this disturbance? Is it Okediji? Or has a rescue attempt been made for my 'guests'?"

Rising from the desk, Kelo, his face grim, his voice level, strained to control his feelings.

"Mr. President, it is my duty to inform you that it is both. Your hostages have been taken from you, and Okediji is in the city. A traitor informed him of the timetable for the attack on your palace, and he has taken advantage of the confusion to attack the city."

Mehendi moved past Bagega, his black face growing even darker with the sudden rush of outrage.

"Who," he hissed, "is the traitor? Who has betrayed me? I will have him and all of his family put to death, a death as slow and painful as I can devise. Tell me!" he commanded. "Who betrayed me?"

Kelo's hand came up with a silenced pistol in it. Almost casually he shot Bagega twice in the face.

"It was I, Your Excellency." Another shot and Mehendi's right elbow was shattered, preventing the president from reaching the pistol in his pocket. "And you've already executed my family."

The blood drained from Mehendi's face, leaving it the color of day-old ash. Kelo grinned and came closer, ignoring Bagega's body. His macabre grin grew wider and wider till it threatened to split his face.

"Now, what was it you said about a long and painful death?" Kelo's eyes almost glowed with anticipation.

Mehendi felt his bowels let loose as he fouled himself. Kelo shook his head gently from side to side as if in sympathy for his leader's loss of control. Moving to the wall, where spears and native hunting gear served as decorations, Kelo removed one of them. Hefting the weight of the panga in his hand, he spoke to Mehendi ever so softly, ever so gently, savoring each word.

"Yes. It is long overdue that you and I should have a talk, a long talk about pain and death."

It was fortunate that Mehendi had had the safe house soundproofed, or the screams that began in the next minutes and lasted through till dawn, when they were no more than wet blubbery sounds coming from a thing that had once been human, would surely have brought the warriors of Okediji to them.

Afterward, Kelo carefully washed himself of the blood, paying special attention to the cleaning of his fingernails.

He had always been a very fastidious man. Returning to the office, he picked up the dead president's bags. Their contents could be used to aid his own people. Opening the door to the outside world, he felt fresh, renewed. He didn't look back at Mehendi's remains. Actually, there was no way that one look could have taken him all in, as his parts were widely separated.

Closing the steel door behind him, he was indeed well pleased. His debt to Hendricks was one he would not soon forget. For without him, this day would have never been so sweet.

TWENTY-TWO

NOVEMBER 1
0612 HOURS

ONCE MORE THE convoy began to move out. Dawn was creeping over the eastern edge of the city. The smoke seemed heavier with the rising of the sun. Dead Askaris littered the streets behind them. Hendricks led the way, his face tense, the muscles working beneath the skin. He didn't like the idea of Okediji getting into the game at this time.

A shadow ran out from around the corner where the Bank of London building sat gray and empty. He almost fired; the pressure on the trigger was at the razor's edge of tolerance. Amazingly, the face staring at him in the spectral glow of the headlights was that of a white man, deathly pale from fear, the eyes overwide in their sockets beneath a shock of light blond hair.

"For God's sake, take us with you!" he cried.

The jeep jerked to a stop, forcing the trucks behind it to slam on their brakes, throwing their cargo into another minor outburst of panic. From around the corner another, slighter figure ran out. It started screaming in sheer terror. It was a girl's scream.

Hendricks rose up in the seat of the jeep, throwing his rifle to his shoulder. Half a magazine spewed out of his FAL, cutting down the two Askaris pursuing the girl. They hadn't had time to register that they had fallen into shit before Hendrick's bullets dropped them.

The girl ran to stand beside the young man. Like him, she was wearing stained and sweaty khaki. She said nothing but her eyes mirrored the same horror. Hendricks knew they had seen things that they never should have. But he had no time to conduct an interrogation. They were white and this was no place for them.

"Get in one of the trucks and move it fast or I'll leave you here. We have no time to spare!"

Grabbing the girl's hand, the young man practically dragged her to the rear of the lead truck. Rough hands hauled them up into the back. Hendricks hoped this would be the last interruption; gunfire was coming closer. Even if Okediji was winning against the Askaris it could spell trouble for them. His file read like a script for a horror movie. If the Askaris broke, which he thought was more than likely, the rebels might head for the airfield and intercept them on the road.

"Put your bloody foot on the accelerator!" Hendricks barked.

Calvin didn't hesitate. The small vehicle leaped forward, followed by the lumbering trucks. They were in a race now. Even without Hendricks telling them, they knew that the game had been changed and new players were coming in. Losing would cost them their lives.

In front of them they saw the streets beginning to fill with people. Terrified blacks hauled belongings with them as they also tried to escape to a place of safety. Hendricks knew for certain that Okediji was near. Blaring horns drove the indigents from their paths. In a panic they trampled over each other, pushing and shoving to get out of the way of the heavy tires of the trucks. They didn't know who the drivers were, didn't care. Death was coming for them in the form of Okediji and his rebels. They had to escape.

The word had passed like wildfire among them: The soldiers weren't holding. Many of them had already fled the city. There was no word from the palace, and the flames coming from it added to their desire to get away. There was going to be a great killing and it would include men, women, and children. There would be no mercy.

The sound of fighting drew ever closer as they moved to the outskirts of the city. Washington swerved his truck to avoid running over a group of women attempting to cross the broad street, dragging or carrying their children with them. He ran over one terrified Askari soldier who had thrown his weapon away and one old man with a halo of puffy gray hair whose legs weren't nimble enough to move him to the shelter of a doorway as the truck jumped the curb to avoid the women. Washington scarcely felt the thumps as the heavy wheels ran over them.

The sun was up. Hendricks cursed the early-morning light casting long reddish-orange shadows across the streets as they reached the boundaries of Bokala and turned onto the road to the airport. This was the last stretch. It was imperative that they do nothing but watch the road, eyes sharp, weapons ready for anything, any movement—a gleam from a piece of oiled steel, a patch of color that wasn't quite right. As far as he could tell, there had been no more vehicles in pursuit behind them, and the road ahead looked clear of any trouble. If they were lucky it would stay that way until they approached the airstrip. Then they could expect some reaction from the survivors of Becaude's attack.

Up ahead the road grew congested again, although they were in front of most of the thousands fleeing the city. From the rear of the trucks the former hostages could see Mehendi's city burning; fire rose over the doomed capital, the smoke blotting out the morning sun. They felt better. The ruin of the city was still, for most of them, small compensation for what they had been forced to endure. The death and torture of the thousands they didn't know didn't concern them. Right now only their lives mattered.

Becaude heard them before he saw them. From the wrecked control tower he put his field glasses back down. It had been a great relief when Hendricks had called in that they were on the way. He, too, had seen the signs of Okediji's approach. Leaning out of the shattered window, he yelled to the men below, "They're coming. Get ready to give support. I hear gunfire. Spread the word. Everyone on his toes. *Allez!*" Pulling his head back inside, he absently shoved a body out of the way to reach the radio. He passed the word to all outlying elements. *Le chef* was coming in.

For now the heat was bearable. What rain they'd had during the night had passed over. On the runways a thin layer of rising fog was swept back in funnels by the whirling engines of the transports. Robinson had got the message, too, and relayed it to his own men. As soon as the trucks moved in they were to load the human cargo and take off immediately. He would be the last to leave, waiting until all of the mercs had boarded. He could also hear the distant crackle of gunfire. Cocking his head, he wondered at how sounds were so deceptive. To him it sounded as if most of the firing was not coming from the city but from somewhere close by.

Becaude raised Hendricks on the radio, his face darkening, creases deepening in his forehead. "*Je comprends,*

Chef!'' To the men around him he ordered, ''Make ready
for a fight. The convoy has come under fire and *le chef*
thinks that Okediji is attacking the city and may come after
the airport. Make certain everyone is in position. Tell Doc
Smyth-Wilson to expect more casualties. There are wounded
and shock cases with the convoy. Everyone to their positions as we rehearsed. This day may grow much warmer
yet!''

For Hendricks it had already grown warmer. Twice they
had to barge through small columns of fleeing Askaris.
The word had obviously spread about the attack on the
palace. He wondered if Mehendi had taken off or if maybe
Kelo had gotten lucky. Whatever the reasons, his trucks
and jeep were a prize to be taken by the fleeing soldiers
and he had taken more casualties as a result. Two of his
men were wounded and two of the freed hostages had been
killed. Several more suffered wounds of varying degrees.
It was five minutes to the airfield, fifteen to safety. Ahead
of him he could see the control tower rising above the flat
field. He thought he saw something beyond it, but it was
only low ground mist. The all of a sudden the brighter
flicker of red rose up from a burning farmhouse. Now he
had no doubts. Okediji was closing in on the airfield. They
might not have fifteen minutes to spare.

The last turn! He could just make out the figures of his
men guarding the entrance to the field. They had taken the
places of the Askaris in the machine-gun bunker guarding
the approach.

Pushing the convoy as hard as he could, he made the
last turn closing on the entrance. As he passed the bunker
he yelled out at them, ''Stay in place until I send for
you!'' Wheels screeched as they hit the tarmac, the trucks
peeling off toward the waiting aircraft.

Becaude was waiting as Hendricks's jeep jerked to a halt

in front of the terminal. Almost at the same instant a 60-mm mortar round exploded at the south end of the field. Okediji was about to make an appearance. "Get your casualties over to the transport!" As he spoke, he saw the wounded from the raid being moved out. Becaude had waited only till he knew the others were on their way before giving the order to evacuate them on the same plane as the hostages. As usual, Becaude was on the job.

More mortar rounds began to range the field. He estimated by their rate of fire that there must have been at least three working, and there could be more coming in as the rebels got organized.

Machine-gun fire was no longer a distant rattle of firecrackers. It was more distinct, authoritative. His men were beginning to return small-arms fire.

"Give me a status report on all sections!" Hendricks commanded.

Becaude gave him the dispositions as the mercs began to tighten up, returning fire against the increasing pressure of the enemy. Duke hustled the hostages out of the trucks to the open bays of the aircraft. A new fear was riding them now, fear that after getting this close something could still happen that would take their safety away from them. They knew that either Mehendi or Okediji was closing in on them. They had to get away. To stay was to return to the terror and death they knew waited for them in the burning city. Several of the men had to be butt stroked in their backs when they threatened to run over some women and children. Others wanted to stay and fight with the mercs. Their offers were refused. This was no time for amateur heroics.

As soon as the hostages were on board, the cargo master took over, shoving them into the canvass seats, yelling at them to fasten their belts and shut up. The pilot locked the wheels at one-hundred percent and gave it full throttle, building the revs to the screaming point.

Duke dragged men back away from the prop blast as shots began to ping off the sides of the aircraft. "Spread out. Move up to the wire and return fire. Keep those fuckers away till they get off the ground!"

Spreading out, they did as he ordered, running at a crouch, zigzagging till they hit the wire perimeter. Then they threw their bodies down and began to return cool selective fire on the enemy. They didn't know who they were shooting at and didn't care. This was a killing time and they had to hold the enemy back or they would have no chance to escape.

Hendricks began directing fire from the captured mortar pits, trying to suppress the enemy fire and give cover to the transport. His problem was where to lay the fire. They were being hit from three sides.

Doc Smyth-Wilson was the last one out of the plane, the cargo bays closing behind him. He'd given what assistance he could, mostly by laying out several doses of liquid Valium to the more panic stricken. As for the wounded, there was nothing life threatening. The serious cases were still on the deck. Only the wounded with a good chance of surviving till they reached Egypt had been loaded on the C-130. The remaining, more seriously wounded would go out with the last of the mercs and he'd work on them in the air. There was still a lot of killing going on and he'd be needed here. With him came Robert K., eyes wide, jaws clenched. He had never experienced anything like this. Around him the world was going insane. The first action had taken place so fast he hadn't had time to register what was happening. All he had seen were mounds of dead black bodies being handled like cord wood. Now there was more firing and he felt his mind whiplashing inside its skull. He knew there was something terribly, terribly wrong.

Doc grabbed him by the shoulder, shaking him hard. "Get your bloody shit together. We still have work to do."

A line of rebels hit the wire. A steady burst of light machine-gun fire set for grazing cut their legs out from under them. At that moment the C-130 began to move. Picking up speed, it headed down the runway, flaps set.

Robert K. saw the Africans go down. Most were dead, but not all. Several were hung up in the wire, screaming in pain, crying out for help. One stood up. His face a mask of blood, he stumbled into the concertina and got hung up, the wire wrapping around him as the steel barbs dug into his flesh. Blinded by his own blood he couldn't see which way to go. His hands were ripped to the bone as he tried to pull the wire off of him only to become more entangled. A merc lying belly down on the runway by Robert K. laughed and shot the man three times in the stomach, blowing his spine out. The intestines wrapped themselves in bloody gray ribbons around the spikes of the wire and still the rebel didn't die. He just hung there in the wire, twisting his own guts out of him as the merc laughed and refused to give the coup de grâce.

Lying on the tarmac beside the laughing merc was an RPG-7 with a rocket in the tube. Stiff-legged, Robert K. walked over to the merc. Doc left, cursing him as he ran to attend a wounded merc at the edge of the wire. Robert K. only had eyes for the laughing man who was continuing to pour fire on the rebels still alive in the wire. He wasn't aware of when his hand took the Browning pistol from its holster and shot the man three times in the back of the head, splattering his brains over the hot tarmac, where they began to steam. Placing the pistol in its holster he leaned over and picked up the RPG. The classes they'd had in Egypt came back quickly as he raised the weapon to rest it on his shoulder, swinging it around the field to where the escaping aircraft was full in the sight. Closing his eyes to avoid the back blast of the initial charge, he pulled against the trigger with two fingers, creating the electrical charge necessary to ignite the rocket's propellant. Even with his eyes closed, there was not much chance that he could miss. The plane was moving only at about thirty knots as it began to pass in front of him. The pilot's total concentration was on the length of strip to the front and the dark dusty puffs cropping up on the runway.

The high-explosive charge in the rocket struck the Plexiglas of the cockpit and exploded behind the backs of the pilot and copilot. They died instantly, the upper halves of their bodies torn nearly in two. The force of the charge threw them against the restraining straps of their seat harnesses. Behind them the radio operator and navigator took three seconds longer to die. With no hands on the controls the aircraft swerved sickeningly to the side of the strip, its front wheels running over a mortar pit and crushing the men in it to a bloody pulp. The nose collapsed and it dug into the earth, props beating themselves into useless pieces of junk against the hard sun-baked soil till they stopped. Screams could be heard coming from the inside of the cargo bay. Dropping the expended tube, Robert K. returned to the body of the merc he had killed and took the dead man's Kalashnikov. He stood very straight as he heard a cry from behind him. He turned around slowly, eyes red from the rush of blood to his head. Doc Smyth-Wilson stood there, face pale beneath a layer of sweat. "What the bloody hell do you think you're doing, you crazy shit?" He barely had time to notice the whitening of the smiling black man's knuckles before half a magazine burst ripped him from the crotch to the chest, tearing his back out of him. Viscera hung like ribbons on white bone fragments. The impact of the fifteen bullets hitting him in less than three seconds kept him on his feet, bouncing him back on his heels as his body shook with the shuddering impact of the rounds. When it stopped, he flew onto his back, then somehow found the strength to roll back over onto his stomach, arms hanging loose beside him, face to the dry earth, mouth open, eyes already dead and fogging.

Calmly, as though he had all the time in the world, Robert K. turned back to the dead merc and began to strip its body of its ammo.

"Say, brother! What it is?" The voice was calm, easy, nonthreatening. Robert K. stopped. He looked over his shoulder to see the face of his brother, who had just witnessed the whole grisly episode of his brother killing the merc and Doc. Robert K. straightened up, the AK in his right hand, finger on the trigger, but the bore pointing at the deck. This was his brother speaking to him. "It's here, man! This is it! They're killing our people. And we are going to stop them. You and me. You're with me, aren't you? You've always been with me. Let's do it. We can take them all out. Our brothers outside the wire are waiting to help us. This is what I was born for. Please Andrew, help me kill them."

The expression on his face was beatific, but at the same time fanatical. The boy was dangerous, a walking bomb about to explode.

Washington moved forward with steady, unhurried steps. "You know I'll never let anyone hurt you, little brother. I promised Momma that I'd always be there. You are my brother and I love you."

Robert K.'s eyes widened, the muscles in his face trembling. A small pool of saliva gathered at the corners of his mouth in a thin froth.

"I'll never let anyone hurt you, little brother. That I promise."

Robert K.'s eyes went wider still as though trying to form a question. A deep shuddering sigh worked its way out of his open mouth. Then he fell into Washington's arms. Holding the body gently, Washington lowered it to the ground, laying his silenced pistol beside it. A shadow passed over him. Raising his eyes, tears running freely he looked up into the stern bearded face of Duke.

He nodded his head at the body of his brother and said in a whisper, "See, Dukey-Doo! I tol' you I'd see he done right."

Duke nodded, saying only, "You did right. I'm sorry it had to be. But now the rest of us need you, too."

Rising, Washington followed the broad-shouldered mercenary back across the field to the terminal where they were beginning to take heavy fire.

Becaude had taken a squad and rushed over to the stricken aircraft. The crewmen were just getting the doors open when he reached them. His men rushed inside, using their bayonets to cut people loose of the straps holding them to their seats. The hostages came stumbling out. Becaude moved them away from the aircraft and forced them on their faces behind a low rise of earth. It wasn't much but it would give them some protection from the enemy rifle fire till he could get them on the other aircraft.

Robinson had stared in horror as the C-130 slewed off the runway and crumbled. As soon as he saw the hostages were being taken off, he began to taxi toward them. He knew what had to be done. He and Hendricks had talked it over during their contingency planning. The hostages came first. It wasn't something he liked but there was no other choice. Taxiing to intercept the hostages, he gave his orders to his crew over the intercom. "Get them on board and close the hatch. As soon as the last one is in we're takin' off.''

From around the field the mercenaries watched the loading of the hostages into Robinson's aircraft. They knew that when it took off they would be left without any way of getting out. Many felt a hollow feeling in the gut but made no protest. They would do their job and pray to the gods of chance that perhaps something would happen. As long as they had their weapons and ammo they were not totally lost. At the thought of ammo most began to count their remaining rounds. There would be no resupply. Even with the captured stocks they would not be able to keep up a high rate of fire for long. Perhaps they would have enough to last the day and the night. After that?

Hendricks watched the transfer. Voice flat and emotionless, he gave his orders over the radio. ''Everyone give suppressing fire to cover the plane.''

Immediately a heavy volume was laid down all around the field as the mercs began pouring out their precious remaining rounds. Duke had returned with Washington. Ignoring the chips flying off the side of the terminal that peppered his body, Hendricks told Duke, ''Take a squad and get to the far end of the field. Make the rebels keep their heads down till they get off. Use one of the jeeps with a recoilless. Now move out!''

''Right, Boss. C'mon Washington, we got some work to do,'' Duke snapped. Gathering four men from the terminal, he grabbed up an RPD light machine gun and several belts of ammo, then slung them over his shoulder. They were gifts from the Askaris who had occupied the building at dawn. They clambered into the jeep and spun off down the strip dodging dust clouds of mortar fire.

Hendricks gave fire assignments to the mortar crews, turning control of them over to a spotter in the tower who gave them their fire commands. He directed them after the enemy mortars. The mortar men began to strip and hustle rounds down the tubes as fast as they could. Hendricks had one man drop random rounds around the perimeter just to keep the rebels nervous. It didn't matter much if they hit anything or not but it would keep some of the rebels down. If they were on their faces, they couldn't fire at the C-130.

Going back inside the terminal he told his radioman to contact all elements and inform them that as soon as the aircraft was off the ground they were to conduct a fighting withdrawal to the terminal, bringing all weapons and captured stocks with them.

The incoming fire was increasing but was not very effective. The suppressing fire from his men kept the rebels from attaining any great degree of accuracy. They were more used to dealing with the less enthusiastic troops of Mehendi. Determined and fierce resistance made them uncertain.

The last of the hostages were being herded, pushed, and shoved into Robinson's aircraft. Around them shots clipped off the tarmac as a light machine gun tried to search out soft targets. Several of Becaude's men went to their knees, laying down fire to try to keep rebel machine gunners busy till the last of the hostages could be loaded. The young couple they'd picked up on the streets of Bokala were among the last to reach the plane. The young man dragged the girl by her hand as shots snapped the air about them. Suddenly she was thrown out of his grip, her body lifted from the runway and hurled several feet through the air.

"*Jan!*" the young man cried out as he ran to her body. He threw himself over her still form as if he could prevent any more bullets from reaching her. She had been stitched up the spine. A hand pulled at his shoulder as one of the mercs tried to separate him from the girl's bleeding corpse.

"C'mon, she's bought it. Get on board!" The young man didn't have to answer the merc. The man went down. The back of his head was gone, leaving a hole that looked as if someone had scooped the back of his skull out. He fell face-down beside the girl, the rifle clattering to the tarmac. Snapping rounds from the shoulder, Becaude ran to them. He tried to tear the young man loose from the girl's body. The last of the hostages were on board and there were only seconds left. His hand was suddenly jerked from the boy's shirt and Becaude found himself staring down the muzzle of the dead merc's rifle.

"Get your hands off of me. I'm not going anywhere!"

If he'd had the time Becaude would have given a Gallic shrug. "*C'est bien*. If that is what you wish. I have no more time. Stay and die with her if that is what you want."

Turning away, Becaude signaled the cargo master to close the tailgate.

The tailgate creaked shut, locking the people inside and separating them from the fight going on out on the field. The brakes were released. Picking up speed, the plane began to move faster and faster down the strip, Robinson driving the engines to red line with full flaps. Machine-gun fire punched holes in the side of the aircraft, letting in bright streamers of light.

Robinson heard a scream from the rear pierce through the roar of the engines. Someone had gotten hit. Ahead of him mortar rounds continued to puncture the runway. Keeping the throttles on full power, he gripped the stick as hard as he could, as if by his own will he could squeeze a few more horsepower out of the engines. At first the transport seemed to settle down lower on the runway. Robinson felt they would never get up to speed. Then he was passing the terminal. On its roof he could see men laying down fire on the far end of the strip with a heavy machine gun hauled up from one of the guardposts. Hendricks was there, standing in front of the doors to the customs counters. Through the Plexiglas his eyes caught Robinson's for just a moment. Robinson saw him raise a hand in a salute, then turn his back to reenter the terminal with his men. He had to shake his head to rid his eyes of the tears that welled up in them, unbidden.

The aircraft was lighter now. He could feel the weight lessening as it began to gain enough speed for the air to provide some lift. Ahead of him he saw Duke and his crew laying down fire with the recoilless rifle. In the distance a burst of smoke and a brief flash of flame spouted into the sky. They'd hit someone's ammo supply.

They were losing runway fast, but the weight was lessening with every yard. He only had a few yards left when the nose at last came up. The plane was free of the earth and returning to its natural environment. He could see small dark figures pointing at them with their rifles and machine guns. But the C-130 was a tough bird, it took a lot to pull one down. As long as the enemy below didn't take out more than two of its motors, he felt certain they'd be able to make it. Then they were up and past the point of danger from ground fire. He kept the C-130 on a steady climb to ten thousand feet, throttling back and easing off the flaps ten degrees at a time. He checked with his crew chief in the cargo bay. He was already treating the wounded as best he could.

Over the intercom Robinson addressed his passengers.

"Ladies and gentlemen. Welcome aboard. Please remain in your seats and keep the safety belts secured. In a few hours we will be landing in friendly territory where medical assistance will be waiting for those who need it. In the meantime please remain calm. Food and drinks will be passed out by the crew in a few minutes. Please do not get in their way as they have much to do. At this moment I would just like to confirm one thing. You are safe and on your way home aboard a United States aircraft.''

The words felt like shit in his mouth. It was as if he were running a flight from New York to Miami. He wondered if those in the rear thought at all about the men they had left behind and what was to become of them. He didn't want to think about them but couldn't help it. Men were dying on the African runway and they were dying because of the people in his cargo bay. He wondered who was of the most value. It was difficult not to turn the nose of the aircraft around 180 degrees and go back for one more look. He felt as if he had somehow betrayed them. It was good that he had orders to follow. They relieved him of the torment of his conscience. He would do as he was ordered and take these people back to his base in Egypt. As for Hendricks and his men, he knew they were lost. For Hendricks, though, maybe this time his ''night of the bayonets'' would end the way the first one had been supposed to.

He pulled the aircraft on up to twenty-five thousand and trimmed her off. There was nothing more for him to do now. He was once more just a cab driver.

TWENTY-THREE

NOVEMBER 1
0700 HOURS

FROM THE TERMINAL roof and windows they gave covering fire to the teams of mercs as they leapfrogged from their positions on the field perimeter. Hendricks moved to the roof. Already a distant speck in the sky, the C-130 was on its way, safe from all the killing. He knew no one would be coming back for them. They were on their own. If they were going to break out, they would have to do it fast or they would be totally cut off by the rebels. They might be able to break out with the trucks and get far enough ahead to make it to the border of the Sudan or Chad. That was their only chance.

Becaude came rushing into the terminal with his men. They threw themselves down behind the windows or took shelter behind the small barrier of sandbags piled up in front of the entrance to the customs section. The truck used to take the hostages to the strip came racing back to the terminal. Becaude had sent one of his men to bring it in. The driver pulled it over to the side farthest from enemy fire.

From the roof Hendricks saw the young man he had picked up in the streets of Bokala. He was carrying the blond girl over his shoulder with an FAL in his left hand. The girl was dead. That was obvious, but why was the boy here? He should have been on the plane on his way to safety.

The firing began to slack off around the field. His men had cleared out of their positions and returned to the terminal, bringing their wounded and their dead with them. Hendricks knew the rebels were waiting for new orders now that the plane and its cargo were out of their reach.

As his men pulled back the rebels moved forward, warily crossing over the wire. If he'd had the men he could have held them there, but he didn't.

The hangars and maintenance buildings were all in flames. He had thought that he might have been able to use the one C-47 still operational, but when his men pulled back someone had blown it. Now it wasn't any more than a smoldering hulk.

He had Duke and Becaude place their men behind the sandbagged barriers in front of the terminal. His men still held the machine-gun post at the entrance to the building. From the roof he had the advantage of height and therefore a good view of the situation. He had the mortars brought back from the firing pits with all the ammunition they could carry and moved up to where they'd be able to provide 360 degrees of fire on the enemy. Right now they were just dropping enough rounds to keep the rebels undercover. It wouldn't last for long though. Ammunition was short for the tubes. He'd given them orders to fire slow. When they broke out he might want to use them for cover.

Moving off the roof and across the terminal, careful to

avoid the open spaces of the windows, he squatted down Indian-style beside Becaude, who sat with his back against the terminal wall, chest heaving from the run across the strip. "We have a bit of a problem, Claude."

Becaude smiled up through a sweaty red face. "A bit of a problem, *Chef*? I would hate to run into what you call a big one. I presume that we are now going to try to make a break for it before we are completely cut off, *non*?"

"That's right. We have the two trucks and your jeeps. Get them around to the front of the terminal but wait until I tell you. If the rebels see us moving them now they'll start firing on them. Gather the men to me and we'll divide things up. But keep a good look out for the rebels to come at us. Now that Robinson and his cargo are gone they may or may not decide we're worth the effort and price it will take to finish us off."

Groaning, Becaude pulled his thick body up and began calling the men to gather in the center of the terminal. As he did this Hendricks went over to the blond young man who was holding the body of the girl in his arms. Near the coffee counter were the bodies of the dead mercs, lying in a neat row, their faces covered by their hats or jackets.

"You should put her with the others," Hendricks said gently.

Looking to where the bodies lay, the young man shook his head and held the corpse tighter to him. Hendricks touched him softly on the shoulder. "Believe me. She will be in good company. Now tell me your name."

"Anthony J. Collier III." He pronounced each syllable as if trying to reassure himself of his own identity.

"All right, Tony, you're with us now and there is much to be done. Take your lady and lay her down with the others, then report back to me. You are going to have a

chance to even the score for her but not if you let yourself
fall apart. Now straighten up and do what has to be done!''

The words were spoken flatly. The mercenary leader
was not offering him sympathy. There was no time for
that. But he was offering him vengeance. That he understood. Nodding his head, Anthony picked up Jan's body
and carried her across to the coffee counter where he laid
her between the body of a Belgian and an American.
Placing her hands over her breasts, he brushed a strand of
bloodstained gold hair from her face and covered her with
part of a green curtain torn from a window.

The FAL suddenly felt very good in his hands. He knew
how to use it. His father had been a soldier before entering
into the business world and had taught him how to use
most small arms. They had an extensive collection at their
country home in Santa Fe, including a semiautomatic FAL.
To date all he'd shot at were targets. He didn't like
hunting but he enjoyed shooting. Now he was going to
have live, human targets to fix in the steel sights, and he
knew he would have no problem in making the kill.

Hendricks watched him. He could see the young man
taking control of himself. He straightened up his spine as
he came to a decision. His fingers tightened on the pistol
grip of the rifle. He could almost feel Anthony shake the
past away from him. He was ready now! Hendricks watched
him as he swiftly checked out his weapon with practiced
hands. The young man knew what he was doing.

The men gathered around him silently. Only the sound
of their breathing broke through the stillness. Outside the
terminal there were intermittent shots. They only served to
accent the situation.

Hendricks let his eyes run over every face there. He
could see the uncertainty in some of the eyes. They were

men who felt abandoned. In others there was only a quiet calm, the calm that comes when one is ready to meet death. He spoke to both groups.

"You know the situation. We are alone and cut off. There will be no aircraft for us. If we are going to get out then we'll have to do it on our own. We have weapons, we have trucks, and you are trained professionals. Act as such and we have a chance. At my signal we will make our break before the rebels make up their minds to assault in strength or shoot up the trucks. Divide yourselves into two teams. As before, the Americans and Europeans. Becaude will take command of the Europeans and I will lead the Americans. Once we are loaded, keep moving. If a truck gets hit, that will be the only reason to stop and pick up survivors. When we pull out we'll head north. Thirty kilometers from here there is a junction in the road. One path goes to the Sudan, the other to Chad. Either one will grant you sanctuary.

"Becaude has the radio frequencies for the base in Egypt. He will contact them as soon as we cross one or the other's borders. Either way it is a run of about two hundred kilometers. Stay alert, save your ammunition, and hit your targets."

One of the men asked softly, "What about the wounded, *Chef*?"

"Everyone goes. We leave no one alive for them. If one is too badly wounded to travel you know what must be done. Now prepare yourselves. We have only a few minutes at most. That is all. Get to it!"

The mercs dispersed, rushing to gather weapons and ammo, checking what rations they had in their packs. Many thanked their luck that Hendricks had ordered them to take extra rations even though the job had been expected to take only a few hours.

Hendricks called Duke over to him. "You and Washington take our truck. We will only need two to take out our people but I want all three. I'll take point in one jeep with a recoilless rifle. And I want you to take the young fellow over there with the FAL with us. His name is Anthony. He's an American so I guess he belongs with you. We pull out in five minutes. I want one other thing. I want this place burned to the ground. Go up to the roof and bring down a case or two of mortar rounds. You can use them, too."

He nodded his head at the line of dead by the counter. "We leave them nothing."

Leaving him, Duke grabbed Jerome and Washington. They went upstairs and came back with two cases of 60-mm rounds. Then Jerome went outside, returning with one of the jerry cans of gas. He handed it over to Duke, who began whistling "Over the Rainbow" under his breath as he began unscrewing the fuses of a couple of the mortar shells. Unobtrusively, he went about the business of turning the terminal into a funeral pyre. The timer was simple, a French device set for a five-minute delay and a backup with a camouflaged tripwire at the entrance to the terminal in case the rebels came in early. It ran to the pin of a white phosphorus grenade. But he wouldn't connect it till the last man was out of the building. Setting the cans down by the counter, he waited till the men began to gather by the windows and doors of the terminal getting ready to run for the trucks.

"*Chef,* do we lay down some covering fire first with the mortars and recoilless rifles?"

"No, Claude. I think we'll do better if we just make a sudden break without giving them any warning. It shouldn't take more than fifteen seconds to get everyone on board and the trucks moving. But as soon as we do, get some machine guns up top where they can fire over the cabs and one in the rear of each truck. I want the flaps rolled up so the men can fire from the sides. When we go out, I want all hell to break loose. Give the rebels what the Americans call the 'mad minute,' all guns firing. Don't worry about ammo. If we don't make it off the field it won't make any difference. Also, when we go, make sure the other vehicles we leave behind won't be in any condition to chase us.''

Becaude left to have a few last words with his men. Hendricks went to the window. One truck was to the left of the terminal, the other just around the corner. One jeep had pulled up behind a shoulder-high sandbag barrier to the right, the nose of its rifle pointing over the wall to the south end of the field. That was the one he'd take.

''Calvin! Get over here with me. You're driving again.''

Calvin had settled down after the action in Bokala. ''Yes, sir.''

Hendricks pointed out the jeep. ''That's the one we'll take. When we get in, head for the road we came in on and turn to the right. Then push, but not so fast that we lose the trucks. I want them about twenty meters behind us at all times.'' Turning around he called out, ''Who manned the 106 on the jeep out front?'' Two men stepped forward from Claude's group. ''All right. You go with me. As soon as we're in the jeeps, load the rifle and get ready to use it.''

Dust motes rose through the air, floating on the growing heat of the day. They tasted of cordite. Mixed with the dust were the smell of fear and the smell of death. The fear came from the unknown. What would happen to them if they failed to break out and were captured? Okediji was known for his brutality—his fiendish skill with his straight razor—where white mercenaries were concerned. His treatment of blacks who fought with them was even more horrible. That was the greatest fear.

The death smell came from the bodies of their own men and the Askaris in the terminal. In a few hours, if they did not get out, the stench would start to grow, sweet and cloying, till it blocked out all other senses. The flies were already gathering in black moving clouds, swarming over the rags and blankets used to cover the dead. But there were enough pools of thick dark blood to satisfy most of them.

Stepping back, Hendricks looked around him. There was nothing more to be done here. It was time to go.

"This is it! Let's do it! *En avant!*" He hit the door with Calvin on his heels followed by the crew that would man the recoilless rifle. The jeep's motor started quickly. Behind him, in a controlled rush for the doors and windows, the mercenaries poured out, hunched over, running to the trucks.

As soon as they were out of the building, Hendricks slapped Calvin on the shoulder. "Let's move it!"

Small-arms fire picked at them. Two men went down, one dead from a lucky shot that entered his neck just above the collar. Jerome was out of the game for good. His body was hauled into the back of the truck with the living. Hendricks had said they would leave nothing for the rebels, not even the dead.

Duke was the last man out after setting his tripwire for the gasoline bomb.

From the rebels across the strip, he could hear shouts. Mortars began coming in. But they were of little effect. The rebels' tubes had been sighted for the terminal. Now that the mercs were pulling out of it, it would take them a few moments to adjust to the new moving targets. By then, if the mercs were lucky, they would be clear and on the road. Then all they'd have to contend with would be any rebel roadblocks or ambushes. It was better than just waiting to die. At least they were doing something.

It had been fourteen minutes since Hendricks's team had come onto the field. As soon as his men were in the jeep, a round of high explosive was slapped into the base of the recoilless rifle and secured by the loader. Another round was in his hands. He moved a bit forward of the tube to keep away from the back blast. The gunner was ready at the sight, finger on the igniter.

They took the turn leading to the main road. Hendricks could see the figures of the men at the machine-gun post. When the first truck passed, they'd jump on board. Twenty meters to go and he'd be past them on the road. The machine-gun post exploded. The delayed blast rocked the jeep. Calvin jerked to a halt. Another explosion and one of the men in the bunker came flying out of it, one arm gone at the shoulder, his face a mask of blood, the uniform on his back on fire. He fell face-down. There was another explosion, this time just in front of the jeep. The rebels had moved up and hit the machine-gun bunker with recoilless rifle fire of their own. Through the dust Hendricks saw something else. A column of armored cars followed by two light tanks were moving up on the road from Bokala. Okediji's men had taken over abandoned vehicles from the fleeing Askaris, using captured men to run the unfamiliar vehicles and weapons systems. To the north he could see men maneuvering through the fields and alongside the road. If they went out that way it'd be a death trap. They were stuck. There was no way out now. Behind him the trucks had also come to abrupt halts. Standing up in the jeep, he waved them back, yelling, "We're cut off here. Try for the north end of the field!"

Without having to be told, his gunner sighted on the leader of the armored cars. Hendricks thought it was a British Saladin mounting a 20-mm and a light machine gun. The high-explosive round of the 106 was more than enough to rip through the three-quarter-inch armorplate on the Saladin's front. The blast blew off one front tire and punctured the hull, sending white-hot steel splinters bouncing around the interior of the car. One man got out alive. The gunner, who was an unwilling guest of the rebels, tried to run for the fields and was machine-gunned by the hull gun of the car behind him.

Calvin whipped the jeep around in a tight circle, racing past the other trucks that were trying to back up to where they could turn around. From the tops of the trucks the merc machine gunners threw out a curtain of small-arms fire, knowing it wasn't going to stop the armored cars or tanks, but it would keep the rebel infantry from moving in on them too fast.

Hitting the strip again, Hendricks saw the rebels had moved out from across the field and were running in small groups to intercept them. One squad of ten men reached the doors to the terminal. He saw the first two men go inside, then the terminal erupted. Duke's tripwire! The men outside were knocked back by the blast, three of them dead. Flames shot out of the windows and then came a rumbling roar as the roof collapsed. Duke had done his job well. In seconds the terminal was an inferno. Clouds of smoke rolled across the runway to mix with the smells of burning petrol, cordite, and rubber.

Nearly all the buildings were in flames or in rebel hands, except for the one workshop. The walls had been knocked down and the insides were a jungle of lathes and machine tools over which twisted steel rafters and corrugated-tin sheeting lay in convoluted heaps. It hadn't burned because there was nothing in it that could be set ablaze.

It took only a moment for Hendricks to realize that they would never make it to the far end of the runway. There were hundreds of small dodging figures all around the field. The rebels of Okediji were coming in for the kill. Behind him the trucks came to the tarmac. Slapping Calvin on the shoulder he pointed to the workshop. "That's it! Pull in there and move the jeep away from us."

To the gunner and his partner he ordered, "Take off the rifle and move it in with us."

He was off the jeep before it stopped. In seconds the two 106 men had their piece broken loose of its mounts and had taken it and the remaining ammo off the jeep. Calvin moved the small vehicle off to the side so if it got hit the exploding gas tanks wouldn't harm them. Then, hunkered over, he ran back under the protective fire of Hendricks, who was laying down short sharp bursts from behind the shell of an old Dodge pickup.

The 106 men tossed out two rounds across the field where a group of rebels had taken cover in the wreckage of one of the hangars. Hendricks and Calvin fired rapidly to give the trucks some cover as they came wheeling in behind them. The men leaped from the backs of the trucks, rolling and dodging as they ran into the ruins of the workshop. They found plenty of cover between the shop machinery and heavy lathes. Becaude had the drivers pull their vehicles away from the shop to the rear of the building, then ran up to join Hendricks.

The firing slackened once more now that the mercs were pinned down. There was no way out. Hendricks knew the faces around him were pale under their coatings of greasy sweat and ash. Each man tried to think of something, anything that would give them a chance to get out alive. Each came up with the same answer. There was nothing.

"*Chef*, I think this time we are in deep shit," Becaude said.

A thin hard smile forced its way onto Hendricks's face. "It's the Congo again, Claude. It seems to have gone full circle."

The firing had died off completely from the rebels now. Whatever was going to happen was up to them. He saw Washington was beside Duke peering out from the bottom of a wrecked lathe. His face was steady, calm. He and the big bearded white man seemed to have some kind of thing working between them. Hendricks approved. It was good to have a friend beside you at a time such as this. It would make the dying easier. No one wanted to die alone. Anthony Collier was by himself. He was crouching in a pile of twisted beams. His face had a hard cast to it. There was death in the eyes and face. He didn't care if he got killed anymore. The young man was now a very dangerous entity. He could snap and go either way. He'd have Duke and Becaude keep an eye on him.

To Becaude, he said, "Check on the men, gather all the ammunition and divide it among them and tell them to conserve their water. When you have done that bring me back a status report. Let me know how many we have and the condition of the wounded. There is no telling how long we'll be here. But as long as we're alive there is a chance. Who knows, maybe there'll be an earthquake."

Alone, he looked across the field to the other hangars and buildings. The enemy was everywhere and getting stronger. The armored cars and two tanks had moved up beside the burning terminal and spread out across the runway in a line. Infantry had moved up between them, a barrier against their trying to break out again. The metal beasts sat there waiting.

The only question now was when they would come or if they would just wait and let nature take them. He didn't think the African mentality was suited to siege warfare. No! They would come this afternoon or in the night. He didn't know when, but they would come. It was now up to Okediji. Touching the handle of his bayonet, he smiled again. This time it was a grim thing, a death's-head smile.

TWENTY-FOUR

NOVEMBER 1
1100 HOURS

OKEDIJI MOVED UP behind a burned-out hangar, taking cover behind the wreckage of one of Mehendi's Migs. Lowering his field glasses he turned to the man beside him.

"This is going to be a great day. It is of course regrettable that they have managed to do so much damage to the equipment, but I suppose that could not be helped. Yes, it will be a most rewarding day and I have you to thank for a large share of it." He smiled benevolently.

Kelo merely lowered his head a bit to acknowledge the words. And with submission is his words he said, "Thank you. I am grateful that I was able to help you in bringing the monster to justice."

Okediji moved a bit to the right for a better look at the mercenary position. Watching his back, Kelo's face gave nothing away, but his mind was not as acquiescent as his show of posture. You will be next, he thought. It is not yet time for my people to rise but they will. The money I took from Mehendi is safe and when the time is right, it will be used against you.

Looking over Okediji's shoulder to the workshop, he felt no real sense of loss for, or loyalty to, the white mercenaries. Their deaths meant little to him.

A movement drew his eye. Even at that distance he knew it was Hendricks. I do owe him something, but it appears that I shall not have the opportunity to repay him, Kelo mused.

Okediji had changed into fresh khakis with a British Sam Browne belt and holster. His epaulets carried the insignia of a field marshal. He had recently decided he deserved a promotion. Since he knew he was in control of the situation, he had taken the time to enjoy himself a bit before going to the field. He felt very good in his new uniform, very much the leader.

From his officers' reports, he knew the mercenaries were pinned down. There was nowhere for them to go. Now he was able to release units from the sacking of the city to join him here. He wanted all the men in his command who could be spared to participate. To witness!

Once his audience was ready, he would begin the final act that would eliminate the white man from his land. That was a good thought: his land. After the many years of struggle and deprivation, now it was his and no one could take it from him. The cities, the villages, the people, the animals, everything was his. Even their lives were his personal property to do with as he wished.

He could not, of course, release all of his units in the vicinity to come to the field, but each would send a representative who could take back the story of what happened here this day. Checking his watch, he saw that it shouldn't be but a few minutes more. His men were streaming in from all sectors converging on the field.

He had not gained all that he wished. The palace was a ruin, the aircraft on the runway destroyed. They would have been useful. And then there were the hostages who had just been taken out of his reach. They had been the most valuable of all. He could have bartered them for much. Still, it was a good day. He had plans for the mercenaries that would give him status among many of the Third World nations. Turning, he smiled pleasantly at the stern face of Kelo.

He owed this man a great deal. He would reward him. Punishment and reward were the secret to continued power. Each must be trusted and believed in. "Serve me well and prosper. Go against me and know pain." That was his code. There was no other way.

Now was the time for pain. His men had arrived and it was time for him to begin. He was growing a bit impatient. Calling an aide to him, he gave his orders. There would be one minute of total fire on the mercenary position, then absolute silence.

Hell broke loose for the mercs. Even with their own mortars and recoilless rifles trying to counter the enemy fire, their effort was feeble at best. From all sides came a hell of fire as the rebels gave the mercenaries their own "mad minute." Shots pinged like hail in a storm off the metal beams of the shop. A barrage of mortar shells walked over them and back again. Men were going down dead or wounded. It was difficult to raise one's head to get off a shot but they managed it. Like moles, the mercs dug deeper into the workshop ruins, forcing holes through the rubble through which they could return fire. Then suddenly, terribly, it was over. The silence was broken by the cries of the wounded and dying, but not all of them came from the mercenaries. They had given back a percentage of what they had received.

The wounded were treated as well as they could be. Once that was done, the mercs took advantage of the silence to reload magazines, take a drink of water, and wait.

"*Mr. Hendricks!*"

The voice reached him across the field. He wondered how it knew his name. "*Mr. Hendricks!*" called the voice again. "This is Field Marshal Okediji speaking to you. Please respond. We have a few items to discuss."

Lowering the bullhorn, Okediji waited. He knew they had no choice but to answer. This was his game and he owned all the pieces.

Pulling up to where he could see across the field, Hendricks could just make out two figures by the burned-out shell of a Mig-15.

"This is Commander Hendricks. What is it you wish to discuss?"

Okediji's voice bounced back at him, full of good humor, amplified through the bullhorn. "Why, I wish to discuss the future of you and your men, of course. It is only through my good graces that you will even have the opportunity to reach the next hour."

"Go ahead. What is your offer?"

"Mr. Hendricks, I do not make offers. However, I am giving you a choice. If you surrender to me now, I shall put you and your men on public trial for the world to witness. After that I will of course have to execute a few of you to keep up appearances, but after a few years in prison the rest will be pardoned and sent home. I know that this option does not seem terribly attractive at this time, but if you will give it a bit of thought and discuss it with your men, I am certain you will come to agree with me. After all, what are your choices? You are cut off. You have many wounded and there is no way out except through death. Therefore, as logical men, it should be obvious to you that my offer is the only choice you have. I will give you until five-thirty this afternoon to decide. Then, if you do not agree to lay down your arms, I will come for you and there will be a great killing and much pain for those unfortunate enough to be taken alive. Though I will not kill all of you, of course. I still need some alive to hold my trial. It will just be done with fewer prisoners, that is all.''

He was right. He did seem to hold all the cards. The number of his men had been reduced to thirty-one still able to fight and seven wounded who were in no condition to do anything. Almost one third of his original force was a casualty. The rest of the wounded who had gone on the C-130 were very lucky. Around him he could feel the eyes of his men as they waited for his answer. Signaling for Becaude and Duke to join him, he held a quick conference with his two trusted deputies. Their heads shook up and down as they agreed to what he proposed.

"Okediji! I have a counteroffer to make. If you will let my men go, take them across the border to the Sudan and let me confirm it by radio with them, then I will surrender myself and my officers to you to do with as you please. To take us all will cost you many lives.''

Laughter boomed back at him from across the field.

"Mr. Hendricks, I do not have to accept any terms from you. I have you in my hand. All that I have to do is close my fingers to squash you like dung beetles. As for taking losses, my men are ready to die for me. That is of no consequence. You are mine. It is I who make the conditions here, not you. Now I will accept nothing less than unconditional surrender from all of you. It is all or nothing. Remember, you have till five-thirty this afternoon to give me your answer. I will call a truce until that time. Then I will come for you one way or the other!''

Hendricks and the men around him automatically looked at their watches. It was eleven-thirty. They had six hours.

Not completely trusting Okediji or the discipline of his men, Hendricks kept the place covered as he moved among the ruins of the shop from one man to the next. There was little he could say that would help them. They had heard Okediji's terms. They knew exactly what was being offered. For some, after perhaps a year in a Bokala prison, they would be brought to trial for the world to stare and gawk at. There were no illusions as to the conditions of black Africa's jail system. Not all of them who surrendered would be alive when the time came for the trial, and then, if for some strange reason Okediji kept his word and released them after ten or twenty years, many would be dead or close to it.

Hendricks had to let each man know that he had a voice in what was to be done. This was not a decision he could make alone. There was no mission now except to save the lives of his men if he could, and if he could not, then he would see to it they had a quick death. One by one each man gave him the right to decide for them. The hardest part was facing the wounded who'd die without hospital treatment. Those who could speak did so, saying only, "You are the *Chef*. It is up to you."

When he came back to his original position, Calvin was waiting for him.

"What's it going to be, Boss?" The smooth-faced Vietnam veteran's eyes were bright. There was fire in them, the kind of fire that he had seen before in the Congo. It was part of the flush that rises when one knows he is on the steps of death and is making his mind accept it. He has become totally and absolutely aware of his own mortality.

Slumping down with his rifle between his legs, Hendricks lit up a cigarette, drawing in the acrid smoke. It tasted of burned petrol and rubber.

Watching Calvin's face between the blue smoky tendrils of his cigarette, he tried to see behind the eyes to feel what the man was going through. Calvin had seen death, violent death, before. But there was something terribly different about being cut off and totally surrounded with no way out. No hope of an airstrike by fighter planes or a bombing run by B-52s. There would be no relief force rushing in at the last moment. They were completely alone with no way out.

"What do you think?" Hendricks asked.

Twisting his body to where he could see better, Calvin said, "I guess that we've bought this one, Boss. I don't think that son of a bitch over there is ever going to let any of us go. He'll hold his trial, and then we'll disappear one by one or maybe all together. I think I'd like it better if all of us went out at the same time. It won't be as hard as dying alone." There—he had said it! "Die alone." The bogeyman was out and Hendricks knew that Calvin had accepted it.

"You're right. He's not ever going to let us go. We die now or we die later. Here at least we make the choice ourselves."

He looked at the sky. The smoke from around the field was clearing, by five o'clock it was going to be bright and clear.

"Anyway," Hendricks continued, "it looks like it's going to be a good day to die."

The muscles in Calvin's jaw and temples worked hard. There was a slight tremble to his hands, which he tried to control by gripping his weapon tighter.

Pointing over to Anthony, he tapped Calvin on the shoulder. "There's someone over there who might need some company. He is completely alone. Maybe you can help him through the next hours.'' Hendricks thought he would give the boy someone else to think about. Responsibility for another would make it easier for them both when the time came.

He was weary, soul tired. The events of the last hours had drained much from him. They had almost made it. The winning or losing had been a matter of minutes, of chance throwing her weight on one side or another. You could plan, calculate, weigh every factor, and still the roll could come up against you.

He knew some of the men were in a state of near-shock. The changes that had taken place in the last hours had been too much. There had been the training, the flight from Egypt, the battles, and the escape of the hostages. It had all gone down pretty smoothly. And now they were here waiting for what the next few hours would bring and there was no way out. They could be taken prisoner or die now. Even the most optimistic of them preferred the latter, knowing it was by far the easier choice.

Hendricks could almost feel the settling down that comes after hard choices are made and accepted. There were subtle shiftings of the body. And there was that look in the eyes, like the look he had seen in Calvin's.

For men who were accustomed to giving death, it was now their turn to cross over. The last great question would be answered. To their surprise some found themselves anticipating the event, tasting it. They wished Okediji would get on with it.

Hendricks knew everything they were feeling. He had been through it before in the Congo during that ''night of the Bayonets.'' He had seen his men prepare themselves to die. Putting out the smoke, he rested, leaning his head forward to ease the strain in his neck muscles. He was ready, too. When he came down to it, there was really nothing to feel bad about. He had lived and he would die. In his time he had seen and done much. And he had taken from life in his own way.

He saw Calvin talking quietly to Anthony. If there was a loss, it was for the young men who would not have the time to fill their lives with memories. But death played no favorites. It took some sooner, some later. At least there was no need to be afraid now. The worst thing was not knowing when one would die or the manner of one's death. Every man here had that question resolved for them. They knew!

Now he would take advantage of Okediji's truce. He lowered his head to his knees and went to sleep. Becaude moved closer to where he could watch over the *Chef*.

TWENTY-FIVE

NOVEMBER 1
1645 HOURS

As HE SLEPT his men counted their remaining bullets one by one. A silence had settled over them as they waited for the hours to pass. Most of the older men did as Hendricks did and slept after taking care of their weapons.

Duke and Washington rearranged pieces of twisted metal and junk to provide them with better firing platforms. Calvin and Anthony told each other their life stories, short as they were. Becaude stayed where he was, where he wanted to be. If the end was to come this day, he wanted to end it with the *Chef*.

Kelo moved back from the runway to watch Okediji's preparations for the final event. He had the officers from his best units select two hundred men to form into a special commando. He named them the Leopards. These were the men who would take the machine shop. To them would go the glory; the rest were to be spectators.

His new elite commando changed from their scraps and rags into new uniforms brought in from Mehendi's supply house for his Askaris. Like children, they laughed in pleasure over the luxury of putting on the new uniforms and boots. Okediji smiled at them as would an indulgent father who had given his beloved children just what they wanted for Christmas.

Neither he nor Kelo had any illusions about the choice the mercenaries would make. They would fight, and that was fine. Okediji knew he would have what he wanted. He wouldn't be cheated of his spectacle. Mercenaries would go on trial and be judged and punished by him for all the world to see. His "children" would bring them to him and there was nothing the men in the machine shop ruins could do to stop it, though they did not know it yet. But they would. They would!

"*Chef*! It is time to get ready."

Hendricks raised his head to look into the dark eyes of Becaude. He smiled.

"The hours fly by when you're having a good time, don't they?"

Becaude smiled back. "They will come soon. We have less than one hour left to Okediji's deadline."

Checking his watch, he said. "Right as usual."

Groaning with stiff knees, he forced himself to his feet, holding the FAL by the foregrip. The weapon was hot from the heat of the day; it would grow hotter still.

He made one last round of his men. They had dug in pretty well, making maximum use of the piles of rubble. They were like mini Stalingrad. He stopped here and there to give a word of encouragement, a small joke, a smile, which fooled no one, though all pretended it did. They were ready. Grenades were laid out, the cotter pins straightened so they'd pull out easier, magazines of ammo placed at easy access.

Their one recoilless rifle was dug in behind a pile of tin sheeting and planks, loaded with canister shot. Once it opened fire the life expectancy of the crew would be measured in seconds. They wanted to get the most out of their weapon before they went down.

Most of the smoke from the fires had drifted away as the fuel got eaten up. Only the stink of burned rubber still hung in the air.

Hendricks saw the trembling of hands as they gripped weapons, beads of sweat gathering under noses and eyes, nervous tics at the corners of mouths. All were signs of fear, but of fear under control. They would do well this day.

Duke and Washington were still together. They gave him a thumbs-up as he passed. The two youngsters, Anthony and Calvin, seemed to have it under control. Anthony handled his weapon with intimacy. He'd spent a great deal of time sighting with it across the field as if impatient for the attack to begin. He would have made a good soldier. Though he had much hate, he didn't let it force him into making any hasty moves. Yes, he would have done well at another time. Becaude looked as he always had, not very concerned about what was going to happen next. He was a fatalist at heart. If it was his time, then so be it.

"What do you think, Claude, should we start the game now and not wait for Okediji?"

Becaude nodded his square head up and down, his thick body shaking with the movement. "*Pourquoi pas?* It does not look to me as if we have much to wait for. The sooner it starts the better it will be for all of us, *n'est-ce pas?*"

Raising his voice loud enough for all to hear him, Hendricks asked, "What do you say, men? Shall we begin the game and make the first move? If we're going to fight

then we might as well get on with it. So what will it be?
Fight now or wait for Okediji to begin it?''

From all around him came the word, staggered at first,
then all together as they began to repeat it in a chant.
''*Fight, fight, fight!*'' It was good. That was all they had
left.

Speaking to Anthony, he said softly, ''Perhaps you have
lost the most here this day. Do you wish to begin it?''

Anthony drew a deep breath. All eyes were on him but
he didn't care. What he would do was not for them. He
looked at Calvin, who nodded his head and then inclined it
toward the field where the rebels waited. ''Take it!'' he
whispered. ''There'll never be another day like this for
you.''

Anthony swallowed, his mouth dry, sticky. Placing the
rifle to his shoulder, he adjusted the sight for range,
checked the wind for drift, then took up his spot-weld.
Hendricks saw him take in his breath, then let it out
slowly, then again, holding a part of it as his finger took
up the slack on the trigger. The boy knew how to shoot.

Anthony had picked his man hours ago. There was a
rebel behind some empty oil drums who had the habit of
sticking his head up every few minutes to look at their
positions. Then it would bob down again.

The distance was about 250 meters. It would be a good
shot if the rifle was properly sighted in and the ammo was
according to specs. Everyone waited. Hendricks raised his
field glasses to his eyes and focused.

Then it came. Anthony took up the last of the slack on
the trigger. The rifle roared back against his shoulder
before he knew he had actually fired. Across the field a
round dot wearing a camouflage snail cap flew back in a
bloody mist. The shot had taken him just over the right
eyebrow. From the mercs came a cheer and a cry of

passion that echoed over the fire. They had sent their answer to Okediji.

After the shot Hendricks swung his glasses around and brought into focus the figure of a tall, well-built man. When he came to the face, he was stunned. It was Kelo. He was standing there with a rebel officer and he had a weapon in his hand. Had he betrayed them? Then Kelo was gone behind the wall of a partially burned-out hangar.

Kelo had taken advantage of the lull in the fighting to watch the men across the field. He was interested in how they would deal with the situation. He saw one large black man in place with a bearded white man. It must have been one of those Hendricks used to speak the Shanga language. It would not go well for him if he were taken alive. He would never make it to trial, though the time of his dying might be much, much longer.

Okediji interrupted his speculations.

"It appears our friends over there have made their decision. I expected nothing less. They think they will cheat me but it will not be. I have already made plans for this eventuality. Come with me. You should have a good view."

From his breast pocket Okediji drew out a police whistle. Wetting his lips, he blew three shrill blasts on it. From around the hangars and buildings and wrecked aircraft his new elite command came forth, dressing themselves quickly into four equal ranks, weapons at port arms. Two hundred men stood smart in the African sun. Everything about them shined, their weapons, their boots, and their faces. With curiosity, Kelo watched what Okediji was going to do with them.

Okediji caught the question on Kelo's face. "They are going to bring me my prisoners."

Another single long blast on the whistle and mortars

began wailing over the machine shop. At first they used high explosives, but no more than ten rounds. It was used just to make the mercs keep their heads down. Then came smoke shells, one after the other, to obscure their vision. One more triple blast on the whistle and his commando moved forward at a trot, not firing. The two rear ranks had slung their weapons over their shoulders, replacing them with finely honed pangas. Kelo put his glasses to his eyes. He didn't want to miss anything.

In the smoke he saw Hendricks signaling with his arms, giving orders to his men. The large black man had moved up behind a lathe, bringing his weapon to his shoulder as the white bearded man with him hauled a light machine gun into a better placement.

The Leopards were halfway across the field when the first volley came from the mercenaries. It was a withering fire from their light machine guns. The first rank began to crumble. The gaps in the lines were filled by the rank behind. They ran over their own men's bodies. Another blast from Okediji's whistle and they began to return the mercenary fire, but they aimed high. They closed to within forty meters now, running fast, ignoring the wounded and dead they left behind them.

The mercs fired the recoilless rifle. A storm of ball bearings packed into the canister round blew arms and legs from bodies in a sweeping fiery scythe of death. Then another round was fired!

Okediji directed his mortars on them. Quickly and efficiently, he called out the adjustments. Two rounds missed, then the recoilless rifle and its crew were gone in a burst of flame, their bodies and weapons mixed into a stew of steaming metal and torn flesh. The Leopard commando was within forty feet now. Great holes had been shot in the ranks but they didn't stop.

The last two ranks were filling the gaps, only pangas in their hands. Their eyes were red with the killing and the lust that comes in battle. Nothing the mercs could do would stop them. The first line hit the jumble of sheet metal and beams that had been a machine shop and threw themselves into it knowing they were going to die. Over their bodies came the next rank, pangas swinging and chopping, coming up red.

Kelo saw the big black man grab one of the commandos and twist his head so he looked back the way he came. Then he dropped the body and disappeared. The mercenaries were using their bayonets and close-combat knives with wicked efficiency but to no avail. They would go down, smothered under the bodies of Okediji's men. Many were taken alive. Okediji would have his trial.

Through his glasses, Kelo saw Hendricks standing up. His rifle must have jammed or run out of ammunition. He was standing in a small clearing with his pistol, calmly shooting every commando who came at him. They never fired back. Then he was down, swarmed over by camouflaged black bodies. Kelo saw a rifle raised in the air, then come down butt first. They had taken Hendricks!

Others threw themselves on the remaining mercs who had no time to reload. They were fighting with blades and fists, but were swamped by the men who threw themselves at them, heedless of their own wounds or deaths. Many of them died, but not all.

Then it was silent. From the machine shop came a long ululating cry picked up by all the surviving commandos of which there were less than fifty. Then the troops Okediji had brought in to witness the capture joined it.

"Uh, uh, uh" was repeated over and over from around the hangars and buildings. The rebels poured forth out of the fields. The chanting had set the rhythm. They moved on to the strip forming into lines that stepped forward, then back. They began to jump. Loose jointed, their bodies acted as whips. They leaped into the air with easy fluid graceful movements, their heads bobbing up and down in the glow of the afternoon sun. They held their rifles as their ancestors had once held their spears and they danced the dance of death and life, for both were the same.

Standing apart, Kelo saw a figure leave the shop and move away from the action. There was something about that figure. He focused on it with his glasses. Now he knew. It was the black mercenary. He was in one of the new uniforms of the commando. He must have changed with the man he had killed. Kelo nodded in approval. Very good. Very good indeed. This one could be useful; he was a thinker.

Okediji had moved onto the field to accept the praise and adoration of his men. The wounded were ignored. Kelo moved to intercept Washington. As he crossed the field, he saw the whites being brought out strung up on poles like gutted gazelles. Their bodies were stripped naked as the warriors danced and chanted around them, running up to touch fingers to the wounds. They tasted the blood of their enemies and wiped the life fluid on their hair, faces, and chests. From this ritual they would gain the bravery of their enemies, taking it into themselves.

Hendricks was brought out, carried above the heads of the warriors. His head was limp and hanging down, but he was alive. The commando were taking him to his conqueror, Leopoldo Okediji, liberator of Bokala, the new king. The dead mercenaries had all been stripped, their bodies hauled to the center of the field. They were put one on top of the other in a bleeding clump of useless, once living flesh! The rebels went for them as a pack of pariah dogs who fed on the offal of the streets.

With their pangas they hacked and gouged great chunks of meat from the still bodies. Many took arms and hands for souvenirs, or—as Kelo thought—to eat later to gain more karma. Heads were tossed playfully from one to the other by Okediji's "children." This was a great day and Okediji was not going to interfere with his "children's" games. They had earned the right to play.

Kelo saw Okediji take Hendricks's head in his hands and look him in the face. He gave orders that the surviving mercenaries were to be taken to the prison in Bokala. There he would question them. A white head rolled by his feet. Picking it up by the hair, Okediji looked deeply into the blue eyes, spat in its face, then kicked it as one would a football, laughing when one of his men caught it in the air with one hand. It was a great, great day.

TWENTY-SIX

NOVEMBER 3
0004 HOURS

THE SCREAMING STOPPED shortly after midnight.

Hendricks wondered who it was this time. A door opened and closed. The sound of a body being dragged came through the thick wood-and-metal doors of his cell. He didn't have to see to know what was happening. They were taking the man Okediji had "trimmed" back to his cell or to a truck at the rear of the prison, where his body would be hauled off to be thrown to the animals or dumped in a nameless grave.

Huddled in the corner, Anthony tried to keep his terror under control, doing anything he could with his hands to block out the sounds of the screaming, which had started three hours before. The mottled side of his face was crusted with dried blood. He had not been given the experience of one of the Barber's close shaves—not yet, anyway.

When they'd brought Hendricks back to his cell, he'd kept his control. He used part of their water to wash away the crusted blood from the artistic slices Okediji had made in Hendricks's flesh. With Hendricks, Okediji had been somewhat more gentle than usual. He would need the mercenary leader as his star subject when they went on trial. He had left the face alone as he had on all he planned on saving.

As for the rest, they were of no more value than the small pleasures they could provide for his men. It was good for them to see that they were the masters and the whites their slaves to do with as they wished. He felt it was very important for the men in his command to know that they were the better, the stronger of the races. There could well come a time when they would go into battle against other whites.

The shuffling faded, followed by more determined steps. The click of hard-soled heels on the concrete hallway came closer. There was a hesitation. Hendricks straightened up. They were stopping outside of his cell door.

The hatch used to slide in food and water opened. From the glow of the fifty-watt bulb in the hallway Hendricks could see it was Okediji.

"My dear friends. How are we this evening? I do hope you are enjoying your visit to Bokala and will be with us a long, long time." Okediji laughed in boyish delight at his humor. "However, I am sorry to say it appears that we have lost one of our guests. He has decided to move on to a quieter existence, which I am certain you will appreciate. He was, after all, a very noisy customer and I am certain that he has kept our other guests awake this night."

Hendricks said nothing, only locked his eyes on those of Okediji, sending out waves of hate. It was all he had to fight with.

The hatch closed, Okediji's laughter mocking as it faded down the hallway. With the thin beam of light the hatch had let in cut off again, the darkness became incredibly heavy, suffocating. The wooden slats of Hendricks's cot pressed into his thighs and felt good. Okediji missed one thing. Sometimes pain can be used as a weapon to keep the mind sharp and to prevent it from falling into the deep recesses of apathy. Hendricks relived every one of the cuts Okediji had made in his flesh. He savored the smile of the Barber's lips as the cold German steel was turned and twisted to extract the maximum amount of pain.

"What do you think they are going to do with us now?" Anthony asked quietly.

There was just enough light seeping through the bottom and top seams of the cell door for him to make out Anthony in the prison clothes of shapeless charcoal-gray pajama bottoms and tops. His body was huddled on his bunk, knees drawn up under his chin, arms around them holding himself.

"I don't know. From what you told me, there may be a chance for you to get out. But you had better decide soon whether or not you're going to tell Okediji about your father. One thing I have learned over the years is that money can open many doors. Perhaps it will open this one for you."

He heard the boy shuffle nervously. "But what about the rest of you? I know that I can get my father to come up with maybe one or two million. Do you think Okediji would let the rest of you go for that?"

Leaning back against the cool stones of the wall, Hendricks shook his head in the darkness. "No way. He's going to have his show and that is one thing that can't be bought. We're the co-stars in his life story. You, he might sell. Us, never!"

There was silence save for the sounds of men in uneasy sleep or trying to control outcries of pain when they moved. He knew Duke and Becaude were two cells down from him. Who was in the next cell, he didn't know. He had tried to talk to him but there had been no response, only whimpering and strange gurgling noises. It was the next day when he found out why. One of the guards with a bit of English and much sign language had delighted in reenacting the event for him and Anthony. The man in the next cell had cursed Okediji during their interrogation. For that, his tongue had been cut out with the Barber's razor. As for his cellmate, he had died, his body sliced into a thousand thin shreds by the razor. It had taken eleven hours. Okediji was a patient man.

Sleep came unwillingly. Around him he saw the Simbas of that dawn in the Congo. He was standing in the ring of his dead, blade in hand, waiting for his moment to join them. He had failed then. He had failed now. It was hard, a torture worse than anything Okediji had done to him. To prepare for death not once, but twice, then to have it snatched away by chance.

His eyes jerked open. The sound came again. *Thhhhhp!* Almost inaudible, but he knew what it was. Sliding across the floor, he put his hand over Anthony's mouth to stop any outcry. "Wake up!" he hissed. "Something's going down."

The food hatch opened, letting in the dim light. A head was outlined in it. "Boss? You there?"

Washington tried to see through the gloom of the cell's interior.

"Yes, we're here!"

Then the door opened. Washington stood there smiling, showing his great white teeth.

Another figure was behind him, a long-nosed pistol in its hand. Kelo looked at him quickly, whispering, "We must go now. There is no time."

Followed by Anthony, Hendricks stumbled out into the hall. "What about the others?"

Kelo shook his head. "Just you and the boy. We can take no others."

Hendricks started to protest, but Kelo turned on him. "There is no other way. I have arranged for you to be taken out. There is no room for the rest, and if I open their cells there is nowhere for them to go or hide their white faces in this land. Come with me and you may be able to do something to save them. Stay and you all die. It is up to you. I do not care. I have lived up to a promise I made to myself. Now come or stay. I am leaving."

Two cells down a voice came to him from behind the bolted food hatch. "Go with him, Boss. We want you to. Then come back and get us or kill that motherfucker for us." Duke moved aside to let Becaude near the hatch.

"*Oui, Chef.* Go with them. We will wait. It will take time for Okediji to stage his spectacle. We will live till you come back. Now, for us, *go!*"

Washington took his arm, leading him up the stairs past the two bodies of the rebels he and Kelo had killed with the silenced pistols. For the first time he saw that Washington was wearing the same camouflaged uniform as Kelo. They went up another flight to the check-in room. Three men lay dead, small black holes draining in their foreheads. In a corner another rebel lay on his side, hands and feet tied, mouth gagged. Hendricks didn't have time to ask why this man had been permitted to live.

Quickly he and Anthony were hustled out into the dark and shoved in the back of a waiting weapons carrier. Kelo took the wheel. Washington rode shotgun, his pistol held on his lap.

In the back Hendricks and Anthony could see nothing. The flap had been pulled down. It was all up to the men in front, but he wondered about Kelo. He had seen him with Okediji. Who was he? Why was he doing this? Whose side was he on, if he had a side? The questions were too much and the pain in his body drained him of the will to think clearly. All that would have to be answered later.

Twice they were stopped at checkpoints. At one they were let through. At the other he heard the small whisper of the silenced pistol working, then the grinding of gears as they drove on. It was an hour before dawn when they pulled off the road, passing huts and bomas surrounded by thorn brush. How long it had taken them to reach there he didn't know. His mind had drifted in and out during the ride. Anthony had caught him once when he almost fell off the bench onto the metal floor of the weapons carrier.

The back flap was opened as soon as they came to a stop.

"We're here, Boss. Let's go." Strong, gentle black hands helped him from the rear of the truck onto the ground. Washington put Hendricks's right arm over his shoulder and half carried him across the field. They were followed by Anthony, the rear being brought up by Kelo, who had exchanged his pistol for an assault rifle. He watched the roads in the distance for any dust trails rising to show they were being pursued.

Another hand came to help, taking some of the weight off Washington.

"All right. Let's get him inside the backseat. Young man, you take the front. Washington, there's a first aid kit and antibiotics in the back. Do what you can for him. It's time to get the fuck out of here."

The voice was familiar. It brought Hendricks back from the edge of blackness. "Robbie?"

"Yeah, I'm here. Now shut up and rest. We're going home!"

Head resting against the rear window, Hendricks saw Kelo standing there alone on the dirt road Robbie used to set down the twin-engined Cessna. He raised the hand with the rifle in it as a salute of farewell. He remembered when, such a short time ago, he himself had done the same to Robinson as he'd taken off with the hostages, leaving them behind.

He still couldn't put his finger on the who, what, or why of Kelo. It was too much. His eyes closed before the wheels left the ground and the small aircraft was on its way out of Bokala.

When his eyes opened, they were over desert country. The sun was midway to noon. His head was clear for the first time since they'd been taken prisoner. Seeing him awake, Washington handed him a thermos full of hot coffee. Gratefully, he put the scalding liquid to his mouth. It burned his lips but it felt good. Robbie looked back over his shoulder.

"Looks like you're going to be all right. We'll be touching down in a couple of hours."

Ignoring the pain in his chest and back, he straightened up, wiping his face with his hands to clear it of the last of the fog.

"Will someone tell me what is going on? And I want to know about Kelo and you, Washington!"

Washington laughed deeply.

"Hell, Boss. All that happened was that I changed into a dead rebel's uniform just before they overran us. I hid behind some trash and they passed me by. Then I just got up and ran with them, yelling for white blood with the rest of them. As soon as I got my chance I cut out and ran straight into Kelo, who recognized me. He grabbed me by the arm, told me to follow him, and keep quiet. I did.

"Later, when we left the field, we talked over the

situation. Then he managed to raise the colonel here on his radio. Between them they set up the escape. Kelo figures somehow he owes you something. He don't really care what happens to the rest. He's just paying back a debt he feels is due you personally. We only took the young white boy because he was in the same cell as you. That's it, clean and simple!''

"What about the man you left tied up?"

"Shee-it! I was the only face he saw, so we left him alive to keep Kelo in the clear about who snatched you. I even left a message in English to him on the desk saying I was one of your men who escaped the field and came back for my leader. That way they won't be looking too close at Kelo.''

Leaning forward, he touched Robinson on the shoulder. "What about you? Won't you get in trouble with your superiors for this?"

Not looking back, Robinson adjusted the trim a bit. "I would if I had any. But after hearing from Kelo, I sent in my resignation after having a talk with the Pentagon. If I get you out with no trouble, they tear up my resignation. If I get caught, then I am just another ex-serviceman who got himself into shit and they don't know anything about it. By the way, I have a message for you from Kelo. He says he'll be waiting for you.''

Hendricks touched the scars and cuts on his chest with a forefinger, running it over the raised ridges where Okediji's razor had sliced into him. He hadn't died and this time he would go back and either get his men out and kill Okediji or die with them. There was no other way for him.

Anthony looked at him from the front seat. His eyes had grown very old in the last few days. He had lost his youth in Bokala. He saw the expression on Hendricks's face. His own grew harder. "I'm going with you. I lost a lot back there, too. Maybe if I go back I can find part of it."

Grasping the shoulder of the boy-turned-man the way he had Calvin's, he nodded his head. He understood.

A black hand went on top of his. A pact had been made! They had all lost something in Bokala and there was only one way to get it back.

From the pilot's seat Hendricks heard Robinson whisper, "Piss on General Forbes and the horse he rode in on. The motherfuckers are going to accept my resignation!"

Then, under his breath, all heard him whisper:

"Vive la mort. Vive la guerre. Vive le mercenaire . . ."